THE MAIN CHANCE

ALSO BY JULES WITCOVER

Eighty-Five Days: The Last Campaign of Robert Kennedy (1969)

The Resurrection of Richard Nixon (1970)

White Knight: The Rise of Spiro Agnew (1972)

A Heartbeat Away: The Investigation and Resignation of Vice President
Spiro T. Agnew (1974) (*with Richard M. Cohen*)

Marathon: The Pursuit of the Presidency 1972–1976 (1977)

THE MAIN CHANCE

BY

JULES WITCOVER

THE VIKING PRESS · NEW YORK

First published in 1979 by The Viking Press
625 Madison Avenue, New York, N.Y. 10022
Published simultaneously in Canada by
Penguin Books Canada Limited

LIBRARY OF CONGRESS CATALOGING IN
PUBLICATION DATA
Witcover, Jules.
The main chance.
I. Title.
PZ4.W828Mai [PS3573.I89] 813'.5'4 78-26867
ISBN 0-670-45112-6

Printed in the United States of America
Set in Linotron Garamond #3

To Barbara
and Jack

THE MAIN CHANCE

1

Noontime traffic clogged lower Connecticut Avenue as after-Christmas shoppers sloshed through a light snow, enduring a cutting wind uncommon to Washington. Michael Webb, in the back seat of a taxi that was making no progress, glanced with impatience at his watch, paid the driver and got out across from the Mayflower Hotel. He started down Connecticut briskly, thinking ahead of what he would write. His interview with the chairman of the House Ways and Means Committee over endless cups of coffee at the Sheraton Park had run on too long; the syndicate in New York would be getting nervous. The chairman was an insufferable blowhard, but he did have the answers Webb needed to finish the next day's column.

As Webb walked along, he saw something ahead that for all his haste caused him to stop. Outside Paul Young's, one of Washington's most prominent celebrity restaurants, a black Lincoln Continental had glided to a halt. Webb recognized the car. He watched the driver walk around the front and open the rear door on the sidewalk side. He saw a tall man, impeccably dressed in a dark-blue business suit, pull himself out. The man wore no topcoat. He looked around as if searching for a friendly face, rubbing his hands to stave off the chill. He smiled at the driver and strode toward the restaurant door.

"Hello, Mr. President," a woman behind him on the sidewalk called out. The man wheeled, broke into a broad grin, and extended his hand.

"Hello, there," he said. "Nice to see you."

Others on the sidewalk stopped to watch. The man moved over to them, shaking hands, smiling, his back to Webb. The other onlookers crowded around the man, some openmouthed in the way people become in the arresting presence of the famous.

"Hang in there, Big Eddie!" a fellow in a hooded car coat called out. Many in the crowd laughed, and the man laughed with them.

"Don't worry, I will," he answered, continuing to shake hands leisurely as the crowd got larger.

"Bastard," Webb mumbled under his breath as he pushed through the gathering of worshippers to the corner of Connecticut and L. He waited for the light to change, then proceeded through the slush to K and across onto 17th, toward Pennsylvania. In a minute or so, he entered the building on the corner of 17th and Penn, the same building that had housed the Committee for the Re-election of the President in 1972—Nixon's infamous CREEP. Michael Webb and his partner, Thomas Wingate Sturdivant, had a corner suite with a cater-cornered picture window that looked out onto the Executive Office Building and the White House beyond.

Tom Sturdivant was working the phone when Webb walked in. That was what writing a daily newspaper column mostly was—working the phone. They were reporters and fact-gatherers foremost, not essayists, but their experience and accumulated sources enabled them to do much of their business by phone. They made a point of getting around town, of seeing and being seen, constantly shoring up their sources; but when deadlines approached they worked the phones. They could call five people in the time they were waiting in the Senate cloakroom to see one source, and because they were on a first-name basis with most of their sources, the phone was good enough. Long hours in late-closing bars across the country had gone into their ability now to dial a number and get a story fully and straight. This was particularly true about Webb. He never said so, but everybody,

Sturdivant included, knew that he really carried the column; his reputation had already been made when Sturdivant had come to him four years earlier and proposed the partnership. The reason Webb had agreed, and everybody knew that, too, was Sturdivant's family connection. It didn't hurt that Schuyler Colfax Sturdivant, the old man, published the revitalized *New York Post* and its affiliated syndicate that would be the column's base—and could assure the undertaking's instant and widespread acceptance in the business.

But this was not to say that Tom Sturdivant did not pull his weight. He was no dilettante; he was one of the young hotshots in the trade, at the time of his pitch to Webb having already won a Pulitzer at the *Post* on his own, four years out of Columbia Journalism School, for an investigation of a Wall Street stock swindle. Pulitzers seldom impressed Webb—he had been denied one for so long on one fluke or another—but he liked the style of this rich young kid. Tom Sturdivant not only had his father's money; he had his combativeness. He could have settled for a life on a beach somewhere, but he chose to work in a business in which his Eastern private-school credentials and manner-isms seemed out of place, especially in tandem with Webb's unwavering gruffness.

The two made a good team; full partners legally, with equal voice about what they would write, and how hard; yet with the older, more experienced man receiving due deference from the younger, oftentimes more innovative one. And they made a striking pair; Webb a stocky man, his brown hair turning gray at forty-seven, with the rumpled intense look of an oldtime reporter; Sturdivant tall, blond and Hollywood-handsome at thirty-three, yet with a hawklike predatory manner that could be unnerving. Webb was a man of contained restlessness; Sturdivant an impetuous raider. They complemented each other in the way they showed themselves to the world—and the way they approached its challenges.

In the beginning, it had been almost like a May–September courtship. But in time the two men settled in. The trouble, if you could call it trouble, was that Webb was becoming a brooder, given to unpredictable moroseness. That, and the drinking, disturbed Sturdivant, and he was beginning to wonder how much longer their professional marriage would last, what future there was for the column, and for himself in it. He liked having and being the best, and would not settle for less. What if Webb's dark moods continued, to the detriment of their enterprise? Sturdivant said nothing about these concerns. A good story always snapped Webb out of whatever it was that was eating him, and they were due for a good one.

Webb took off his overcoat and tossed it on a chair.

"Guess who I just saw going into Paul Young's?" he asked his partner.

"Spiro T. Agnew."

"No, but you're close. Our old friend Ed Hacker, looking and acting as presidential as ever."

"It figures," Sturdivant said, holding his hand over the mouthpiece of his phone.

Webb sat down at an old Underwood typewriter, slipped some paper into it, and started to write the column.

"Where's Nora?" he asked as he typed, not looking up.

"Still at lunch, I guess," Sturdivant said.

"Well, I need her to check some stuff for me on this energy piece. Ways and Means is throwing the monkey wrench in again. It looks like no bill next year. I'm going to get the column out before New York has a tantrum."

"We still have two hours."

"I know, but you know how they are. They all want to get out early up there at the end of the year, to go to parties and all that. I just hope Nora didn't decide to cop an extra hour today."

Sturdivant started talking into the phone. Webb dialed the number of a local delicatessen and had a sandwich sent up, then went back to the typewriter.

At Paul Young's, the first rush of the lunchtime crowd had already packed the lobby and spilled over into the long bar beyond. The maitre d', portly and self-important, held forth at the entrance, a barely tolerant Saint Peter. As recognizable figures came up, he fawned and directed them down a wide staircase to their tables; as the anonymous GS-10 civil servants and gawking tourists approached, he merely noted their presence with irritation, like so many fleas.

The man who had attracted the crowd outside was working his way through the jammed lobby now, still shaking hands as other diners recognized him and gave way. His face was red and animated, from the wind and adulation that had whipped around him outside. When the maitre d' spied him, he pushed aside the unknown petitioners in front of him and greeted the man warmly.

"I've been expecting you, Mr. President," he said, leading him down the stairs. "I've saved a table for you in the far corner."

"No, if you don't mind, John, I want to sit right out here where I can see people," the man addressed as Mr. President answered.

The maitre d' rushed over to a foursome about to sit down, whispered to them harshly, and they stepped back, looking over to the staircase. He returned and ushered the VIP to the table.

"Leo Manasian will be joining me," the man said.

As soon as the maitre d' had moved away, other patrons were up and around the table.

"It's good to see you, Mr. President. How are you . . ." "We're still with you, Mr. President. . . . Don't let them get to you, Mr. President." "Keep fighting. We haven't forgotten you."

The former president of the United States, Edwin Abbott Hacker, smiled at the encouragements. After two years on the shelf, they still liked him. Some of them anyway. Not those bastards in the liberal wing of his Democratic party, of course, nor the vultures in the press who had been largely the cause of it all. But that feeling for him was still out there. He knew it. There wasn't a time when he went out in public that this same thing didn't happen. The Sunday before, when he had taken his regular box seat at RFK Stadium for the Redskins game, half the crowd stood and applauded him. Some booed, too, but that was politics.

Leo Manasian—squat, disheveled, harried—came bustling over to the table.

"Sorry I'm late," he said as he sat down. "I wanted to get those polls together to tell you about."

"Well," Ed Hacker said, after the well-wishers had moved off, "how do they look?"

Manasian glanced around nervously. "Is this a good place to talk? Why don't I ask John for a table in the corner?"

"Don't worry," Hacker said. "I've looked around. There's nobody near us but the hoi polloi. I like it here. Go ahead."

Manasian, still uncertain, spoke in a whispering, conspiratorial voice. "The numbers look good. We ran a fifteen hundred sample, a full national slice, and it's remarkable. After all you've been through, you still have a solid thirty percent favorable."

"Yeah?" Hacker said. "And what's the bad news?"

"Well, it shows forty percent unfavorable, but there's another thirty up for grabs—real soft on you. And that's in a vacuum. When you get up against somebody, anybody, it's bound to break out better."

"What else?"

Manasian leaned forward, a smirk on his face. "The attitudinal breakouts are great. About thirty percent are glad you got bounced the way you did, but only twenty percent are sure in their own minds you were guilty of anything. And sixty percent—get this—think the press did a job on you."

Hacker's eyes, deep blue and expressive, brightened. "Perfect," he said. And then he too leaned forward. "Well, what do you think?"

"I say, 'Go,'" Manasian replied, softly but with a look that would have done justice to Mark Hanna, or, better yet, Peter Lorre, the old actor to whom Manasian bore a striking resemblance; flat, fishy eyes set in a round face that carried a perpetual scowl and worried look. They could have been a pair of Mafia hit men planning a contract.

The two men, their heads together now, continued the conversation, keeping their voices down. Manasian was still nervous; he never could understand why Hacker insisted on meeting in such public places.

Well, no, he *could* understand it; he just didn't appreciate it. The fact was that Hacker, ever since the federal prosecutors had plea-bargained him out of the White House on charges of campaign irregularities and influence-peddling, needed public attention and approval. When he had copped the plea to avoid indictment and certain impeachment, the pundits had said and written with relish that his shame would banish him forevermore from public view. But that expectation only proved they didn't really know Ed Hacker.

From the very beginning, it should have been clear that repentance and sanctuary were not the way of this man who had risen to the presidency at the center of public debate and controversy. His dramatic televised farewell from the East Room of the White House had, after all, set the tone of his forced exile; his party's liberals and the press, he told the country, "have achieved through connivance, distortion of the truth, and the poisoning of public opinion against me what they could not accomplish at the ballot box."

Throughout, he had minimized the severity of the allegations against him. It was true that the charges did not approach the obscenity of the Nixon crimes. In the context of the post-Watergate morality, however, they were sufficient to trigger the congressional inquiries and Justice Department investigation that were his undoing. Okay, Hacker acknowledged, he had been careless about identifying contributors to his campaign in the Democratic primaries two years earlier. And, he admitted, maybe he hadn't been technically eligible for all the federal matching money he took, the money that had enabled him to outspend his opponents. But politics was a tough game; everybody knew that, and everybody played hard ball. Why, he lamented, had he been singled out? And as for the charges that he later rewarded his big oil benefactors with veto power over key appointments to the regulatory commissions, he steadfastly argued that nothing had ever really been proved. It was a railroad job, pure and simple, he insisted, and the people knew it. They knew that politics was rough-and-tumble, that mutual back scratching was part of it. Ed Hacker had never made a secret of his willingness to get along with people, the big and the small. The whole secret of his success had been that. And they had hanged him for it.

Ed Hacker like Nixon before him surrendered the presidency, but his parting shot was not lost on the faithful. Almost at once after his resignation, they rallied to him. Everywhere he went he was applauded, greeted with shouts of encouragement and displays of continued confidence. And so it became his custom—unlike the self-confinement of Nixon—to go everywhere, to stick his forced departure in the teeth of his accusers, his "persecutors," as he and some indefinable segment of the electorate saw them to be. He salved his political and emotional wounds in the warm public approbation of the True Believers who stuck with him. In the reigning cynicism about politics in general, it was easy to accept the notion that Ed Hacker—open, glad-handing, a bit roguish but charismatic Ed Hacker—had been punished, cut down, for being too successful with the people, too straightforward with them. As for the snickers of contempt from those not thus persuaded, Hacker ignored them for what he convinced himself they were—the continued manifestations of old grudges against him. He was a foe who played the game too hard, too relentlessly for their liking, and he had a special something going with the voters that, not understanding, the nonbelievers resented.

In a gossipy town like Washington, Hacker's thirst for constant public approval ran risks. Manasian was conspiratorial by nature anyway, but holding such a critical political conversation in the middle of Paul Young's really brought out the paranoia in him. He leaned toward Hacker until he was all but whispering in his ear; a veteran of the Joe McCarthy days would have been reminded of committee counsel Roy Cohn, dark and brooding, with his mouth to the ear of the Wisconsin bully, while cringing witnesses sat before them in the Senate Caucus Room. As he talked, Manasian swept the dining room with his eyes, on guard for any reporter or other political enemy who might be within listening range. He saw none, but his vigilance continued undiminished.

"Okay," Manasian said finally as he picked up the check. "It's all settled then. Saturday morning, in plenty of time to make the nightly news and the Sunday-morning papers. We'll have to use Lafayette Park across the street, because press conferences are barred from the front. The mansion will be in the background anyway, and the point that you're fighting to get back in will be made just as well. It'll be a perfect visual, and I've already gotten clearance. I knew you'd say go."

"Should we tip off anyone?" Hacker asked.

"Why?" Manasian said. "Better to make it a bombshell. I've already told all of our people to button up, but they'll be here as always to give you a send-off. We haven't forgotten how to do those things."

"Okay," Hacker replied. "I'll leave it to you. I'm going to stay in the apartment from now until then, working on what I'm going to say, and keeping out of sight."

"Good," Manasian said. Very good, in fact. It would be hard enough to keep a lid on this one, he knew, without having Hacker popping in and out of the most prominent watering spots in town, as was his habit, just to have his ego massaged. The two men rose, again triggering a rush of well-wishers, autograph seekers, and backslappers. As they headed for the stairs, both nodded pleasantly to a group of four very good-looking young women, secretaries in some downtown agency, no doubt, out for their one martini and chef's salad, and for conversation about who was doing what to whom in the office, and to what end.

Nora Williams, lunching with three old friends from school, sat poker-faced as Hacker and Manasian left. Then, after a few moments, she casually glanced at her watch, remembered that she had to be back at her desk early, and excused herself. The others expressed disappointment, because she more than any of them was plugged in, by the nature of her job. Whether she knew what was going on in town or not, they believed that she did, and she didn't bother to disabuse them if it made them happy. But the fact was she never told anybody what she knew until they first read it in the column. That was a cardinal rule, and it never occurred to her to breach it.

Nora Williams was what used to be called in the newspaper business a legman, and still is. The news business is too traditional to allow such a ludicrous accommodation as "legperson." She was the legs, and the eyes and ears, of Mike Webb and Tom Sturdivant. Had one of them been sitting in Zeibert's, Hacker and Manasian would have had coffee and retreated to some other more secure haven. More than any other members of the press, Webb and Sturdivant were held especially responsible by Hacker for what had happened to him, and the journalistic community clearly agreed, having awarded them every available prize for their columns disclosing and documenting Hacker's campaign and later acts of political sleight of hand.

So Nora Williams' advantage, beyond her professional sense of news, was her obscurity. Most men noticed her for her striking good looks—tall, wiry yet delicate, dark-haired, alert—but did not identify her as part of the Webb-Sturdivant team, as she and the two columnists considered her to be. She had been trained as a reporter and they used and paid her as one, behind the trappings of office secretary. It was a convenient, easy, and effective cover, and if it bothered her professional pride at times, she knew it was a productive ploy, and it wouldn't be forever. She was twenty-nine, and whenever she cared to she could land a reporting job on her own with one of the good papers. If she wanted to. But she didn't know if she wanted to, because she was in the middle of top-notch Washington journalism right where she was, and she got along so well with Webb and Sturdivant. With Sturdivant especially, as their best friends knew.

Nora Williams hurried out of the restaurant and headed with long, loping strides down Connecticut toward Pennsylvania, her coat open despite the weather. She could not restrain a broad smile now, and as she moved along, almost sprinting, men returned the smile and watched in amusement as she passed, wondering with pangs of envy what it might be to have so obviously stimulated her. She turned into the CREEP building—that was what she liked to call it—got into an elevator and watched the floor numbers light up in sequence as it climbed. At the eighth floor she burst into the carpeted corridor, running now, swung open the door that said "Webb and Sturdivant," and breathlessly encountered the two men at work. They looked up and stared at her. For a long moment, she just stood there, inside the door, beaming.

"Well?" Webb finally asked, impatiently.

"Coax me," she said, but neither of them responded. "Boys, I am about to tell you something that's going to get me a raise."

"Don't bet on it," Webb said, in his studied gruff way.

"Let's hear it first," said Sturdivant, tolerantly.

"Guess who's going to announce his candidacy on Saturday?"

"Never mind the games," Webb cut in. "It's an hour to deadline."

"Okay. Would you believe Edwin Hacker?"

"You've been smoking dope on your lunch hour again," Webb said.

"It's true, Mike. He and Leo Manasian were sitting at the next table at Paul Young's and I heard the whole thing. They thought I was some dumb secretary."

"With big ears," Webb said, smiling now.

"They've got polls saying its do-able," she said. "And they're going to announce in Lafayette Park, with the White House as a backdrop."

"Saturday, eh?" Webb said. "That would just get him under the filing deadline for New Hampshire."

"I can hear him now," Sturdivant interjected. " 'Two years ago, my political enemies conspired to turn me out of that great house across the street. The time has come for me to ask the American people to stand up and be counted on that conspiracy.' "

"Hard to believe," Webb said.

"Why?" she asked. "I heard it all, I'm telling you." She recited the polling figures for them, to demonstrate that her ears had been open.

"I don't doubt you heard what you heard," Webb said, backing off a bit. "I saw Hacker going in there."

"Why couldn't it be?" Sturdivant asked, supporting her as he usually did.

"Because it would destroy the party."

"Since when would that bother him?" Sturdivant asked. "As long as he can vindicate himself in the eyes of all the haters in the country who believe he got screwed, what's to stop him? I wouldn't sell him short, either. Look at the reaction he gets wherever he goes. He can still turn on the old malarkey."

"It's disgusting," Webb said.

"Maybe so, but it's real."

The bearer of the tidings broke in. "Are you two clowns going to sit here and argue about it all afternoon? If you don't want it, I'll take it over to the *Post* or the *Star,* or the Times bureau, and get myself a good job while I'm at it."

Webb looked up at her. "Cool off, sweetheart," he said, using an expression that dated him and that he knew irked her. "We'll have to make some checks, that's all." He turned to his partner. "Who'd know for sure who still talks to us?"

"That's the problem," Sturdivant said. "We're poison to the whole bunch of them."

"Why not check with the Park Police?" she offered. "They'd need a permit to use Lafayette Park, and I heard Manasian say he'd gotten clearance."

"Of course," Webb said. "You call them, will you, Nora? And be as casual as you can."

She picked up the phone and quickly confirmed that Manasian had obtained a permit in the name of Citizens for Hacker for Saturday morning.

"I'd still like to hear it from somebody on the inside," Webb said.

She frowned.

"Wait a minute," Sturdivant said. He took his phone, put a finger to his lips, and dialed.

"Hello, Phil? This is Tom Sturdivant. . . . Yeah, fine. . . . Listen, Phil, can I ask you a favor? Could you check your flights from Minneapolis for Friday afternoon and night and see if any of the old Hacker crowd is booked into Washington? . . . No, I'll hold on if you don't mind."

Mike and Nora listened intently to the one end of the conversation they could hear. Tom, the glint of conspiracy in his eye, held up his hand for quiet, though nobody was saying a word.

"Yeah, Phil. . . . Oh, yeah? Well, that's interesting. . . . No, nothing I can tell you about. And forget I called, okay? . . . Thanks, Phil. I owe you one."

Tom hung up the receiver and broke into a broad grin. It was the kind of cops-and-robbers, gumshoe journalism he loved.

"Let's go," he said. "Phil Cohen at Northwest says they got a call this morning from Manasian blocking out fifty seats from Minneapolis to Washington National for Friday night."

"These guys always have to have their cheering section, and Hacker especially," Mike said. "You want to write it," he asked Tom, "or should I?"

"I'll do it," Tom said, eagerly. "You can finish up the energy piece and we can hold it for tomorrow's file. Nora, put down all you can remember about the conversation, will you?"

As Tom wrote and Nora worked up her memo to him, Mike went to the files and dug out background about other presidents who had tried to re-enter the White House after leaving office: Martin Van Buren, as the Free Soil candidate in 1848; Grover Cleveland in 1892, the only president to make a successful comeback; Theodore Roosevelt as the Bull Moose candidate in 1912. No previous president, of course, had tried to come back after having been forced to resign. Even Nixon, for all his chutzpah, never was so bold, but he had been completely discredited. Not like Hacker, still a good old boy to so many; a rogue, maybe, and a hustler. But not a serious abuser of the Constitution.

Mike's memo to his partner was characteristically thorough. He gave him, in fact, more than Tom needed to flesh out the column on Hacker. Mike pointed out, for instance, that while Cleveland had lost the electoral vote and the White House to Benjamin Harrison in 1888, after Cleveland's first term, he had never really lost popularity, having won the popular vote in that election too. When Tom read this detail, he laughed to himself. That was authentic Mike Webb; behind the old-time newspaper journeyman there dwelled a lover of obscure political history. In the column on Hacker, Tom made brief reference to Van Buren, Cleveland, and Roosevelt in a paragraph near the end and let it go at that. They were reporters, not historians.

Webb and Sturdivant—and Williams, the invisible partner in the byline—were onto a live one. Tom spun it out on his typewriter, Mike read copy as each take was finished, and soon Nora was dispatching the column by Telecopier on a closed circuit to the syndicate in New York:

Washington, Dec. 27—Former President Edwin Hacker, in an effort to erase history's black mark against him, has decided to seek the White House again next year.

According to sources close to Hacker, he will declare his candidacy at a dramatic press conference Saturday morning in a park across the street from the White House, which he was forced to leave in disgrace two years ago to avoid prosecution on charges of campaign irregularities and influence-peddling.

U.S. Park Police confirmed that Leo Manasian, Hacker's old political chieftain in the White House, has obtained a permit to use Lafayette Park on behalf of a group called Citizens for Hacker, obviously the embryo campaign committee for the unprecedented bid by a deposed president.

Manasian is known to have blocked out 50 airline seats from Hacker's hometown of Minneapolis to Washington on Friday night, the eve of the announcement. The former president's old friends have always been on hand for past declarations of candidacy, and this time, apparently, will be no exception.

Hacker is said to be armed with private polls indicating a core strength of about 30 percent remaining for him in the American electorate, despite the nature of his departure from the White House, and a large segment of voters, approaching another 30 percent, undecided about him. Also, the polls are said to underscore considerable public agreement with Hacker's long-standing contention that the press and liberals in his own party engineered his removal, and to reflect considerable public uncertainty about Hacker's guilt.

The former president will be the first member of his party to declare his candidacy for the White House, which will be vacated by President Shoup at the completion of his abbreviated term as Hacker's successor. Shoup pledged,

14

on being elevated from the vice-presidency, that he would not seek a term of his own because of his advanced age. He is now 73.

Hacker's candidacy is certain to throw the Democratic party into turmoil and internal warfare. So far, only a number of long shots have indicated a desire to run. Hacker's move may well trigger a drive by the party's liberal wing to consolidate behind one strong candidate to oppose him. Otherwise, a danger exists that a large field against him could enable Hacker to parlay his core strength into low-plurality victories in a string of primaries early next year. . . .

The column went on, but that was the meat of it.

"Okay, Nora, you got lucky," Mike said when the column had cleared in New York and was on its way to Webb and Sturdivant's three hundred client papers around the country. One of them was the morning *Washington Post,* and there, more than in any other outlet, would the impact be felt, because it was the Bible of the Washington political community. And that, no doubt, was where Edwin Hacker would see the story—and be infuriated. The thought was unspoken but shared now by Mike, Tom, and Nora.

"Let's go downstairs," Mike suggested, still talking to Nora. "I'll spring for two drinks. No more. Because if you or Tom or I have any more, especially you, the story will be out before we can get it into print ourselves."

"I ought to call George," Tom said, like a small boy with a secret. "He'll hit the ceiling."

"Let him hit the ceiling when he picks up the *Post* in the morning," Mike said, reining in his partner. "We don't want him babbling it all over the Hill tonight, before the eleven-o'clock news."

"I guess you're right," Tom said. There was no one in the United States Senate who loathed Edwin Hacker more than did Tom's brother George. It would be asking too much of him to sit on this news, even for a minute.

The columnists and their legman, they quite proud of her and she of herself, took the elevator from the eighth floor to the lobby. It was now late afternoon and the ride turned out to be a local. At each stop, as new passengers got on, Nora looked impishly at her colleagues and tightened her lips in exaggerated assurance to them that she could keep a secret. From the lobby, they walked around the corner and to the far end of H Street, to the Class Reunion, a press hangout, sometimes also frequented by—intruded on by, the reporters thought—administration types from the White House and the EOB. Tom walked with an aristocratic swagger and bounce, in the style of Fred Astaire; the other two had to hurry to keep up with him. He was always, literally, a young man in a hurry.

"Why are we going here, with the place always rotten with reporters?" Nora asked when they reached the bar.

"It's called living on the edge," Mike said. "It's no trick to keep a secret while having a few pops at the Hay Adams, with all those stuffed old Republicans sitting around like they're near death. You walk out of the Class without spilling your guts, you're doing something."

Inside, the bar was dark, with small groups of reporters sitting at tables and more standing along a long bar, presided over by a young and sassy Irishman named Jack Bailey, a practitioner of the bartending style of touching up the customers with friendly derision, leavened with frequent drinks on the house.

"Here they come, the dynamic duo," Bailey said, conspicuously treating Nora as the invisible appendage. "They must have a live one," he said to everyone within earshot, which in his case was everyone in the place. "Otherwise, they wouldn't be seen dead together."

The dynamic duo waved and took a table at the rear, against a wall that sported an old blown-up photo of Charles Van Doren, the celebrated quiz-show corner-cutter of the late 1950s. The bar was full of such campy art: a Jimmy Carter blowup as an Annapolis graduate; Jerry and Betty Ford on their wedding day; Joe McCarthy in heat; Edward R. Murrow at his World War II mike; Nelson Rockefeller giving an upstate New York crowd the finger, with Bob Dole grinning in the background.

The coconspirators downed their first drinks without saying

anything. Even before the scotches hit their mark, however, each had that warm feeling that a clean beat on a major story always brought to professionals like these three. Only they, outside the inner circle of Ed Hacker and the syndicate processors of the column in New York, knew what they knew. It pained them to keep it to themselves while their colleagues sat all around in blissful ignorance, about to get their professional tails burned. But inwardly they savored it. They thought that this, after all, was why they spent their lives as they did. And the news they were about to convey to the world was certain to mean more excitement—and political throat-cutting—in Washington and the nation than had been seen since Hacker's departure. They thought, also, how Hacker would react when he learned he had been scooped on his own bombshell by the very bastards who had done him in the last time around. It was too delicious.

They had a second drink, and then, in spite of Mike Webb's admonition, a third and a fourth together. Only after the fourth did Tom Sturdivant and the legman go off to do what they usually did—have dinner at some inexpensive little place like the Calvert Café, which she preferred to his oftentimes pretentious Rive Gauche and Jockey Club tastes, and then make love, leaving Webb to do what he usually did, which was to have a fifth and a sixth, and maybe a seventh drink, and then home, his lips as tightly sealed as at the start. And, if he was lucky, get to sleep. That, he thought, would make it about as perfect a day as he could hope for anymore.

2

Uncertainly, Mike Webb struggled out of the cab in front of his California Street apartment building, a reconstructed relic, and peeled off two singles for the driver. He stood for a minute looking up to the fifth floor. He saw no lights. Then he walked across the circular driveway, into the lobby, and over to the elevator. By mistake, he pushed the button for the fourth floor but did not notice, recognizing his error only when he got off and his key failed to fit the apartment door. He rang for the car again, went up another floor, and tried again. This time the key fit easily and he let himself into the dark apartment. He removed his shoes and was walking quietly into the bedroom when a light suddenly came on in the living room behind him.

"It's two o'clock," Ruth Webb said, evenly. There was no anger in her voice, no tone of remonstration. It was as if he had phoned for the time and one of those robot-sounding telephone-company operators had responded. She was curled up in a deep chair, her hands folded in her lap, her dark-blond hair streaked with gray catching the light of the reading lamp she had just switched on.

"I couldn't sleep," she said, again in a monotone from which he could read nothing. She turned her face, a plain but lively face that wore her forty years well, and looked at him. "I was worried about you," she said.

"I've been celebrating a big story," he said, flatly, the earlier buoyancy gone.

"Oh?" That was it. She always spared him the obvious lines, like "So I see." If there was bitterness in her, she was not one to inflict it on him randomly. She was too disciplined, and too generous, for that.

"We found out Hacker's declaring for the presidency on Saturday."

It was as if he had told her the sun had set in the west again that day. He looked at her, a bit exasperated. "Aren't you surprised?"

"Nothing surprises me in politics. Except I'm surprised, after all this time, that it seems to surprise you."

"I didn't think he had the nerve."

She laughed quietly. "Shall I make you a cup of coffee?"

"No, thanks," he said. "I just want to get to bed . . . . Are you coming?"

"No, I think I'll just sit here awhile longer. I couldn't get to sleep now."

Webb walked wearily into the bedroom and sat on his side of the wide double bed. Slowly he stripped off his jacket, tie, and shirt, and then his trousers and socks, and let himself fall back on the bed. In a moment, however, he rose, picked up his clothes, and put the shirt and socks in a hamper. He carefully arranged his trousers and jacket on a hanger and hung it in his closet, draping the tie over the hanger. The actions gave him away as a traveling man, a man accustomed to too many nights in hotels and motels, conscious always of the need to get another day out of an unpressed suit, of surviving on the campaign trail. He walked to the bed and let his head go back on the pillow again, swinging his feet up and stretching them out. His stocky frame seemed in repose less fleshy, and he looked closer to his forty-seven years than he did clothed, when he embraced the appearance of the older, unkempt, harried newspaper hack. He lay there, eyes open in the semi-darkness.

After a while, Ruth Webb came in, combed out her hair, took off the chenille robe she wore over her nightgown, and noiselessly climbed into her side of the bed. She was short, but trim and firm—disciplined in that way too; she looked as she always had, from the first days he had seen her in a small off-Broadway theater, playing Ellie Dunn in *Heartbreak House*. At that time, she had thought nothing would ever replace her interest in the stage. But Michael Webb had changed all that, and she had willingly left it behind for him. As he lay beside her, she glanced at him for an instant. His eyes were closed. To her, he always seemed at these times stripped of his pretensions of invulnerability. She studied him silently, stoically but not unkindly, then turned her back and went off to sleep.

When at last he heard the sound of her slow and regular breathing, Webb opened his eyes again. He lay quietly for a long while and then, sighing heavily, swung the covers away and rose. He walked into the living room and to a window overlooking California Street. He lit a cigarette and watched the solitary police officer near the corner who was standing guard outside the embassy of El Salvador. For months now, they both had witnessed the passing of the nights, and Webb felt an uncomfortable affinity with the man, whom he did not know and had no real desire to know. He had always deplored idle time; he thought that nothing was more unbearable than to be a sentry over it. In the navy, years before, the deadly-still night watches had been agonizing for him. He was not one, like others, who could give himself over easily to fantasies that would speed the passage of time. Rather, he would more likely brood about himself, about his lack of achievement if he was not, by his own lights, achieving, or about the purpose of his compulsive pursuit of achievement if he was. He would endure the night in this way, inflicting relentless self-examination upon himself while awaiting daybreak, impatiently.

If he had been one of the night people, one of those who functioned best while the world slept, it would have been much better for him. And had he fancied himself a writer, he might have filled the void that plagued him by passing the night hours at his typewriter. But he did not delude himself about that; his strength was in his ability to extract facts, in his rapport with important people who talked to him, who told him things they did not tell others. That was what set him apart from most of his competitors.

Webb felt a sting in the fingers of his right hand. He looked down and found that the butt of his cigarette had burned to the end. He pinched it out and deposited it in an ashtray, then returned to the window and his shared vigil with the policeman below.

On nights like these, Webb could barely remember that there had been a time—and not all that long ago, either—when he had slept well. It had been a time of hard work and sense of accomplishment, of taking on a new role and shaping his talents to it. The steady success of the column with Tom Sturdivant had satisfied his compulsion for work, had brought him more money and esteem—even celebrity—than he had expected or needed. But for months, the old restlessness had returned, the drifting. It was as if some mechanism within him would not permit him to sit back, to rest on his record. He had always liked the story about the constituent who told the politician that after many years he was not going to vote for him. The politician, dismayed, recited all the favors he had performed for the man over the years; to which the man replied: "But what have you done for me lately?" That was how Mike Webb constantly felt about his own work; he never let up, no matter what the earlier accomplishments. And he was tired, there could be no doubt about that. The sleeplessness was a double ordeal for him.

This story today, though. That would help. It promised to breathe life and interest into what had appeared to be a routine campaign ahead. Because he and Sturdivant had been instrumental in disclosing the details of Hacker's deceptions and graft, the political community and much of the reading public would be looking to them to "get" the former president again. And that, certainly, would be the way it would be expressed: "get" him. That made him uncomfortable; at his insistence, he and Sturdivant had never conducted themselves nor written the column in a vigilante style. But Sturdivant did hate Hacker with a vengeance, and it would take some doing to rein him in this time. Webb contemplated the next weeks with more than the anticipation of a committed reporter. He saw the emerging story about Hacker's candidacy as a personal catharsis; perhaps, soon, he would be able to sleep again.

Mike Webb watched as the police guard began his hourly turn around the block. As the man walked out of sight down California Street toward Connecticut, Webb lit another cigarette, went to an old writing desk that doubled as a bar, and poured himself a scotch. He walked over to the bookcase, pulled something out, switched on a floor lamp, and settled down into a high-backed chair. He skimmed the book for a few minutes and then laid it aside. He turned off the lamp and sat there, sipping the drink, the ash from his cigarette the only visible sign that a man was there in the darkness awaiting the first light.

It was still dark when George Richardson Sturdivant's phone rang. He awakened with a start and lifted the receiver quickly in the hope the ringing would not disturb Edith Sturdivant, snoring peacefully if inelegantly at his side. He made the move expertly in the blackness, like a man who had been obliged to do it often.

"Did I wake you up?" his brother Tom asked.

"No, I always get up at five-thirty," the senator mumbled wearily.

"Well, I've got some news you'll want to hear."

"Hold a second," George Sturdivant said. He put the receiver down, got up, and walked quickly into the living room, slipping into a burgundy velvet robe as he went. He was the kind of man who cared about how he looked, even when there was no one around to look at him. And he looked elegant all the time—tall, erect, square-jawed, with eyes that were constantly darting about. He picked up the phone in the living room. "Okay, Tom. What is it?"

"Ed Hacker is running."

"Running? For what?"

"For president, what did you think?"

"You've got to be kidding."

"Read the column this morning and you'll see if I'm kidding." Tom, himself in bed, propped up on one elbow with Nora Williams stirring at his side, related the story.

"That," George Sturdivant said when he had finished, "is a disaster. It will kill the party. It will kill me for re-election if he heads the ticket."

"What are you going to do about it?"

"What am *I*? Is that why you're calling me at five-thirty? What can *I* do? If he runs, he runs. We just have to hope all those other guys who've been dropping hints can get together behind one of them."

"George, there's only one way that will happen."

"And that is?"

"If you run yourself."

There was a long pause before the senator answered. "No, thanks. The Senate is a fast enough track for me. Besides, you know how many times I've already said I absolutely won't be a candidate."

"That was before all this. Nobody can expect you to stick to that. Nobody will want you to. You're the only one who can force the others into line behind you."

George Sturdivant paused again. "I don't know. I'd made up my mind against it . . . . Call me later." He hung up and returned to bed. Hacker in the White House again. Even the possibility of it. The idea was revolting. More than that; intolerable. He debated awakening Edith to tell her the news, but decided against it—not so much out of deference to her as out of his own preference for another hour's sleep. In a moment he was off. To be able to do this was one of George Sturdivant's greatest strengths. It insulated him from the pressures others put on him. And so he was a hard man to persuade to do anything he didn't want to do. If he really didn't want to.

"He doesn't think he'll do it," Tom Sturdivant told his bed companion, "but he'll do it. He just has to be lobbied."

"And who's going to do the lobbying?" Nora asked, through her drowsiness.

"I am, for one."

"Why? What's it to you?"

"What's it to me? Do you think I want to see that crook back in? Why do you think we worked for a year getting the goods on him?"

"I thought it was because it was one hell of a story."

"Well, sure, it was that. But the man was a menace, Nora. *Is* a menace."

"So? Let him run. It means another good string of stories for us."

He reached over and took her in his arms. She was always as warm as toast in the early morning.

"Do you know what the trouble with you is?"

"I didn't know there was any trouble. You said I was perfect."

"The trouble with you is that you listen to Mike too much. He gives you that line that the story is everything and you buy it. The fact is, there *are* good guys and bad guys in this world, and Ed Hacker is a bad guy."

"And it's not enough for you to find out what a bad guy he is and then write about it. You have to get your brother to run against him."

He let go of her and leaned back on his pillow, exasperated. "And you're telling me it's none of my business. You're telling me it's unprofessional to get involved in shaping the events I write about."

"Yes, that's what I'm telling you."

"Well, I'm sorry. I don't have the same, narrow, Roaring Twenties, Front Page outlook that Mike has. I didn't go into the column to be just another reporter. We've got clout now, and my brother happens to be an influential senator, and he also happens to be the one guy who can pressure the other Democrats into line. If I can get him to do it, I'm going to."

"And what about the column?"

"What about it? We keep writing it."

Now it was she who was exasperated. "You think it's perfectly okay to split your time writing the column and then going out and manipulating the story you're on?"

24

"You have a quaint way of putting things," he said. "Your lips move, but Mike's words come out."

"Well, how are you going to get around him on this?"

"Listen, as long as I hold up my end of the column, what gripe does he have?"

She smiled, leaned over, and kissed him lightly on the neck. "This," she said, "is going to be fun to watch."

Ed Hacker was always up first. He went to the door of his apartment at the Watergate, opened it a crack, picked up the morning paper, and strode into the kitchen. Even when he was alone in a room, he carried himself with an outward sense of self-importance, as if he had been born president of the United States—the member of a royal line. He fixed himself some orange juice, drank it, then switched on an electric coffee maker and put an English muffin in the toaster. He was consciously proud of himself as he did it, patting his firm stomach. For a man of fifty-eight he was in terrific shape, and as he reminded himself of the fact he walked over to a full-length mirror in the living room, opened his terry-cloth robe, and looked at himself—tall, tan, solid but lean. He gave his reflection his best stump smile, revealing a full, even set of flashing white teeth.

"Ed Hacker," he said aloud to the mirror, "you are a beautiful hunk of man. . . . And you're going to be looking at yourself in all those magnificent mirrors in the White House again this time next year. . . . No, make that January twentieth." He laughed and walked back into the kitchen. He sat at the breakfast bar and poured his coffee, casually picking up *The Washington Post* and glancing over the front page. When he saw it, he nearly spilled the coffee over himself and the paper.

The editors had moved the Webb-Sturdivant column onto page one. "Hacker to Seek Comeback," the headline just under the masthead said.

Hacker whistled under his breath. "Son of a bitch!" he said. "How the hell did they get it?"

He wheeled around and picked up the phone on the breakfast bar, dialing rapidly.

"Hello, Leo? . . . Well, is he there, Margaret? . . . I don't care what time it is. Yes, this is the president. Wake him up."

He sat there impatiently, looking at the column again, fuming.

"Leo? Have you seen the *Post?* Well, those bastards Webb and Sturdivant have the story. . . . How do I know how they got it? You tell me. . . . No, I'm not saying you leaked it, but somebody did. . . . Yeah, it says about the Lafayette Park permit and everybody coming from Minneapolis. It had to be the Park Police or the goddamned airline. . . . Well, what do we do now? . . . All right, call me later."

Hacker hung up. He smelled something burning. He pulled the blackened English muffin from the toaster and tossed the two halves angrily into the sink. He was slicing another open when Mildred Hacker came in, wrapping an old silk robe around her, looking wan. She was tall and thin—emaciated, almost—with sleek greyhound features, and she moved with an aristocratic preciseness.

"I'll get that for you," she said, taking the muffin and knife from his hands. There was no "good morning," no peck on the cheek, or any other demonstration of affection or even recognition, and he in turn said nothing. Several moments passed in silence, and then she spoke again. "What was all the commotion about? You woke me up."

"Sorry," he said, not sounding sorry. "Webb and Sturdivant have my announcement in the column."

"Does it matter?" she asked. "The world was going to know about it in a few days anyway."

It was clear from the way Mildred Hacker spoke that the decision of her husband to run again did not thrill her. She had thought that when they had been forced to leave the White House, that had been the end of it; she could put aside the play-acting once and for all. She even contemplated divorce for a time, but the truth was she was afraid even to mention the possibility to him. Afraid. That was the proper word.

She was not sure when she had stopped loving and started fearing him.

"It matters," he said. "It takes the edge off. We want to work up visible support around the country to make sure this thing is taken seriously."

She allowed herself the faintest of smiles. "Surely," she said, "you're not afraid to be a laughingstock? With your thick skin, you have nothing to worry about. After what you've been through."

What *you've* been through, she said. That was how she insisted he understand how it had been. It was *his* humiliation, not hers, she wanted him to know. And when he refused to be humiliated, it infuriated her nearly as much as the resignation itself.

"Well, my dearest Mildred," Hacker said, "you've always known it takes an armadillo to survive in politics, and that's what I am. And whether it discomfits you or not, I'm going to stick it back in their teeth. What grates me is that of all the smart-ass reporters in this town it had to be those two who came up with the story. But I live for the day when I stand on the Capitol steps and take the oath again. I want to see both their faces looking up at me from down there in the press section."

She laughed. "What a worthy motivation for high public service," she said. "Too bad the history books will be denied knowing about it. It would be an inspiration to millions of mothers' sons."

"Well," he said, eyes twinkling, "I'm nothing if not honest." And he laughed now.

There was a time for Mildred Hacker when that roguish charm overwhelmed her, made her think he was the most attractive man she had ever known. Over the years, she had seen it work in small crowds and large; it had been the magic that had brought them political and social success. But it had also been the magic that brought other women into his life, and it had come in time to be the central deceit of the man she had married. He was not, after all, a harmless charmer; that so many others could still see him to be so one-dimensional baffled her. Others might laugh at the idea of Ed Hacker seeking the presidency again; Mildred Hacker was not among them.

As they sat at the breakfast bar, the phone rang. He picked up the receiver.

"Yes? Who? . . . All right, I'll talk to him. . . . Hello. . . . Yes, how are you, Herman? . . . Sure, I remember you. I still have the hard hat you gave me in the Oval Office. . . . Yes, it's true. . . . Well, I appreciate that. I knew I could count on you and your boys. Why don't you get up a group and fly in from Cleveland for the announcement Saturday? I'll want you up on the platform with me, of course. . . . Good. See you then. . . . Oh, wait a minute. There's a friend of yours here who wants to say hello to you."

Hacker grinned mischievously at his wife. She gritted her teeth at him and shook her head violently no. He laughed silently and thrust the receiver at her. She kept shaking her head, tears coming to her eyes. But he held the phone out and she finally took it.

"Hello? . . . Yes, hello, Mr. Polanski. . . . Of course I remember you. It's good to hear from you. . . . Yes, isn't it exciting? . . . How's your lovely wife? . . . Well, of course. I'll look forward to seeing both of you Saturday. . . . Good-bye."

Mildred Hacker, solemn-faced all at once, handed the receiver back to her husband. An amused grin cracked across his face, but he said nothing. She got up from the breakfast bar, turned, walked into the bedroom, and quietly closed the door behind her.

3

Saturday mornings in downtown Washington customarily have a ghost-town quality. Government, for the vast majority of the bureaucracy, is an eight-to-four or nine-to-five affair, Monday through Friday, with the immense white-collar work force fleeing to the Virginia and Maryland suburbs for the weekend. It is a time that true Washingtonians like best, a time not appreciated by those who merely use the city as a means to earn a livelihood, who withdraw and leave the parks, the wide streets, and the neighborhood restaurants to the city dwellers. In the springtime and summer, the weekend evacuation of the bureaucrats is offset somewhat by the tourists—the gapers with their Instamatic cameras and their walking shorts and sunglasses. They clog the Washington Monument grounds and the Smithsonian, and form long lines at the White House for the privilege, after an interminable wait, of a quick shuffle through the semi-public lower floors. But they are confined largely to the sightseeing circuit—from Capitol Hill, down Pennsylvania and Constitution avenues beyond the White House, to the Lincoln Memorial, and, in recent years, the Kennedy Center. The devotee of the other Washington can easily avoid them.

On this Saturday morning, however, the crowd on the north side of the White House, across Pennsylvania Avenue, had filled Lafayette Park by eleven o'clock. It was a beautiful day, crisp but clear—"Hacker weather" some of the assembled reporters called it, in their cynical conviction that the gods have perverse tastes in mortals and intercede for their favorites. The television crews had moved in three hours earlier, setting up their cameras and other equipment on a makeshift wooden platform facing the front of the White House, to provide a proper setting for the occasion. A panoply of microphones was rigged on a smaller speakers' platform draped in the mandatory bunting of political occasions, and a large banner stretching between two high poplars overhead proclaimed: "Put President Hacker Back Where He Belongs." The banner nicely framed the White House itself in the background. The public-relations agency hired by the Hacker campaign took considerable pride in coming up with this visual underscoring of the campaign's pitch, but, the fact was, the circumstances dictated the arrangements. Senators and former senators announced their presidential candidacies from the stately Senate Caucus Room, as in the manner of the brothers John and Robert Kennedy, Eugene McCarthy, Scoop Jackson, and others; that was *their* cliché.

Tom Sturdivant and Nora Williams were about to enjoy a leisurely breakfast at her bilevel apartment off Connecticut Avenue. She was, to his initial surprise and continuing joy, a marvelous cook, whose own joy came in preposterously elaborate preparations for the most informal meals. On this morning, as he read the *Post* and the *Star* in bed upstairs, she was concocting some exotic mixed-fruit drink, using fresh oranges and lemons squeezed by hand, and preparing poached eggs with Hollandaise sauce, garnishing the plates with lettuce and parsley. As she worked, she chattered incessantly to a parrot she kept in a huge cage at the foot of the stairs. Tom could gauge her mood by listening in on these mostly one-way conversations with the bird, for they were most animated and original when Nora was feeling good. The parrot was young and untrained, and Nora labored endlessly to extract a few simple words from it. For all her trouble, the most she could generate were outrageously shrill gawks, but she would reply to them as if she understood, laughing uproariously as the bird squawked variations of its monotonous message. It delighted Tom for her to behave so uninhibitedly when he was around. He had no doubt she held such ludicrous conversations with the parrot when he was not there, and he felt it was a measure of how fully she accepted him now.

He once asked her why, when there were only the two of them, she always took great pains with their meals together. "You have to be good to yourself," she told him, "because you can't count on anyone else to be." The remark told him much about her skepticism, and about her independence. And while he admired her for it, at the same time he felt robbed of the comfortable feeling that she depended on him. Ever since she had come to Washington, and he had met her that first day after Mike Webb had hired her, he had always been part guide and protector to her, though the other developed rapidly as well. But in spite of all that, she remained steadfastly in control of her own life; he admired that in her, but wished there were less of it where he was concerned.

Tom Sturdivant's own independence derived less from inner strength and determination, and, knowing that, perhaps he resented hers the more. She respected his professional performance more than the circumstances that had so readily positioned him to demonstrate it. She sometimes called him "the Yalie" in Webb's presence, and in private, in moments of playfulness or anger, she would refer to "Daddy" and all the perquisites he derived from having a father prominent in New York society and powerful in the newspaper business. But the important thing, to him and her, was that he was very good at what he did. In her view, he had risen above his advantages. When he had gone to Webb and proposed the column, the fact that the elder Sturdivant could provide the necessary base for it certainly was the major sweetener. But Webb had been in the business too long himself, had spent too many years at late-night rewrite desks and ultimately establishing himself as a Washington journalistic institution, to take a flyer with a rich boss's kid. Tom Sturdivant's work, his tenacity, especially demonstrated in his Pulitzer, won Webb's attention and respect.

Without this ingredient, the team of Webb and Sturdivant surely never would have happened. And without it, the less visible team of Sturdivant and Williams would not have been consummated either. "You're lucky to have old Mike carrying you," she would occasionally jibe him. But Webb's willingness to throw in with the younger, much less experienced Sturdivant was an essential reinforcement of Nora's own judgment of the man she warily, cautiously, if at the same time emotionally, let so completely into her life.

Having finished with the papers, Tom got out of bed, slipped on his robe, and walked quickly downstairs. He found Nora in a long white-cotton nightgown, transparent in the morning sunlight, with the parrot now perched comfortably on her shoulder. She was putting a vase of flowers on the table preparatory to serving breakfast, and he smiled at her doing so, but said nothing. He kissed her softly at the back of her neck, avoiding the darting beak of the bird, and put his hand on her flat stomach. She went about her business as if he had not done so, not out of any rejection but more in an acknowledgment of the naturalness of it. It had been one of their good nights and now it was going to be one of their good days. She put out breakfast and they sat close together as they ate. She poured coffee for both of them and they leaned back contentedly.

"So you think George will do it?" she asked him.

"I don't think he wants to. He doesn't have the fire in his belly."

"That's what comes of being to the manner born," she said, smiling.

"Well, he's been in the Senate twelve years," he replied. "That takes some effort."

"That, and having a name like Sturdivant."

"I thought you liked George. I thought you thought he does a good job."

"I do, and he does. But he's not exactly up from the streets, you'll have to admit that."

"If that's what it takes, maybe you should see if you can get Mike to run."

She laughed now, and leaned over and kissed him. "I can always get to you," she said. The parrot squawked, as if in agreement.

They finished breakfast, and after they had cleared the table together, and after she had put the bird back in its cage, she took him by the hand and led him upstairs. In the bedroom, she unceremoniously pulled the cotton nightgown over her head, tossed it on the bed, and walked toward the bathroom.

"Are you coming?" she asked, looking back with the slightest trace of a smile.

"Absolutely," he said. "Wouldn't miss it." He dropped his robe on the bed and moved, with his slightly arrogant jaunt but unhurriedly for once, into the bathroom behind her.

She pushed back the shower curtain just enough to climb into the tub, then bent and turned on the water, adjusting the faucet to a warm flow. He stood and watched her, admiring the soft curve of her back as she bent over, and then, before she straightened up, he climbed into the tub behind her, gently pressing himself against her. She did not change position, but instead continued nonchalantly to adjust the water. She turned on the shower, letting the spray soak her dark hair, and looked up at him, reaching her arms high overhead and then easily around his neck. He bent his head and kissed her lightly and brought his arms down to draw her up to him from beneath. She moved easily with him and they tasted each other, softly at first, he exploring the corners of her mouth, and her closed eyes, moving down to her neck. She responded naturally, her hands on his shoulders, and he raised her slightly and entered her as the shower cascaded down on them. They pressed together, their lips finding each other, until they finally held fast for a long moment, and it was over. They stood holding on, he caressing the features of her face, she still with eyes closed. Finally, she opened them, as if just awakening, and smiled easily at him.

"Okay?" she asked, playfully.

"Okay," he said, still not in control, but with a half-smile.

They separated and she picked up a bar of soap, turned him around and began soaping his back, then turned him again and did the same for his chest. Then she handed him the bar.

"Now me," she said, and she waited, smiling and closing her eyes as he soaped her all over with gentle hands. They rinsed off and climbed out of the tub. He took a towel and dried her thoroughly, like a child, and she darted off into the bedroom. He tied the towel around his waist and walked in after her. He stretched out on the bed and watched her as she began selecting her clothes for the day. The first time he had seen her this way, in a hotel room in San Francisco during a party convention, he had been deliciously surprised at her wiry voluptuousness. Fully dressed in her fashionably understated style, she seemed much slimmer, boylike, almost prim. It was, he soon came to know, an intentional masquerade, a facade she constructed to make certain she was accepted for her ability alone. It was that, but it also was, he came to understand, a confident coquettishness, as if she were playing a huge joke on the world by camouflaging this sensual side of herself. Seeing and knowing her first in that world, and then beholding her behind the facade, heightened the revelation and the excitement for him, and she knew it and exploited it.

"You are," he said, slowly and emphatically, "most assuredly a bitch. And a tease. And it's wonderful."

She turned to him, lowered her lashes demurely, and blinked them quickly. Then, suddenly, she threw herself across the bed and pinned him down beneath her. She put her lips to his ear and whispered, "Yes, isn't it?" And she laughed uproariously, rolling over on her back beside him. He moved toward her but she was too quick for him. She scampered off the bed and was at the closet again.

"Enough's enough," she said. "We've got to get going. What shall I wear?"

Mike Webb was already at Lafayette Park when their cab arrived shortly after eleven. They worked their way through the crowd to where he was standing beneath one of the portable loudspeakers mounted in the lower branches of a tree.

"They're all here," Webb said to his partners. "The right-to-workers and the right-to-lifers and the right-to-kick-the-press-in-the-assers. Waiting for their marching orders from the leader." He gestured among the crowd, where placards held aloft proclaimed such verities as "Don't Make Me Join a Union" and "Abortion Is Murder" and "Who Ever Elected Walter Cronkite?"

"Have you talked to George again?" Webb asked Sturdivant.

"Not since yesterday. He said he wants to take a reading on this thing today. To get a feel of how serious Hacker is."

"Is a boa constrictor serious about eating a pig?" Webb said. "If George is going to do it, he's going to have to move. If he doesn't strong-arm or bluff those other guys out of the race fast, it's going to be a disaster on the left."

Suddenly, cheers went up from the crowd as the same black limousine that had appeared in front of Paul Young's earlier in the week pulled to the curb. Edwin Hacker bounced out, Mildred Hacker with frozen smile in place at his side. Together they made their way through the well-wishers who crowded around them, while Leo Manasian cleared a path to the speakers' platform. With him was a spectacular-looking blond woman in her mid-thirties, stylish in a fitted dark brown coat, yet flashy in the manner usually associated with affluent Republican matrons from the Midwest—bouffant hair lacquered and exactly in place; large rings on three fingers of each hand. She carried a briefcase.

"That's Bea Morrison, Hacker's personal secretary," Tom told Nora. He winked exaggeratedly when he said "personal," and Nora signaled her comprehension by winking back. On her own, she recognized another member of the entourage, Greg Commager, a slick, plastic-looking pretty boy in a three-piece suit who had been the White House press secretary in the Hacker administration. He could have been Ed Hacker's son, and doubtless would have loved to be. As he strode behind the former president toward the platform, he smiled and waved to reporters he knew—and knew detested him—as if *he* were about to become the candidate. He was as shameless as Hacker himself.

Hacker worked the crowd easily, but was jostled in the growing enthusiasm. "It'll be good to have the Secret Service back today," Hacker said as they walked. That had been one of the things that grated on him most; that Congress had gone out of its way after his resignation to pass legislation denying him that protection and other entitlements of past presidents. It hadn't done that to Nixon. To Hacker, the action was proof that his forced resignation had been pure politics-playing. He had said from the day he left the White House, even in the face of such overwhelming evidence, that he had been railroaded, and there was no doubt that he intended to sing the same tune as a candidate.

From the start of the rally, it was clear that Hacker would not be inhibited by standards of taste. As he climbed onto the platform, the hired band struck up "Ruffles and Flourishes" announcing his arrival, and then, unabashedly, "Hail to the Chief." The crowd, numbering several thousand packed into the center of the park, roared its approval. The usual introductions were made, and then Senator James Brattle of Oklahoma, a short, squat little man with the vapid eyes of a snake and a tight smile, introduced Hacker—"the man who should *still* be the president of the United States, and *will* be the *next* president of the United States!"

Hacker rose from a folding chair, his arms aloft, his hands tightened into fists, and walked to the microphone, like Douglas MacArthur wading triumphantly ashore in the Philippines. He signaled for quiet but let the cheering go on, let it roll over him and over the crowd, and most important over the live television audience of millions lying just beyond the red eye of the cameras fastened on him. He called his wife to his side and ostentatiously kissed her, not for one second disturbing the plastic smile locked on her face. Then he routed her back to her seat, like some wind-up walking doll, and returned to the lectern, his hands raised for silence. Nora glanced at Bea Morrison, standing to one

36

side of the platform with Leo Manasian. She was impassive during this public demonstration of marital accord, as if she were accustomed to the exercise.

"My fellow citizens," Hacker began, "I stand before you today— across the street from the house you once voted I was entitled to call home for at least four years—to declare my candidacy once again for the presidency of the United States."

Again the band broke into "Hail to the Chief" and the crowd cheered and applauded, placard-carriers pumping the air with their signs.

"This," said Webb to his colleagues, "is right out of a bad movie."

Hacker again signaled for silence, but halfheartedly. He let the cheers die a natural death, and only then proceeded:

"Four years ago, I embarked on a crusade to lead this great country of ours out of an age of political immorality, an age that saw an assault on many of our most cherished institutions and beliefs: the right to work where you want, for whom you want; the right to walk the streets of our cities in safety at night; the right to send your children to the schools of your choice; the right to sleep securely at night in the knowledge our national defense is second to none; the right to conduct your own business as you choose, without the interference of the federal government; finally, but surely not least, the right to life itself—to keep the social planners and the parenthood planners and the atheistic butchers from playing God with the lives, born and unborn, of millions of American babies."

Hacker delivered all the cheer lines, venomously, but at the same time tempered them with that disarming boyishness that was his trademark.

"It is no secret why I am standing here today in this park, rather than sitting in my rightful place in the Oval Office just across this street," he intoned. "What you and I see as our inalienable rights have been usurped by those who have forgotten the basic tenets of individual rights on which this country was founded." He paused to let the cheers come on. "And in this usurpation, the willing and even eager ally has been the press, the whole communications media—that interlocking monopoly that uses our airwaves and our printing presses in a never-ending effort to brainwash the American people. Who are these people who select what you and I should read, or see on television? Who ordained them to be the judges of performance and morality for a whole country?"

"Yeah, who?" somebody in the crowd shouted.

Hacker nodded in the manner of a Southern black preacher before his enraptured congregation, and pressed on:

"They sit in their lofty towers in Manhattan and their editorial offices and studios in Washington and tell us what is good for us and what is bad. But what they tell us is always good for *them,* and usually bad for *us.* They try to tell us how to vote, and when the way we vote displeases them, they use their power to void that vote."

He had them now, and every accusatory line evoked some loud response from the fired-up audience.

"I stand before you today as the duly elected president of the United States, against their wishes. I stand before you today as a deposed president of the United States, in accordance with their wishes. As I said on that day two years ago, that day when I was driven from that great house across the street by their trumped-up charges, I am the victim of a press run rampant. They did not like me, who was your clear choice to be your president, and so they got me."

"Right!"

"Well, in the months ahead, starting in New Hampshire, I will be asking you to state that clear choice once again. In terms so loud, so unmistakable, that they will not dare reverse your will a second time. Ladies and gentlemen, in our system of government the people choose the president, and today I offer myself as the vehicle through which the powerful few in this country can and will be so reminded!"

"I never thought two years ago I'd be standing here today listening to this crap," Webb said. "And wondering whether it might wash."

A man in the crowd turned to him, a sneer on his face. "Don't worry, Webb," he said, "it'll wash, all right. People are sick and tired of bastards like you telling us how to run the country. You went too far this time, getting him. You wait and see." And the man stormed off.

"The voice of the people," Webb said.

As Hacker concluded, among much cheering and applause, Leo Manasian and Bea Morrison were immediately at his side. The band struck up "Hail to the Chief" yet again and the crowd surged forward around the former president. Secret Service agents, whose superiors had read *The Washington Post* like everyone else, moved in to provide protection for Hacker, the declared candidate. That had been a legacy of the Robert Kennedy assassination in 1968. Lyndon Johnson, even as Kennedy lay dying in the Hospital of the Good Samaritan in downtown Los Angeles, had ordered it, and Congress swiftly appropriated the necessary funds. Now the scene was joyful, and Hacker savored it to the hilt, greeting old friends and supporters, including Mr. and Mrs. Herman Polanski all the way from Cleveland.

Manasian, meanwhile, consulting with the head of the Secret Service detail, looked around and saw something that made him frown. He went over and whispered in Hacker's ear. Only then did the candidate turn and make his way to Mildred Hacker, who was sitting in the front row of folding chairs, alone, forcing a weak smile. He brought her over to the center of the platform, and as he did Nora watched her. With no sign of recognition, the former first lady passed Bea Morrison. Neither spoke nor looked at the other as the agents led them in a foursome with Hacker and Manasian through the crowd to a waiting limousine. Hacker steered his wife into the rear seat first, then got in beside her, with Bea Morrison following, so that he sat between them. The candidate and his secretary looked out at the waving crowd, but Mildred Hacker stared straight ahead as the car pulled away behind a police escort.

4

Tom Sturdivant was in a cab bound for Capitol Hill. He and Mike Webb had decided on the angle for Monday's column on the Hacker announcement, and Webb had gone back to the office with Nora Williams to write it. As the cab left Lafayette Park, Sturdivant took out a pad and read over the notes he had made during Hacker's speech, underlining the points and the phrases he thought most likely to irk his brother George. He was sure George had watched on television, but he anticipated, nevertheless, he would have to make a hard sell to him on running.

Tom Sturdivant knew that his brother liked very much being in the Senate of the United States. Its clubbiness suited him; an exclusive fraternity of special privilege and prestige, yet without the wearisome burdens of bureaucracy that bore down on wielders of influence in the executive branch. Tom had often heard George say that he had one of the one hundred best jobs in Washington, and the young brother feared that persuading him to give it up would be difficult. Unless, of course, George Sturdivant really wanted to be president. Or couldn't abide the thought of Edwin Hacker in the job again. Tom knew that both conditions were true. So it would be a matter of leaning on those two pressure points.

The cab moved routinely through the light Saturday-afternoon traffic up Pennsylvania Avenue, past the Department of Justice, the FBI building, and the National Gallery of Art, where, he remembered, some of his father's collection was now on loan.

His father. There was another pressure point to which George Sturdivant was vulnerable. But Tom was hardly the one to push it. From the beginning, he had been on the outside. The death of his mother at his own birth had made it that way. In the twelve years before Tom was born, George Sturdivant and his father—and Tom's three older sisters—had developed a closeness that was enduring, and that Tom afterward was never able to infiltrate. For one thing, there was little time or opportunity. In the way of the power-seeking widower on the rise, Schuyler Sturdivant assigned the rearing of the boys to a series of exclusive schools in New England and then abroad, before bringing each home in turn for his destiny at Yale. George was always a couple of schools ahead of Tom and they saw little of each other or of their father. George could cope with the situation because he had had those twelve close earlier years with the old man; Tom seemed always to be in the process of catching up—in school, and more important, within the family, with his own father.

After Yale, the elder son naturally went on to Harvard Law School and then into politics, winning and serving three two-year terms in the New York legislature before successfully running for the Senate. It was a path the younger son would have preferred, too. But by now he had had enough of competing with his brother's record. Tom looked elsewhere and, in his perhaps unconscious desire to earn the approbation of his father, turned to journalism. Both brothers, others duly noted then and later, unabashedly took advantage of their father's connections—George within the Democratic party that was one of the old man's lifelong passions; Tom as a reporter for the family newspaper. The two were, after all, the heirs to the family name and position, so why not?

In their relations with each other as well, the family was the glue that bound the brothers, rather than how each felt about the other. For all that, they did share trust and mutual respect, and in many ways depended on each other, though neither would have listed the other among his most intimate "friends." And so, when either sought to move the other, the strongest lever inevitably was the family. Perhaps later, if he himself could not persuade George, Tom would seek their father's intercession. But that was not in the regular pecking order of the Sturdivant family. George could go to the old man directly, but not Tom.

The cab pulled up at the Old Senate Office Building. Tom paid the driver and ran up the front steps two at a time. He strode through the rotunda, down the left corridor with his Fred Astaire élan, his heels clicking smartly on the marble floors, to his brother's office. The staff was off for the weekend and he ambled through two outer offices, and unannounced into the senator's private suite.

George Sturdivant sat behind a large, clean oak desk, his hands in his trouser pockets, his feet up, deep in thought, frowning. He looked up and saw a carbon copy of himself, taking the twelve years away; less puffy around the blue eyes, the long, straight blond hair fuller, but his brother without doubt.

George Sturdivant swung his feet off the desk, got up, and reached over, shaking Tom's hand. If it was an uncommon formality between two brothers, it was also a commentary on how they stood with each other. George sat down again and propped his feet back on the desktop. Tom slouched into a chair across the desk and deposited his feet up, so that they sat there sole-to-sole, one the mirror image of the other.

"Well," Tom asked, "what did you think?"

The senator did not answer at first. Then, after looking off to the side, he turned his head and said, in a soft, controlled voice: "That son of a bitch. That low-life son of a bitch."

Tom permitted himself the barest smile. He said nothing. In another moment, his brother went on: "I cannot *believe* the man's gall. As many times as I've seen him, I'm never really prepared for it. The blatancy of it."

Tom weighed whether he ought to comment but decided against it. He suspected at once that the Hacker chutzpah had done his work for him, and he was right. George Sturdivant suddenly swung his feet off the desktop and, looking directly at Tom, brought his right fist down hard on it.

"Goddamn it, I'm going to do it!" he blurted, his voice rising for the first time. "I can't sit by and let that son of a bitch get away with it!"

Tom smiled broadly. "Good," he said. He had hooked his fish without effort and would do nothing to lose him now.

The senator began to pace the floor behind his chair, striking his fist into his open palm. Again, he turned to his brother. "What about you? What are you going to do about it?"

Tom was momentarily puzzled. "Me? You're the politician, George, not me. I'll get involved in my own way. It was pretty effective the last time around, if I may say so."

"This isn't going to be an investigation for fraud, like two years ago," the senator said, sitting down. "This is going to be a political campaign. Hacker going one-on-one with the great, gullible unwashed. A hyped-up pitch by his old Madison Avenue swifties. And you're going to be reduced to analyzing speeches."

"Well, what would you have me do? Quit the column and write speeches for you?"

"No." George Sturdivant leaned forward across his desk. He caught his brother's eyes with his own. "Not quit the column and write speeches. Quit the column and run my campaign."

Tom Sturdivant drew in his breath. "George, you're kidding."

"No, I'm not. That's the only way I can do it."

"What do I know about running a presidential campaign?"

"What did John Mitchell know?"

"Very funny, brother."

"I mean it. It takes brains and imagination to run a political campaign, not experience. That's been proved time and again. Mitchell, Gary Hart, Hamilton Jordan. All winners, and they started with a clean slate. They didn't try to fight the last war."

"Why should I do it and give up the column?"

George Sturdivant again caught his brother in his most riveting look. "First, because I'm your only brother and I'm asking you. Second, because you don't want to write a column the rest of your life. It's a killer. Mike's not going to last forever, and then what?"

"Then I get another partner or I do it myself."

"And you think that will satisfy you?" The senator leaned farther forward. "Listen, Tom, I know you've always had a yen for politics. If we can pull this off it will mean eight years in the White House, not just four. You know that. And I'm ready to commit to you right now that you'll be chief of staff. You'll be the Ham Jordan, the Dick Cheney—"

"The Bob Haldeman. Yeah, thanks a lot."

George Sturdivant tried exasperation. "Look, Tom," he asked, "do you want to be the neutral observer all your life? You call me before dawn and tell me I have to put my career on the line to make sure this guy doesn't get back in. And when I ask you to do the same, you act as if I'm crazy. The only way I can undertake this thing is if I have somebody I absolutely trust and can rely on to protect my ass in a very tough business. And you know that nobody in this office is up to a presidential campaign."

"What about Marty?" Tom asked. "Rudy? Frank?"

George shook his head. "They're all legislative types," he said. "They know how to get a bill through committee. But outside of New York not a one of them knows a county chairman from a choirboy."

"There *is* a difference," Tom conceded. "Well, how about all the old pros in the party?"

"They're not loyal to *me*. What's it to *them* if I make an ass of myself? I don't want to have to worry about the rats deserting a sinking ship at the first sign of trouble."

"But what kind of clout could I have running a campaign for the first time?"

"You'd have as much as I, as the candidate, would give you. You're my brother, don't forget that. And don't forget Bobby Kennedy. There's never been another campaign manager like he was for Jack."

"I'm not that tough."

"Don't tell me that. You can be as tough as you have to."

Tom mulled over the idea. "I don't know. I'll think about it. I'll have to let you know."

"All right, but don't procrastinate. If we're going to consolidate the left, we have to move."

Tom smiled. "For a man who didn't want to run yesterday, you're sure in a hurry today," he said.

"Well," the senator said, "Hacker works on me that way. And if it's going to be done, it has to be done fast."

"I'll call you."

"Fine."

Tom got up and started out. It did not seem to occur to either of them that in all this talk, not a single word had been said about what George Sturdivant would be running *for*. The fact was, he wouldn't be running *for* anything; he would be running against Hacker, against the prospect that a president thrown out of office in disgrace could not be permitted to reclaim it. What George Sturdivant was *for* could come later. He could assemble the necessary brain trusts, the party ideologues, and the power-seeking academics, and they could put together "his" issues. And then the media magicians could be brought in to package and project them for maximum voter acceptance. There was plenty of time for all that. What had to be conveyed at once was the signal, the word to the political community that George Sturdivant had decided to "go," so that alignments could be made.

As Tom reached the door, his brother called him. "Tom," he said, "there's one other thing."

"Yeah?"

"The old man wants you to do it."

The two brothers looked hard at each other.

"What is that supposed to mean?" Tom asked.

"It means only that he wants you to do it."

"You talked to him about it? Before you asked me?"

"Of course. Why should that surprise you?"

"And what did he say? That he'd take away the column if I didn't play ball?"

"Of course not. But you know how unpredictable he can be—when he's crossed."

Tom stared at his brother.

"Like I said, I'll think about it."

"Fine."

Tom opened the door and walked out, his jaw set.

George picked up the desk phone, dialed, and waited. "Dad?" he said. "I laid it on him. I think he'll do it. . . . No, that's not why. That just got his back up. He'll do it because he's a Sturdivant. And because he wouldn't mind running the country. Same as me." George Sturdivant laughed into the phone, then said good-bye and hung up. "Same as you, old man," he said aloud.

After the driver had dropped Mildred Hacker off at the Watergate, he took her husband, Leo Manasian, and Bea Morrison on to the new Hacker headquarters on Connecticut Avenue, just below Dupont Circle. Another crowd had gathered there and the candidate stood on the hood of a car and spoke briefly, invoking the same cheer lines about the villains who had turned him out of the White House. Then the three made their way to the rear of the ground-floor headquarters. They pushed through scores of volunteers, mostly matronly women who left off their stuffing and licking of envelopes to greet their hero; past long tables with campaign buttons, bumper stickers, and literature that had somehow materialized almost overnight but gave evidence of the efficiency of the newly mobilized Hacker staff. In the rear, a private office and sitting room had been arranged, in keeping with the requirements of a former president.

"How do you like it?" Bea asked the candidate.

"Well," he said, putting his arm casually about her waist, "the Oval Office it ain't. But I guess it will do." He turned, looked the room over, and then, watching Leo's expression as he spoke, said to his secretary: "That sofa. Does it open up?"

She and Leo both laughed.

"You and your one-track mind," she said, pushing him off, but playfully.

She walked to a well-stocked bar at the other side of the room and, without asking what they wanted, made drinks for the two men and herself.

"You are without a doubt," Hacker said, "the perfect woman. Isn't she, Leo?"

"I'm really not qualified to say," Leo replied, "but I certainly wouldn't dispute it." A hack's answer worthy of a diplomat.

"Well, I'm qualified," Hacker said, trying to grab her again as she twisted away.

"God, I'm glad I didn't know you when you were in your prime," she said. "You're hard enough to handle now, when you're an old man."

"Old?" he said, with feigned offense. Quickly, he pulled his shirttails out of his trousers and bared his stomach. "Look at that," he said. "Flat as a pancake. Flatter than yours."

"Yes, Lyndon," she said. "But where's the scar?"

"Lyndon was pot-bellied compared to me," Hacker said.

Leo Manasian finished his drink in several gulps. The horseplay made him nervous. He set the glass down and headed for the door.

"You two obviously want to be alone," he said. "I've got work to do. I'll see you later."

When he had closed the door behind him, Hacker went over and locked it, then walked to Bea and held her. This time she did not push him off. The playfulness was gone.

"I wish," he said, "it had been you up there with me."

She frowned. "Oh, come on, Ed," she said, "you don't need to go through that routine with me. How has Mildred been about it?"

"She's been as usual," he said. "Bitchy when we're alone, but a trooper in public."

"I don't know why she continues to put up with you," she said.

"Why do *you?*"

"Don't fish for compliments," she said. "I dislike it when you do that."

"Who's fishing?"

"I put up with you because you have such a flat stomach," she said, lightening the tone.

He smiled and kissed her in a familiar way. This time she did break away and went to pour two more drinks.

"What is she going to do about the campaign?" Bea asked.

"She says she'll go along on the first primary, through New Hampshire, to keep the tongues from wagging."

"I suppose that's best," she said.

"I'm sorry, but I think it is."

"Don't be sorry. I made my bed—as they say."

Hacker walked over and put his arms around her. "As they say," he repeated. She laughed and reached behind her to take his hands.

"What's the matter?" he asked. "Are you nervous here? The door's locked. Anyway, everybody knows by now never to come in on me without knocking. I'm a former president, remember?"

"No, I'm not nervous," she said. She walked over to the sofa and began taking off the cushions. He watched her quizzically as she did so. She turned to him in the process and, smiling, said: "You asked if it opened up, didn't you?"

It was late afternoon when Ed Hacker returned to the Watergate apartment. He heard his wife moving about in the bedroom. In the living room, he turned on the television set, watched a college football game for a few minutes, then strolled in where she was and lay down comfortably on the bed, his hands behind his head. He watched her as she busied herself putting some clothes in a suitcase.

"Why are you doing that already?" he asked. "We won't be going to New Hampshire until next week."

"I'm not packing for New Hampshire," she said.

"No? Well, what then?"

"I'm packing for good, Ed. I've had it."

A look of weariness came over him. "Oh God," he said, "are we going to go through this again?"

She did not respond, but kept packing.

"What is it this time?" he asked, impatiently.

Again she did not answer.

"Is it Bea?"

"What do you think?"

"Come off it, will you, Mildred? You've known about her for four years. I'd think you'd be adjusted to it by now."

At last she left off what she was doing and turned to him. "Adjusted? How am I supposed to be adjusted to it? When you parade her in front of people in my presence—the way you did today?"

"Mildred, Bea happens to *work* for me. Did you expect her to stay home for the announcement?"

Mildred Hacker did not reply. She resumed her packing, taking down a second large suitcase from a closet shelf. Her husband made no attempt to stop her.

"And New Hampshire," she said finally. "I suppose she'll be up in New Hampshire?"

"Certainly. I'll need her up there."

"Need her. You make me laugh. Well, then, you won't be needing me."

He rose and swung his legs over, sitting on the edge of the bed. "Look, Mildred, I don't want to argue with you about it," he said. "You have to be there with me. You agreed you'd go to New Hampshire, didn't you?"

"I didn't know she'd be up there."

"The hell you didn't. You don't give a damn whether she's up there or not. You're just happy to have an excuse to back out of the campaign. To have something to hold over me."

She continued her packing. "Why is it so important for me to go? You're always saying I don't have any feel for politics anyway."

"It's important because all those millions of hicks out there think it's important," he said. "God, I wish sometimes I were a liberal, a goddamned intellectual. They never seem to get hung up on those things. They're too busy trying to legalize abortion and marijuana to give a damn about whether or not your wife is campaigning with you."

She smiled for the first time. "Why don't you just become a liberal and kick me out?" she said. "Maybe there would be some votes in it for you."

"You'd love that, wouldn't you? You could go out as the wronged woman. Maybe then you could run against me. That's getting to be all the rage, you know."

She tried to snap the lock shut on the large suitcase. Still he made no move to stop her. As she struggled with it, in fact, he finally rose, went over, and snapped it closed for her.

"Do you want me to carry them down to the lobby for you?" he asked. "And I'll call you a cab while I'm at it."

"Very funny," she said, obviously taken aback by his seeming willingness to have her go.

"It'll be my pleasure," he said, bowing to her in an exaggerated fashion.

She glared at him for a long moment, then put her face in her hands and slumped into a chair. He smiled and went back to the bed, resuming his relaxed position with his hands behind his head, elbows out. He said nothing as she sat there, her head bowed in her hands.

"The good, old-fashioned woman," he said, watching her. "When things get a little tough, turn on the tear ducts and wash all the problems away."

She looked up at him now, not attempting to hide her contempt. "You rotten bastard," she said, quietly, evenly.

He laughed. "No nicknames, please. The neighbors might hear you." He got up from the bed again, walked over, and picked up the two suitcases she had just packed. He opened one, dumped its contents on the floor, then did the same with the second.

"You sure keep this bedroom a mess," he said. "You'd better clean it up. Leo and Bea are coming by to pick me up for that Teamsters' reception over at the Hilton, and I may want to run her in here for a few minutes before we go. You wouldn't want her to think you're a lousy housekeeper."

"You wouldn't do that," she said.

"No, but it sure would make you feel the martyr, wouldn't it?" He smiled again, turned and walked out into the living room. She heard the television set go on again, and in a moment the sounds of the football game. Wearily, she went over and lifted the two suitcases to the bed. She locked them, empty, and replaced them in the closet. Then she began to pick up the scattered clothing, folding it with care and arranging it in piles on the bed. She was dry-eyed as she took each pile and carefully replaced it in a large bureau next to the closet. When she finished, she went over to the bed and stretched out on it, looking at the ceiling.

Mildred Hacker lay there, with the sound of the television set coming from the other room, until at last she heard the doorbell ring. She quietly but quickly half-closed the bedroom door and stood behind it, listening to the muffled voices outside until the television set was switched off and she heard the front door close. Then she opened the bedroom door and walked to a window in the living room, overlooking the front entrance to the Watergate and, off to the right, the Kennedy Center.

Outside, it was beginning to get dark; a chill wind obliged the few pedestrians to raise the collars of their coats and lean forward as they walked into it. She could see into some of the rooms in the Howard Johnson Motor Lodge on the opposite side of Virginia Avenue. It was from there that the collaborators in the Watergate break-in had watched in horror as they saw their colleagues surprised and arrested in the "third-rate burglary" that had brought down another president. She let her eyes drift from one room to another, catching for a few moments at a time the disconnected scenes being played out in the various rooms; a fat man sitting before a television set in his underwear; two youngsters bouncing on a bed, ignoring a frazzled mother; the tantalizing shadow of two forms behind a closed drapery with silhouetting lights on behind it.

Presently, just below her, Leo Manasian, Bea Morrison, and Ed Hacker appeared on the sidewalk. Manasian flagged a cab and took the front seat. Hacker helped his personal secretary into the back and moved in beside her. Mildred Hacker watched the cab pull away, then she turned and walked to the television set. She switched it on. The football game was still in progress and she watched it for a long time, though everyone knew that the former first lady, unlike her outgoing, sports-loving husband, detested football.

5

The moment Mike Webb entered the Class Reunion, he spied Greg Commager sitting alone at the far end of the bar. It was very like Commager to do his drinking in a place where he knew he wasn't wanted. He had made a career of rubbing people the wrong way. Most press aides—flacks—for politicians tried to blunt the adversary relationship with one kind of conciliatory line or another, from the old "I used to be a newspaperman myself" to just plain sucking around, offering tidbits of information, mostly useless, in the hope of ingratiating themselves with reporters. Commager was refreshing in one way at least: he was a pure, unadulterated pitchman who made no pretense about which side he was on. He had never worked on a newspaper or in a radio or television newsroom. He was a certifiable devil to the reporters; that is, he majored in public relations at Northwestern, hustled himself a job with one of Chicago's largest and most prestigious advertising and PR firms upon graduation, and had spent his twenties and early thirties distorting the redeeming social virtues of everything from beer to bathing beauties to low-tar "safe" cigarettes.

"Hiya, Mike boy," Commager called out when he saw the new arrival. "It looks like we're going to be doing business again."

"Drop dead," Webb replied, walking past him to a table in a far corner.

"Still the personality kid," Commager said, turning to Jack Bailey, the bartender, who shot a look of disdain his way and moved to the other end of the bar. Bailey poured a scotch on the rocks and took the drink over to Webb, placed it in front of the columnist, and sat down at his table.

"Can you beat the nerve of that bastard?" he asked.

"Can't beat it," Webb said. "Never could."

"He's been waiting two years for this," Bailey said. "The worst thing about Hacker running again is we're going to have to put up with him."

Webb frowned. "No, Jack, the worst thing about Hacker running is Hacker running. This flea we can ignore."

Greg Commager had caught on with Ed Hacker through clients of his firm who were big givers to the first Hacker campaign. His days as press secretary in the West Wing of the White House were an endless exchange of vitriol and verbal viciousness, the likes of which had not been seen since Nixon's Ron Ziegler. The few Washington reporters who did not despise him were the most blatant right-wing apologists who themselves were looked upon by their colleagues with contempt. Commager seemed to relish this distinctive place he held in the hearts of the Washington press corps. It was a badge of honor of sorts, his bona fides with Hacker in the former president's own continuing war with the Fourth Estate.

It had always riled Webb that Commager had somehow managed to escape indictment for his part in the myriad conspiracies within the Oval Office to head off the Hacker resignation. Commager, by the very nature of his role as spokesman and official stonewaller, had had to have intimate knowledge of Hacker's misdeeds, but the Justice Department had never moved against him. Webb had his own ideas about that, too, but once Hacker was out of office, the column had gone on to the new president and other stories. Still, it grated on Webb to have Commager hanging around.

Bailey, the amateur politician, tried to get the resident expert talking. "You don't think Hacker's got a shot, do you?" he asked Webb.

"Why not? If all the nice, calm, rational voters stay home and all the zealots go to the polls, and if there are four or five candidates on the left against him, sure, he's got a shot,"

Bailey leaned forward, glancing first in Commager's direction. "I hear George Sturdivant may go, to get the others out."

"Really?" Webb asked. "Where did you hear that?"

"Just kicking around the bar. I think most of the others would run for cover if he did. All their flacks come in here, and the last couple of nights they've been chewing their nails over what Sturdivant will do. All except Jim Simons, Walter Grafton's guy. He says old Walter ain't gonna be scared off. He's waited too long and he's paid his dues in the Senate and he wants his shot."

"Yeah," Webb said. "That sounds like Walter. He can't be nominated, not at his age. But he could screw it up nicely for George."

"What does Tom say about his brother?" Bailey asked.

Webb looked at him and smiled. "What are you," he asked, "a bartender or the new Jack Anderson?"

"Just asking," Bailey said, grinning and shrugging his shoulders. "A barkeep is only as good as his information."

"And his scotch," Webb said, shaking his empty glass and handing it over. Bailey sighed, got up, poured a refill, and brought it back to the table.

"I'm supposed to know everything that goes on in this town," Bailey said. "Are you trying to ruin my reputation?"

Another voice broke in. "What reputation?" Commager had materialized at the table.

"Private conversation," Webb told him. "Get lost, Flack." He said it unmistakably with a capital letter, for maximum contempt, but Commager shook it off.

"Mind if I sit down?" he said, sitting down.

"Yes, I mind," Webb said. "I don't consult with horse thieves, body snatchers, or ex-White House press secretaries who ought to be in the slammer."

"I don't blame you," Commager said, "I wouldn't, either."

There was an awkward pause, then Commager, leaning back, tucking two fingers into the pocket of his blue pin-striped vest, spoke again: "I have to congratulate you for busting the story the other day," he said. "It certainly didn't hurt us to have the boys who did us in announcing our candidacy. It gave us instant credibility, PR-wise. Nobody thought there was anything funny about it. Thanks."

Webb knew he was right, and it irritated him that it had worked out that way. "PR-wise," he repeated, disgustedly. "Why the hell don't you learn to speak English?"

"I make myself understood," Commager said. "When we start riding your ass in this campaign, you won't have any trouble understanding us, and neither will your readers."

"Punk threats from a punk," Webb said, trying to control himself.

"We're going to ride on your back right into the White House again, and you know it," Commager said. "Compared to you, Judas Iscariot will look like the Good Samaritan when we get through. Our polls show people believe you railroaded us the last time, and we're going to make hay with that."

Bailey saw the blood rising in Webb's face and he intervened. "Who do you see going against you?"

Commager laughed. "Stop playing games with me. I know it's greased to get Sturdivant in. Who do you think you're kidding?" He looked hard at Webb. "Everybody knows you went after us in the first place to clear the way for your partner's brother. You spend a few weeks throwing rocks at Grafton and those other clowns, they cave in; Sturdivant takes over and goes one-on-one against us. Well, that suits us fine. We can get a lot of mileage out of the relationship between our opponent and the column that screwed us out of the presidency."

Bailey grinned at the preposterousness of it, but Webb did not.

"You think you can get away with such bullshit?" Webb asked.

"Why not?" Commager answered. "You have to admit, it fits in nicely with our whole conspiracy theory. Our folks are very big on conspiracy theories, you know." He laughed again. "Before we get through, we'll have people blaming you for both Kennedy assassinations and Martin Luther King thrown in for good measure. One thing about having the haters on your side: their capacity for believing the worst about their enemies is infinite."

Tom Sturdivant was well into the darkened room before he saw that Commager was sitting with Webb and Bailey. He turned toward the bar, but Commager spied him and called out. "Come on over," he said. "We were just saying nice things about you."

"I don't drink with male whores," Sturdivant shot back.

"Is that any way to talk about your partner?" the impenitent Commager asked.

Sturdivant continued toward the bar, and Commager got up.

"Okay, okay. I've done enough damage here for one night. I wouldn't want to break up such a beautiful marriage." He bowed and walked past Sturdivant to the far end of the bar, where his drink guarded his barstool. Sturdivant gave him a contemptuous look and joined Webb and Bailey at the table.

"What was that all about?" he asked.

"Just your basic Commager," Bailey said. "Trying to endear himself to the press."

"A none-too-subtle shot across our bow," Webb added. "He's got it all figured—about George getting in. It's all a plot we concocted two years ago. We got the goods on Hacker just to grease it for your brother next year."

"Yeah," Sturdivant said. "That would be the way his mind works."

Webb was unusually solemn. "And the way the minds of millions of God-fearing American voters work."

Bailey stared at him. "You're not serious, Mike."

Webb took a long slug of his drink. "I'm serious," he said. He turned to his partner. "And we better get serious about these guys. They know the mood of the country toward us—not just the column, all of us—and they mean to tap it for all they're worth."

"Son of Spiro Agnew," Bailey put in.

"Exactly," Webb said. "We forget too easily what Agnew was able to generate against the press. And look at Hacker. Two years after he's out on his ear, with an airtight case against him, and he's treated like a hero, just as Agnew was. People stand up and applaud when he appears in public. It's still out there, and Hacker intends to tap it."

The bar customers were calling to Bailey, so he left the table.

At once, Sturdivant leaned over to his partner. "Mike, we've got to talk."

"Okay, start talking."

"Not here."

Webb, assuming Sturdivant was onto a story, suggested they go back to the office. Webb paid the bill and they walked around the corner. It was dark now, but Nora Williams was still at her desk as they entered.

Sturdivant stopped short. "I don't want to talk in front of Nora," he whispered.

Webb was surprised. "Why not? You got something new going you want to tell me about?"

"Of course not. This is just between you and me."

The two men walked quickly past her, nodding, and went directly into a small private office they usually used only to interview jumpy subjects. The jauntiness was out of Sturdivant's step. He closed the door behind him. It was the first time since Nora Williams had worked with them that she had had a door shut in her face.

"What the hell's going on here?" she demanded, to the empty outer office. Then she picked up her briefcase and stormed out. "Who do they think I am?" she said to nobody. "Some goddamned, bird-brained secretary?"

In the private office, the atmosphere was already too tense for either of the men to have been alerted by the door slamming behind her.

"Well, what's so important that we had to step on Nora like that?" Webb inquired testily.

"I was just up to see George. He's interested, all right."

"So?"

"But there's a catch."

"A catch?"

"He wants me to run it for him."

Webb said nothing at first. He picked up a cigar from the desk in front of him, unwrapped it, lit it, and took a long pull. He sat on the corner of the desk, not taking his eyes off his partner's face, gauging him like a boxer feeling out his adversary in the early going.

"I see," he said.

Sturdivant stood watching him, trying to read his reaction.

"And what did you say?" Webb finally asked.

"I said I'd think about it."

Webb was up off the desk so fast the motion hit Sturdivant like a blow from Webb's fist. "You said you'd *think* about it? What in hell is there to think about?" He stood facing his partner. His fists were clenched.

Sturdivant was clearly startled. "Take it easy, Mike," he said. "I only said I'd think about it."

"*Only* said you'd think about it?"

"Yes, that's all."

Webb turned his back and walked to the window looking out on the Executive Office Building. Then, in a soft voice, he continued: "You only said you'd think about it. And what, may I ask again, is there to think about?"

"Well, we don't want to see Ed Hacker back in the White House after all we did to get him out of there."

"And so you think the best way to keep that from happening is to become a professional politician? What's wrong with the way we got him out of there the first time? Is good old-fashioned, hard-nosed investigative reporting suddenly passé?"

"We got lucky the last time, Mike, you know it," his partner said—a rare flight into self-deprecation.

"Lucky—and we worked our asses off," Webb said. "That's what it always takes."

"What makes you think we'll get lucky again? The guy's been out of office two years, doing nothing."

"I don't know whether we will. But that's the way we have our impact. You know and I know that Ed Hacker didn't stop being a crook when he left the White House. We've got our lines out, and a lot of information will be coming our way simply because of our track record on him the last time. If you want to keep Hacker out of the presidency, you're sitting in the best seat to do it right where you are."

Sturdivant moved uncomfortably in his chair. "That's not the only consideration," he said, a bit airily now. "George *is* my only brother. And he *is* thinking about running for president. That doesn't happen every day in a family."

Webb turned and faced him. "And this *is* your only column. But you think you can do more as a professional pol, about which you know absolutely nothing, than you can as a reporter, which you've been with some success. Come on, Tom, quit kidding yourself."

Sturdivant was just as exasperated now. "I know I'm not a professional pol. But George says he needs me. You know those guys in his Senate office. They know the Hill and not much else. And he doesn't trust any of the old pols. He says they've all gone in the tank for one hack or another in the past. He says he needs somebody completely loyal to him, and I can't argue with him on that."

"Oh, you can't argue with that. You can just taste it, can't you? Big man running a big presidential campaign. And after that, big man at the White House, running the country."

"That doesn't matter to me, you know that."

"No, I *don't* know that. I thought you were a newspaperman. I thought you wanted to do it from the outside. Make things happen from the outside. Aren't you big enough in this town?"

"Mike, back off a minute. You make it sound like I want to defect to the enemy. You always see these things in such textbook terms.

Always them against us. I swear, sometimes you sound like Jimmy Stewart in some old Grade B movie about freedom of the press."

"Maybe that's because I feel that way."

There was a long, awkward silence. The last exchange came off as callous ridicule, and Sturdivant had not intended to go that far. But Webb *could* be such a damned boy scout.

"Mike, he's my *brother*."

"Yeah. He's Jack Kennedy and you're Bobby. And just because you've covered a couple of campaigns you think you can move right in and run one. Even if you could, which I doubt, what happens afterward? I suppose you become attorney general. Or, better, chief of staff at the White House. A Yalie Ham Jordan. Is that it?"

"It was mentioned," Sturdivant said, lamely.

"And if you lose? I keep the column going until you get it out of your system, and then you come back and we pick up just as we were?"

Sturdivant didn't reply.

"Except that by that time, the column's got a hole in its credibility like a cannonball hit it broadside from ten feet away. No thanks, buddy."

Sturdivant stood up. "Naturally, Mike, I couldn't expect you to keep the column open for me. . . . But even then, that might not be possible."

Webb's eyes flamed. "What do you mean, not possible? Do you think I need *you*? I was making it fine in this business long before you came along with your Pulitzer Prize and got me into this thing. Don't kid yourself, buster. I can go back to being a reporter anytime—the *Times,* the *Post*—anywhere. And I don't need you to keep the column going. I can cut it back to three a week, or find myself another boy. There are plenty of eager beavers out there who would die for the chance."

"I know that," Sturdivant said, apologetically. "It's just that . . . the column might not be there."

Webb stared at him again. "And what is that supposed to mean?"

"Well, George talked to my father about me joining him. And he's all for it. It may even have been his idea. You know how he's always talked about having a Sturdivant in the White House—"

"So that's it," Webb interrupted. "The old man threatens to knock the column off the syndicate if you don't go along."

"Nobody said that."

"He didn't have to say it."

"That has nothing to do with it, Mike."

"Why doesn't it? Do you think we couldn't move over to another syndicate?"

"I guess we could."

"You *guess*? Do you think your old man has been carrying us all this time? Is that what you think?"

"No, but it hasn't hurt to have a New York base. It's guaranteed us a regular pickup by the networks and the newsmagazines."

"The hell with a New York base. Let's stop playing games, Tom. You don't have the guts to break off from your family. You never have."

Sturdivant turned on him. "Did it ever occur to you that I have no desire to 'break off' from my family, as you put it? What's wrong with being part of a close-knit family? A family that accomplishes things? This country owes a lot to my family."

Webb slumped into his chair behind the desk.

" 'This country owes a lot to my family,' " he echoed, in a mincing voice. "Where have I heard that before? Did it ever occur to you that maybe it's the other way around?"

"Sure it has. And that's why public service appeals to us so much."

"Bullshit!" Webb stormed. "Public service. What a condescending way to talk about grabbing for power! Why don't you admit you got into the news business for the power, into doing a column for the power, and now you just have a shot for a much bigger slice of it? Don't talk to me about your brother and Family!" He said that, too, with a capital letter.

There was silence again.

Finally, Sturdivant spoke: "I haven't decided whether I'll do it yet."

Webb glared at him. "Yes you have. You just can't get the words out. Have you thought about what Nora will say?"

"No. I can't let that be a factor. If she loves me, she'll understand."

Webb's eyes shot to the ceiling. "*Now* who's talking like Jimmy Stewart? Do you think she's some kind of dumb robot broad? She sleeps with you because she thinks you're one hell of a reporter."

"How do you know why she sleeps with me? Did she tell you?"

"Tom, don't be more of an ass than you are already. The girl's got a love affair going with the newspaper business. You happen to be the handy vehicle for it."

"You don't know what you're talking about."

"Well, we'll see."

"I didn't say I was going to do it."

"No, but you will." Webb paused, then went on: "It's just as well. Commager is already onto George running, and he's going to stick it in our ear. He's planning to build his whole antipress pitch on George's tie-in with the column that put the skids under Hacker. You might as well be working with your brother straight out. Commager's going to make it sound that way, in any case. And that's more baggage than the column can carry, with or without your old man."

Sturdivant began to rub his palms together. "You're pushing me, out," he said, waveringly, his customary brashness gone. "You want me to do it."

"If that's where your head is," Webb said. "You're no good to me, or to the column, if you're thinking the way you seem to be, from what you've just been saying."

Sturdivant reddened. "Don't push me, Mike," he said. "I don't like to be pushed."

"Except by your brother, or your old man," Webb said, evenly, watching his partner.

Sturdivant got up slowly, walked to the door, and opened it. "Shove it," he said, in an uncommonly quiet voice. "Take your goddamned column and shove it. I'm going out and make my brother president."

6

Nora Williams was upstairs washing her hair when Tom Sturdivant let himself into the apartment with his key, and so she was not aware he was in the living room working his way into her bottle of scotch. They were to have dinner, but he was early. She came downstairs with nothing on but a towel wrapped around her head, talking to the parrot, which was watching her from its cage. When she saw Tom, she gasped.

"What's wrong?" he asked. "This isn't the first time I've seen your beautiful body." He said it with a touch of possessiveness that annoyed her.

She sat on the lower step and held her head in her hands. She was shaking. "Why do you do things like that?" she asked. "You know how I hate to be startled." She began to sob quietly, and he went over to her.

"I'm sorry," he said. "I wasn't thinking. I didn't expect you to come down like that." He put his arm around her, but she pushed him off, walked over to a coffee table, picked up a cigarette, and lit it. She made no effort to cover herself; it was not that. He knew she felt completely at ease with him in that way. It was just that her sense of privacy abhorred such unannounced intrusions. She drew on the cigarette, not looking at him, and then picked up a robe lying on the sofa and, without haste, slipped it on.

"I'm sorry," he said again.

"It's okay," Nora said, irritably. "But remember, you don't live here."

"I'd like to."

"Maybe you would. But you don't."

She had regained her composure, and it was quickly hardening into hostility. She sat on the sofa and glared at him as he stood in the center of the room.

"Look, Nora, I said I was sorry. Are you going to make a federal case of it?"

"No . . . But I want to know who the hell you and Mike think you are, closing a door on me. I'm not your goddamned receptionist."

"Oh, so that's it. We were having a confidential conversation, that's all."

"Since when? Since when do you two have confidences that exclude me? That wasn't the arrangement when I took the job, and you know it. Was it about me? Was that why?"

"Of course not. If you would just keep your pants on—"

"I don't wear pants."

He smiled. "Yes, I know," he said. "That's what I like most about you."

She drew her robe more tightly about her. She did not think he was being funny, and she was not amused.

"I had to talk to Mike alone, that's all," Tom said. "I came right over here to tell you about it. Don't be bitchy. I don't need it right now."

Nora said nothing, but kept glaring at him, waiting.

Tom took a long swig of his drink, and her expression suddenly changed from anger to apprehension. That was not like him. He said nothing more.

"What is it, Tom?" she asked, in a worried tone.

"You're not going to like it," he said.

"Tell me."

"I'm quitting the column."

Her eyes widened, but she did not respond.

"George has asked me to run his campaign and I'm going to do it."

He waited for her to say something, but she just continued to look at him.

"He says he needs me."

Still nothing from her.

"I don't want Hacker in the White House again."

Nothing.

"The column won't be enough this time. This is going to be a political campaign, not an investigation of corruption. . . . Mike doesn't need me. He said so. . . ."

"Terrific," she said. She said it flatly, disdainfully. It was her favorite word. Usually she used it to convey her enthusiasm, but this was distinctly not one of those times.

"I told you you wouldn't like it."

"It doesn't matter if I like it. You like it."

"I don't *like* it, Nora. It just seems the best way for me to go right now."

"Yes, it will open new worlds for you. You can go to the National Press Club for lunch and cozy up to all the flacks. You can tell them you used to be a newspaperman yourself."

"There you go again. Your mouth moves and Mike's words come out. The newspaper business is not a monastic order. It's just another way to make a living."

"Sure. Like selling shoes. But you didn't win the Pulitzer and get to be somebody in this town on your own by selling shoes."

"Is that what's important to you?" he asked. "Getting to be somebody?"

"It's a hell of a lot better than just being born somebody."

"Well, George is my brother and I care about what happens to him."

The family thing again. She never knew how to deal with the damned family thing. For something to do, she got up and walked to the kitchen, put water in a kettle, and turned on the gas under it.

"I see," she said. "It's not to save the country from Hacker. It's to put the family in the White House. That's an even more noble calling. And of course you'll go right in there with George."

Tom refilled his glass, still standing. "Anyway, Mike practically pushed me into it," he said.

She lit another cigarette. "Don't tell me that," she said. "You went in there and gave him all the same mealymouthed alibis you're giving me, and he hit the ceiling. What did you expect?"

"I didn't expect otherwise from him. But I thought you—"

"You thought I'd curl up and purr at your feet? Did you think this wouldn't affect things with us?"

"I knew you'd be upset."

"Upset? God, you're inept with words for a writer. You're only throwing your career away, that's all."

"Don't be so melodramatic."

"Don't you be so goddamned casual about it."

They lapsed into silence. Finally, he walked over to her, putting his arms around her with his drink still in his right hand. That irritated her too.

"It's done," he said quietly. He could feel the tension in her. "Nora, I want you to come with me."

She pulled back. "As what?" she asked in a low, even voice. "Your full-time mistress?"

"As my legman," he said, trying to smile. "I'm going to need somebody I can trust, who can tell me what's going on inside and outside the campaign."

"No, thanks. He's not my brother."

"What are you going to do then?"

"Just what I've been doing, I guess. I'll have to talk to Mike. He'll be taking on another guy. There isn't a good reporter in town who wouldn't give his eyeteeth to work with him. You won't be hard to replace . . . unless you're taking Daddy's syndicate with you . . . Is that it?" She pulled away from him altogether.

"I don't know what's going to happen with that," he said defensively. "George talked to my father about me, and he made noises about squeezing me if I refused to go with George. But it was just a threat, and, besides, there's no reason for him to take it out on Mike now."

"Unless he wants to make the point that without you the column is nothing."

"I'll talk to him, if you want."

"If *I* want?" Her eyes widened again. "If *I* want? You wouldn't mind having Mike in your debt, would you? You've never liked all the talk about him being the heavy on the team."

He turned, walked to the sofa, and sank into it. "Boy, you're really high on me tonight, aren't you?"

"No, not very. I wish you'd leave now."

"I thought we were having dinner."

"I'd rather not."

"Not tonight, or not ever?"

She paused, then went over and sat beside him. She took his hand. "Not tonight," she said. He kissed her and she held on for a moment, then broke away, not in anger this time, but in obvious sorrow.

"I'll call you tomorrow, okay?" he asked.

"Okay," she said, and allowed herself the weakest smile.

After he had let himself out, Nora took the parrot from its cage and perched it on her shoulder. She poured herself a drink from the opened bottle of scotch and took it upstairs with her. She took off her robe and, the bird flying up, she sat on the edge of her bed, looking at herself in a mirror on the wall across the room. The face she saw was drained of color, making her large, dark eyes look even larger. A wave of shock came over her to see that what Tom was about to do could affect her so visibly. The parrot settled on her shoulder and pecked at her neck. She seemed not to notice.

Tom Sturdivant's decision should not have made that much difference to her, she told herself, if she loved him. But it was suddenly crystal clear that it made all the difference. In the last months she had fitted him into an idealistic image that she knew was not really him—the rich New York prodigy who was putting his advantages aside to change the world, or at least a small part of it. But now the reality had shot unexpectedly to the surface.

It was an old story with her; high, perhaps impossible, expectations, self-delusion about each man she hoped would fulfill them, then jolting disappointment when the illusion was shattered. Part of it was her narcissism; she knew how she looked and she was not going to waste herself on the wrong man. Each time, she had denied this self-assessment, but it was central to her inability to give herself fully to anyone. That, she knew, was behind her playfulness with men. It disarmed and delighted them, but it also enabled her to keep even the most physically intimate relationship under control.

She had told herself long ago that she wanted to end the game, make it all work with someone, cherish him and at the same time devote herself to her work. She was angry at Tom Sturdivant for demonstrating to her how she had judged wrongly once again, and at herself for playing her special game with yet another man, with the customary outcome. They would continue to see each other, of course, and be together, but she could not tell for how long. And she knew it would not be with the carefree mood that had made it work.

She took a sip of her drink, looking deeply into the glass. Then she resumed staring at herself in the mirror, dry-eyed and empty. The parrot squawked, but she did not answer.

Mike and Ruth Webb walked to the bar in the foyer of the Kennedy Center at the ballet's intermission. He ordered a glass of champagne for her and a double scotch for himself. That Mike Webb was a devotee of the ballet was one of those seeming incongruities about him. His colleagues would more likely have pictured him in a box seat at a baseball game with a beer and a hot dog. But at either event, the ballet or a baseball game, the Webbs would have seemed an odd pair—he with sagging shoulders and a look of perpetual weariness; she still with the prideful carriage of one who had been in the theater, who had been accustomed to admiring eyes. About him there was a carelessness, as if he had gotten dressed in the dark. She always had to remind him not to wear black shoes with a brown suit—if, indeed, he insisted on wearing the brown suit she could not abide. She, for her part, was always impeccably turned out, usually in elegant styles that only accentuated her husband's casualness. The contrast would have embarrassed some men, but Webb seemed not to notice. Although his wife was painfully aware of it, she had long since ceased worrying about his appearance and concentrated on her own.

"Are you enjoying it?" she asked as he took the plastic glass of champagne from an aloof bartender and handed it to her.

"I've seen better and I've seen worse," he said, distractedly. "Look, do you mind if we skip the rest? Let's go upstairs and have something to eat."

"All right, if you insist. But these tickets cost fifteen dollars apiece," she said.

He didn't reply. He finished his drink and she hers, and they walked down the foyer and around to the elevators. They took one to the top floor and Act III.

"I thought you couldn't stand this place," she said as they entered.

It was true that Webb greatly disliked both the overrated, overpriced food and the ostentatious elegance of the place—the chandeliers and the swirling drapes and the bowing waiters in their tuxedos, with their too-heavy French accents and above all their condescension.

"Well, we're here," he said.

The maitre d' recognized Webb at once, to his greater chagrin. "Ah, Monsieur Webb, so nice to see you again," the man said, sweeping his fluttering hand toward a table. Many were empty, with all the performances in the theatre and halls below still in progress. Webb ordered a single scotch for his wife and another double for himself.

"You're in a hurry to get there tonight, aren't you?" she asked.

"Tom walked out on me today," he said, abruptly.

Her eyebrows arched. "What? Do you mean you sat through the whole first act without telling me that?"

"I didn't want to spoil it for you."

"What happened?"

"His brother is going to run. He put the arm on Tom to manage it for him. George and the old man."

"And what about the column? What about the syndicate?"

"I don't know. If they drop it I can sign on with somebody else. I'm not worried about that."

"Why do you have to do it at all?" she asked. "Why don't you just get out of it?"

He grimaced. That again. "That would make you happy, wouldn't it?" he said, wearily.

"Yes it would."

"Well, it wouldn't make me happy."

"How do you know until you try something else?"

"Look, Ruth, are we going to have the same conversation for the thousandth time?"

"Why not? At least talking about leading a normal life keeps me going."

"We're here tonight, aren't we?"

"Yes. Thank you. For one act."

He ordered another round of drinks and they sat there, looking at each other.

"Well," she finally inquired, "what are you going to do?"

"I'm going to continue with the column, of course."

"And get a new partner?"

"No."

"You can't do six columns a week by yourself. You'll have to cut back to three."

"No."

"Then you'll kill yourself. And me."

"I've decided to do it with Nora."

His wife looked up from her drink. "That kid? What makes you think she'll stay on doing research for you with her boyfriend gone? She'll go with him."

"You didn't get me, Ruth. I said I'm going to do it *with* her."

Ruth Webb stared in disbelief at her husband. "You mean make her a partner? Give her Tom's spot?"

"That's it. She already is a partner."

"You're crazy. She's never been a reporter on her own here. This is a tough town. You don't even know if she can write under pressure. If she weren't sleeping with Tom she wouldn't be working with you at all."

"Don't be ridiculous," he snapped back. "I hired her, remember? She's damned good. And she deserves it."

"Oh, I see it now," she said, watching his eyes avoid hers. "You just want to get back at Tom. You think this is the surest way to humiliate him. And you're willing to pull yourself down just to settle the score."

"I think it will sell," he said, defensively. "There hasn't been a successful man-and-woman column in politics for years."

"And you, the great feminist, are going to lead the way. Mike, sometimes you're so transparent it's embarrassing to me. You're angry at Tom now, but you'll cool off, and then you'll see how ridiculous this idea is."

He said nothing.

"Besides, what makes you think the syndicate will buy it? The girl's a nobody, an unknown."

"They'll go along with whatever I say. It's my risk, not theirs. If they don't like it, there are other syndicates."

"Well, *I* don't like it," she said.

"Why not?"

She did not answer him. A waiter came and Webb signaled him wordlessly for another round of drinks.

"What does it matter whether I like it or not anyway?" she said when the waiter had moved off. "Why do you bother telling me? If you're going to do it, you're going to do it."

"I'm going to do it."

They ordered dinner, ate without further conversation on the subject, and went home.

Nora Williams was lying face down across the bed on top of the blankets, the parrot perched on the back of a chair, when the phone rang. She raised herself up, her large eyes puffy, and looked at the clock on her night table. It was just before midnight.

"Nora?" Mike Webb asked. "Did I wake you?"

"It's okay," she said drowsily.

"Have you talked to Tom tonight?"

"Yes; I know all about it."

"Well, what are you going to do?"

"You're asking me? What about you?"

"I mean, are you going with him?"

"Of course not. The question is: Do I still have a job with you?"

"Be in the office on time in the morning. We'll talk."

"Mike, tomorrow's Sunday."

"Okay. Make it at eleven, then."

"I'll be there," she said, puzzled.

The building-maintenance man, grumbling aloud at the unexpected Sunday chore, had already scraped Sturdivant's name off the glass on the office door and was making it read "Webb and Williams" when Nora got off the elevator and came down the hallway. When she spied it, her mouth dropped open, then broke into a dazzling grin. She raced through the door and caught Webb from behind as he stood reading the AP ticker. She threw her arms around his waist and held on.

"Does this mean," he asked, deadpan, "that you'll take the job?"

7

Tom Sturdivant had not been sleeping well since the touchy conversation with his brother and the scenes with Mike Webb and Nora Williams. His attempts to phone her were unavailing; either she was not home or she wasn't answering, and he did not want to call her at the office and risk getting Webb. Besides, on reflection, it was best to let things settle for a few days. He told himself in his returning self-confidence that she would come around and accept what he had done.

The sound of the *Post* newsboy in the predawn hush alerted him. Wearing only pajama bottoms, he waited until he heard retreating footsteps; then he opened the door of his apartment and picked up the paper. He scanned the page-one headlines as he strolled back into his bedroom; another mass suicide by a fanatical religious cult; another rise in the consumer price index; another stupid trade by the Washington Redskins, certain to enrage the fans for the tenth time this year; a story on Senator George Sturdivant's formal announcement of candidacy against Edwin Hacker. Tom Sturdivant read that one through, turning as the story jumped to the inside, where it was confirmed that he had left the column and would be running his brother's campaign. His eye caught a small box next to the story.

The New York Post Syndicate announced yesterday that nationally syndicated columnist Michael Webb will continue his daily column with a new partner. Nora Williams, who has been an editorial assistant to Webb and his former partner, Thomas Sturdivant, for the last four years, will replace Sturdivant. In response to inquiries, the Post Syndicate said the choice was Webb's. The syndicate said the new arrangement would cover the remaining year in Webb's contract. Williams, 29, is a graduate of Michigan State University and was a researcher at Newsweek magazine in New York for four years before joining Webb and Sturdivant.

"What?" Sturdivant said to the printed page he was staring at. He threw the paper onto the bed and reached for the phone, certain that Webb also would be awake.

"Mike," he said, "what in hell are you doing?"

"Why not?" Webb answered, irritably.

"Because she has no experience as a columnist."

"Neither did you when we started. Neither did I, for that matter."

"But we'd been writing for a long time. "She's been just a . . . researcher," Tom said.

"Yeah? Is that what you call her, to her face?"

"You can't do it, Mike. You're asking too much of her."

"What's it to you, Tom? You're not even in the business anymore. Why don't you just go off and elect yourself a president, as you put it, and leave the news business to us less ambitious types who are staying in it?"

The conversation ended curtly. Tom began dialing Nora's number, then put the phone down. It was not yet seven o'clock. Hurriedly, he showered, shaved, got dressed, and hailed a cab to her apartment. He took out his key, then thought better of it and called up on the intercom outside the locked front door of the building.

"Yes?" Nora said, sleepily.

"This is Tom," he said. "May I come up? I need to talk to you."

She seemed caught by surprise. She hesitated for a moment, then said, "Sure," and she pressed the code numbers on her phone that sprung open the lock on the door. He raced up the two short flights of stairs to her apartment and knocked. He felt a tightness in his throat. She was there waiting for him, wearing tan shorts and a black blouse that she obviously had just slipped on. She was barefoot and apprehensive, even frightened, by his sudden appearance.

They were both tense. They reached out tentatively for each other, but she was defensive, and at the last moment turned her head and kissed him on his cheek. They walked into the living room and sat on opposite ends of the sofa. She watched him as if he were about to leap at her. She was so nervous that he asked her a question that would never have occurred to him otherwise.

"Are we . . . alone?"

"In the apartment?" she replied incredulously. "Yes . . . except for the bird."

"Then what's the matter?"

"Nothing. I just didn't expect you," she said.

"Well, I'm sorry. I just came over to congratulate you. There's a story in the *Post* this morning."

She smiled, but barely. "Thank you. It certainly was a surprise."

"I guess you must feel pretty good, replacing me."

"I'm scared to death," she said. "And I'm not really replacing you, Tom. I know that. It can never be the same between Mike and me as it was with you two. But if Mike wants to give me the chance, why shouldn't I grab it?"

"Because it's too conspicuous a place for you. You'll be too vulnerable. Anything good you do, Mike will get the credit for, and anything that's not good, you'll get the blame."

"I know it's a gamble. But why shouldn't I take it?"

"Because you don't have to."

The uneasiness was slipping away now, and her temper was rising. "And what am I to do then? Continue to be a glorified researcher the rest of my life?"

"No," he said. "You can marry me."

Her mouth fell open. For all the time they had been together, they had seldom explored that possibility. She had told him it was something she wanted eventually, especially the children part, and sometimes when she was depressed about the condition of her life, she would ask him where they were heading. But she did not often press the matter, because most of the time it was her own career that was uppermost in her mind.

"Say something," he said as she sat there, seemingly in shock. He was not accustomed to being refused anything.

"I don't know what to say," she said, a look of fright, edging on panic, on her face.

"Say yes," he told her, softly, expectantly.

She seemed very disoriented, breathless, his suggestion like a totally unanticipated blow to the stomach. Her eyes began to dart about the room, as if she were seeking some route of escape. He got up and moved over next to her, and she reached out and threw her arms around him, clutching at him. She was shaking now, and beginning to sob.

"What's wrong, Nora?" he said, holding her, not looking at her face, turned away from him.

"I don't know," she managed to say. "I'm suddenly so frightened. . . . I don't know what to do. . . . Tell me what to do, Tom."

He released her and turned her face to look at him. "You know what I want you to do. But what do you want?"

She looked at him, the panic still there.

"I don't know. I don't know what I want. . . . I don't want to have to deal with it. . . . I can't marry you. . . . Not now."

"Why not?"

"Because . . . I don't know, it scares me to death, just the thought of it."

"I thought it was what you wanted."

She looked down at her hands and did not respond.

"Is it what I've done? Quitting the column and going with George?"

"I don't know. That's part of it, I guess. And the other."

"The column, with Mike?"

She nodded, not looking at him.

"I have to try it," she said, still looking down, avoiding his eyes.

"I'd never be happy if I didn't try it and find out . . . about myself."

"And what about me?"

She looked up. "What about you?"

"I mean, what about you and me?"

She reached over and pulled his face down to hers. She kissed him, but in a distracted way.

"Tom, please don't push me," she said. "Too much is happening all at once. Can't we just go on as we have, until things settle down a bit?"

"Are you saying no, Nora, or maybe?"

"I'm saying I can't talk about it, now, Tom. Please?"

She kissed him again and held him fast. She was still shaking, and he tried to comfort her, bewildered and disappointed himself, yet finding something in himself willing too to put off a resolution. He could feel the desperation in her, and she sought to use his closeness to somehow drain it out of herself. The resistance that her words had just conveyed vanished in how she drew him to her, and in a moment they were together on the sofa, with the morning sun streaming in on them.

The parrot, stirring in its cage, emitted a low, tentative squawk and in the midst of their lovemaking, Nora began to talk to it. "Good morning," she said, cheerily, as if nothing unusual was going on, as if nothing special had been said earlier, as if Tom were not even there, let alone intertwined with her. "Want to come out and play with us?"

He laughed in spite of the tenseness of the situation. Her shifting moods were unnerving, but they captivated him. He addressed himself to distracting her from the bird, and they spoke no more of where they were going. That, he understood clearly, would have to wait.

8

Most of the seats on the Hacker charter were taken when Mike Webb and Nora Williams got aboard at National Airport. It was the first week in January, and the first campaign trip to New Hampshire by a deposed president seeking re-election was an irresistible magnet to the press corps. There were enough takers for the available seats at first-class fare plus one-half, the exorbitant going rate, to pay for the plane charter and give the candidate and all his hangers-on a free ride. For a contender who complained that the media were the ruination of the country, and of his own fortunes, taking advantage in this way was a nice and satisfying twist.

Hacker was not yet aboard. The newspaper, radio, and television reporters, and the television cameramen, soundmen, and other assorted technicians were busy amusing themselves and getting an early start on the plane's liquor supply. Later in the campaign—after the primaries and the conventions at which the two party candidates would be chosen—the entourages would be much larger, requiring two planes for each nominee. One would be for the candidate, staff, and reporters, the other for the technicians—"the animals," in the vernacular of the writers. They had long ago earned the name by their primitive focus on alcohol and women, and their atavistic techniques in dealing with each. In their pell-mell pursuit of the stewardesses, and of the liquor in their jurisdiction, they came on like so many inmates just released from years of solitary confinement. Little wonder that the animals' aircraft was known as "the zoo plane," and for the stewardesses the duty on it was an experience in blatant body-grabbing. Some took to it with delight; others quickly asked for transfers; a few tried to cope with the situation with studied iciness, but it was like trying to hold off a tank attack with a flyswatter.

Barney Mulvihill, Mike Webb's best friend and former wire-service colleague, now the political writer in Washington for the Chicago *Sun-Times,* sat on the aisle about halfway back and waved Webb to him.

"I risked my life and saved you two seats," he said, taking his coat from the window seat and his typewriter from the seat in the middle. Nora moved in to the window and Mike took the seat beside Mulvihill.

"So you finally concede it takes two of you to keep up with me," Barney said.

"Nora has never been on one of these circuses," Mike said. "I thought I'd better break her in."

"What are you, her father?" Barney asked in mock disappointment. "I have the contract for breaking in young broads."

Nora laughed. She was thrilled to be going to New Hampshire for the primary and she didn't mind being called a broad by Barney. She knew that he had no other name for women and that he used it in her case with affection.

Barney Mulvihill would never have been elected sweetheart of the feminist movement. He took his politics, his politicians, his liquor, and his women straight. Although he was a reporter of infinite sophistication and discrimination, he chose to market his knowledge and his style in the robust trappings of the old, hard-nosed and irreverent reporter in *The Front Page.* He was a big man, well over six feet tall, barrel-chested, with thick, curly gray hair that fell recklessly over his always animated eyes. He was a physical force unto himself. He puffed cigars ferociously, drank whiskey voraciously, and talked about women lustily—all in a way that veneered his seriousness and commitment to his work. He kept up a running monologue—on the campaign, the candidate, and his colleagues in the press corps—that was funnier and sharper than most of those colleagues were able to write. Indeed, many of them blatantly stole his best lines and used them in print, without embarrassment. He never seemed to mind, because he was always able to come up with something better than most of them could steal, even from him.

The effortless way Barney Mulvihill operated, having a great time and still turning out some of the best copy written on the campaign trail, left others not only in admiration but, in some cases, in frustration. The younger generation of "journalists"—they called themselves that—thought his manner—he was a great mimic, and singer of songs, and teller of what in his day were called ribald stories—was not in keeping with the importance of their calling. They were supposed to be better schooled, better bred, and altogether more serious. They were constantly talking about the need for the press to probe beyond the candidates' speeches and press releases and the "inside baseball" of campaign-staff squabbles and into an exploration of "the underlying issues of paramount importance to society." Mulvihill, once asked by an eager-beaver fledgling "journalist" what he thought was "the underlying issue of paramount importance to society" in a particular campaign, looked at his somber interrogator and replied, "Do you mean, is the candidate queer?" He took great pleasure in deflating such pomposity, and in turning aside that segment of the press—ever-growing—that seemed more interested in covering the press than the candidate and the campaign. But he dealt with "the paramount issues" in the context of the real people who ran for public office and those who worked for them, rather than in any rarefied, antiseptic atmosphere that had little place in the rough-and-tumble of political power-seeking as it actually existed.

As Mike and Nora settled in, Barney waved his massive arm for a stewardess. "Could you give me a refill," he asked, "and bring a couple of Bloody Marys for the old guy here and his daughter?" The stewardess looked at Mike and Nora and, apparently believing Barney, went off to fetch the drinks.

"What's happening?" Mike asked.

"They've laid on the whole bit," Barney said. "All the local pooh-bahs are meeting the plane in Manchester. I hear Amos Cormier is running a front-page editorial in the *State News* blasting you for driving our esteemed former president from office, and taking note that Tom's gone to work for George. He spells out the whole plot: how you're going to write the column with one hand and run the Sturdivant campaign with the other, through your lackey. That's Tom."

"Great," Mike said. "A great way to start."

Nora sat there, saying nothing but taking everything in.

When the drinks came, Barney passed one to her. "Shut up and drink," he said. "And just watch me. Do whatever I do."

"Everything?"

Mike broke in. "You're safe," he said to her. "The only thing he can do that you can't do, he can't do because he can't find anybody who'll do it with him."

Barney shook his head. "Sad, but true," he confessed.

In the front of the plane, Greg Commager came bounding aboard, officious and busy, with Leo Manasian, Bea Morrison, Ed and Mildred Hacker behind. Manasian and the candidate sat side-by-side in the front, first-class compartment reserved for candidate and staff, and the women took seats alone on either side of the aisle, several rows apart. Just before the plane took off, Commager walked back to the press section, amid much hissing and booing.

"Thank you, thank you, paying customers," he said. "President Hacker wishes to convey his appreciation to you for taking us with you to New Hampshire." More hisses and boos, mostly good-natured. Commager was such a total boor that he could be entertaining in his boorishness. "Gentlemen, gentlemen," he said, nodding as he came down the aisle, warding off the taunts and catcalls like a goalie under fire. "And lady," he said as he came up to Nora. "Could I offer you a better seat up front, with a better class of company?" He gestured toward Mike and Barney.

Nora smiled sweetly at him. "Fuck off," she said.

Commager did not miss a beat. He continued down the aisle, greeting the assorted derision with an even grin that told its recipients that the sentiments were returned in full measure.

Barney nodded his head toward Nora and told Mike: "Good broad."

En route to Manchester, Hacker himself strolled back to the reporters' section and held forth in the aisle. He joked and traded banter with them as if they were not the thieves and blackguards who, he was already telling the country, had stolen the White House from him. When he spied Barney Mulvihill, he bowed low, grandly, as in some medieval court. "Your Royal Highness," he said, mockingly. "I'm honored to have your presence on this humble adventure. I take it as a sign you believe I'm still a winner."

"Mr. President," Barney said, varnishing the title with sarcasm, "you're still what you've always been." And he let it go at that.

Hacker looked right past Mike, but stopped when he caught a glimpse of Nora. He brightened, reached over Barney and Mike, and took her hand. "My dear, it's a pleasure to have you with us. Maybe we can talk a little later. I'm always ready to give a young reporter a hand, especially when she's as handsome as you." As far as Hacker was concerned, Mike was not there at all. Nora smiled sweetly again. Recalling her brief answer to Commager, Barney and Mike held their breath.

"Thank you, Mr. President," she said, and that was all.

When Hacker had moved on, Barney leaned toward her. "Thank you, Mr. President," he mimicked. "And I just got finished saying what a great broad you were."

"A flack is a flack, and a former president is a news source," she said, shrugging her shoulders.

Barney leaned back and said to Mike: "Smart broad."

As the plane approached Manchester, Nora excused herself and went to the rear of the plane to talk to a woman reporter she knew. When she was gone, Barney looked at Mike with a wry expression.

"What's the matter with *you?*" Mike asked.

"Nora's a helluva researcher, and a looker, but why did you do it?"

"Because she can be damned good—and we're doing the column the way I want it done."

"That's the only reason? Not because you want to burn Tom? Or something else?"

"Like?"

Barney hesitated. "Mike," he said, finally, "it just doesn't look right. The girl has no real news experience."

The discussion clearly made Mike uncomfortable. "She worked for me for four years," he offered. "She had to learn *something.*"

Barney allowed himself the faintest smile toward his old friend. "I'd just be very careful about appearances if I were you," he said.

Mike was not amused. "Barney," he said, in a rare show of irritability for him, "why don't you just mind your own business?"

"Okay, pal. Just trying to alert you to the sensitivity of the situation."

It was snowing lightly when the jet set down in Manchester, but it was a pleasant, dry snow. The endless pines that covered the mountains off to the north hung heavy with whiteness. A high-school band in bright orange uniforms, with prancing majorettes in wispy skirts over white leotards, struck up a lively march as a large collection of local Democrats stood waving at Hacker, who was peering out from the front cabin. It was a crowd of hooded parkas and puffy goose-down ski jackets; of big fur hats, stocking caps pulled over ears, and red wool hunting caps with earflaps down; of heavy boots with corduroy trousers tucked in; of mittens and an occasional wool mask, with only eyes and nose exposed. It was, Barney remarked, too cold for sensible people to be out. But even in politics-hardened New Hampshire, the arrival of a former president was a special event.

Mike pointed out to Nora the assorted political notables: the mayors of Manchester and Nashua, the state party chairman and his wife, the party chairmen of Hillsborough, Rockingham, and Belknap counties—names that she had read in the column but to which no faces had ever before been attached. "You ought to introduce yourself to all of them," he told her. "They can all be helpful."

"Okay," she said. "But why don't you introduce me?"

"Because I'm your partner, not your nursemaid," he said, smiling. "It's better to establish your own relationship with these people. One thing to remember: these folks are politicked to death every four years. They're wary of everybody—candidates, pollsters, campaign workers, and especially us. They've had it all up to the ears. Don't try to con them about anything."

Nora listened intently, like a rookie quarterback being sent into a varsity game for the first time. Barney could barely suppress a smart-aleck remark, but he made the effort.

The press and television reporters and technicians filed off the plane first. As they waited for Hacker, about a dozen newsboys ran up and handed them Friday-morning copies of the *New Hampshire State News*, with Cormier's editorial across the top under the headline: "Hacker to N.H. Today to Reclaim Stolen White House." The editorial was all Barney had said it would be:

President Edwin Hacker, still the elected Chief Executive of the United States of America no matter what political larceny has been perpetrated against him by the knee-jerk, liberal Eastern Establishment press, returns to the Granite State this morning to launch his courageous bid to recapture the White House. With him, ironically, will be a host of the same journalistic jackals whose naked distortions and contrivances two years ago smeared this great and good American and contributed to the advancement of global communism by driving from the world scene one of its most effective arch foes.

Columnists like the notorious Michael Webb, a spider who has entangled more than one patriot in the strands of lies he spins, may not be paid agents of the Soviet Union. But they might just as well be, for the service they perform to the Communist conspiracy by seizing power from men like Edwin Hacker.

Faced with the prospect of Hacker's re-election this year, Webb's longtime partner in libel, Thomas Sturdivant, silver-spooned son of Schuyler Sturdivant of the New York publishing empire, has joined the staff of his brother, Sen. George Sturdivant of New York, in a direct effort to defeat Hacker in the New Hampshire primary. And in a thinly veiled deceit, Thomas Sturdivant's close "companion" of recent years, a young woman named Nora Williams, has been selected as stand-in for Sturdivant in the Webb-Sturdivant syndicated column, presumably until Sturdivant has dabbled in the game of politics long enough to undo Edwin Hacker again. The newspaper business is a rough game itself, and anyone who has been involved in it knows that a mere girl in her twenties does not get the plum of a syndicated column on her journalistic talent alone.

We do not foist the Webb column, which is undiluted garbage, on our readers. Those who do see it elsewhere are forewarned that this "arrangement" is likely to produce an unbroken series of favorable reports on George Sturdivant and gutter attacks on Edwin Hacker, to the point where it will be impossible to tell where the campaign propaganda leaves off and the Webb-Sturdivant-Williams column begins. . . .

The sheer outrageousness of Amos Cormier's editorials always amused the visiting Washington-based reporters. Nora, reading this one as she stood on the tarmac, said it was the most ridiculous thing she had ever seen in a newspaper. But Barney cautioned her.

"Don't kid yourself," he said. "This guy has clout up here. Manchester and the tight blue-collar knot around it, all the textile and shoe and other factory workers, have been reading Amos Cormier's editorials for breakfast every morning for most of their lives. They see the world in the same conspiratorial terms he does. For every voter who's laughing at him, three or four are shaking their heads and saying he's right."

"I can't believe that," Nora said. "This stuff is undiluted garbage. I could sue him for what he said about me."

"Sure you could," Barney said. "And draw even more attention to him. He'd love that."

At last, Hacker bounded down the stairs, his wife dutifully behind, and shook hands with the local notables. Then he moved swiftly to the airport fence to greet the modest crowd that had been assembled by the advance team. The Secret Service agents, who had joined him from the moment of his declaration of candidacy, were now in full control, and they were easy to identify: double-knit suits, trim haircuts, blank, searching eyes. They methodically scanned the crowd like a pack of humanoid radars.

"Look at the SS boys playing spook," Barney said to Nora, nodding toward the agents. "If I ever catch you with one of them, you're out of the union, understand?"

She obediently shook her head and suppressed a laugh. "They're wired, aren't they?" she asked, observing the conspicuous plugs in their ears and the tiny hand-mikes they palmed. "How does it work?"

"One wire from the earplug goes under the collar and another from the hand-mike runs up the shirtsleeve, to a small battery-operated radio transmitter strapped to the belt at the small of the back," Barney told her. "Broads have been electrocuted screwing around with those guys."

As Hacker worked the fence, Barney and Mike fell in closely behind, watching him perform his press-the-flesh specialty and keeping an eye on the people who reached out to him, taking particular note of the occasional oddball. The agents focused on the crowd, to the left and right of the candidate as he moved along the fence. Their eyes swept furtively and their lips whispered surreptitiously into the hand-mikes to some invisible superagent responsible for this contingent of a dozen government-issue body protectors.

As Mike and Barney pushed in close to the candidate, one of the agents stuck out his arm stiffly and blocked their way. They gave him a dirty look but respected the barrier. The "SS," as the reporters derisively called them, took themselves and their job seriously; the worst of them affected a bully-boy posture, not unlike junior safety patrollers at the street corners of America lording it over their schoolmates. The newer recruits especially were full of themselves, and of the idea that they were responsible for the safety of a presidential candidate.

In the campaign pecking order, they saw themselves as part of the staff, superior to the "newsies," as they contemptuously referred to the irreverent band of scribblers who were able to drink and horse around at will, while the agents were required to toe the line in a military way while on duty. They made up for it, of course, when they were not working, hustling the stewardesses as avidly and often more successfully than the media "animals." They were loyal to the candidate they served, not only in the performance of their official role but often politically and emotionally, especially with a man like Ed Hacker. The old law-and-order pitch went down well with them, and most were happiest when assigned to the hard-liners. In the past, the George Wallaces, the Spiro Agnews, and the Barry Goldwaters had been their favorites, because then their essentially dreary work became a labor of love. They served the George McGoverns and the Mo Udalls efficiently, but without the commitment they brought to the other assignments. The "newsies," for their part, reciprocated in spades the agents' animosity toward themselves, dismissing them as mindless automatons, in a manner that failed to appreciate their legitimate function.

Nora stood flat-footed as the candidate and the accompanying agents and reporters moved down the line. Suddenly, Hacker broke off, wheeled around, and climbed into a black limousine that was waiting at the fence, with two state troopers on motorcycles as escorts. The agents dashed to other cars in front and behind Hacker's car and the pool reporters—one from the AP, one from UPI, one from each of the networks and from the "specials," the daily newspapers sending their own correspondents—climbed into the next two cars to monitor the candidate at close range. The rest of the reporters raced to the press bus at the end of the motorcade. Mike was about to board when he turned and saw his new partner rooted on the tarmac. He waved to Nora impatiently and she finally came running. She was the last aboard the bus and walked a gauntlet of catcalls down the aisle to where Mike and Barney had saved her a seat.

"You almost got left behind," Mike said, in a tone of mild parental displeasure.

"Yeah, you better get your head in the game," Barney said, smiling.

"You left me standing there," she complained. "Why did you bother to go over to the fence? The pool was right there."

"Because you never know," Mike told her. "There's always the death-watch aspect to these things, as grisly as that sounds. You never know when somebody in the crowd is going to pull out a gun and short-circuit the whole process. Barney and I have seen for ourselves how unexpectedly it can happen. We were both there in Dallas, and in L.A. with Bobby; I was in Laurel with Wallace and in Memphis with King; Barney was in Sacramento and San Francisco with Ford. And when it happens, there's nothing like it; nothing as immediately terrifying—short of a battlefield."

She looked at him. "You *like* it?"

"No, of course, we don't *like* it. But to be there is to have brought home to you the brittleness of the whole system, the whole fabric."

Barney broke in. "Don't make it sound so goddamned noble, Mike," he said. "It's our fire engine coming out of the station, that's all. It goes, and we go after it. We hope it's a false alarm, of course. Remember in Miami with Reagan in 'seventy-six, when that guy pulled a toy gun on him? The adrenalin rush is the same whether the candidate gets shot or doesn't. But you want to be there."

"Not me," Nora said.

"No," Barney said. "You're a goddamned columnist now." His tone was suddenly harsh, and she flushed. She decided it was best to drop the subject.

The entourage drove from the airport to the Sheraton Wayfarer in the town of Bedford, just outside Manchester. The Wayfarer, a long, rambling motel that grows new wings every few years like a deer putting on antlers, is the nerve center of the New Hampshire primary. The networks come in early and book scores of rooms from late December through the primary in late February, and one or more of the candidates always uses the place as his headquarters. It is ideally suited for both candidate and the media, because it has an excellent restaurant, a lively bar and quiet rooms, some looking over a picturesque waterfall and pond. Also, it is just off a main highway from which the whole state is accessible. One can settle in at the Wayfarer and get to most parts of the state and back by car in a day. In a life in which such things as dependable laundry service and a mail drop take on inordinate importance, the Wayfarer is as close to a home as one can expect.

In a large conference center on the other side of the pond, accessible through an old covered, wooden bridge, the Hacker faithful had been collected for the New Hampshire kickoff of the campaign. About three hundred people were there, screaming their heads off, when Hacker came into the hall and onto the stage, his arms held aloft. The press entourage crowded in at long tables set to one side. The New Hampshire chairman for Hacker, a former senator who had retired to the ease and prestige of the federal bench through the good offices of the candidate, went directly to the microphone and introduced him as "the man you elected four years ago, and will elect again, as president of the United States, Edwin Hacker!"

Hacker, beaming, took the cheers, then began:

"I can't tell you how good it is to be back in New Hampshire. Four years ago, you good people started me on the road to the White House by giving me a stunning landslide victory. It isn't necessary for me to recite how I was later deprived of the presidency. You all know the story. I suppose that's why I'm here today. And why you're here. To demonstrate that the choice of a president is in the hands of the American people. Not the press or a few politicians."

The wire-service reporters, the stenographers of the trade, scribbled furiously in their notebooks, though it was the same old Hacker pitch.

90

Mike held a notepad and pencil in his hand from habit, but didn't bother to take anything down. That was one of the perks of writing a column.

"Because this is the case," Hacker continued, "I am announcing here that I propose as a candidate to make my views known not through the slanted prism of the traditional press conference, but through what I call a people's conference. You are the voters, not the gang of media celebrities who have trooped up here on my heels." Many heads turned toward the press tables, amid an audible murmur of hostility. "And so I want to answer *your* questions, and let *them* listen to what's on the minds of the people.

"You will see microphones in each of the four aisles here, at the front and halfway back. A member of my staff is at each of them to keep things running in an orderly fashion. Please step up with your question and identify yourself before asking it, and I'll try my best to answer. You can ask about anything you like. I've always said I have nothing to hide. Let's show the press how democracy really works."

As if on signal, individuals rose from their seats and moved to the microphones.

Mike and Barney, at a press table in front, turned around and watched, then looked at each other. "The fix is in," Mike said. His friend nodded.

The first questioner was a man who identified himself as Paul Trombley from Manchester. "I run a small clothing store on Main Street," he told Hacker. "I voted for you the last time and I'm going to vote for you this time. But what good is it for us to vote for a man like yourself and then have the special interests down in Washington just turn the results around? Just throw them out as though they never happened? What guarantee is there that if we elect you again that the same gang that got you the last time won't try it again? And won't succeed again?"

The crowd erupted in applause and cheers at the question, as if it were an answer.

Hacker smiled modestly, held up his hands for silence, and addressed the "unsolicited" question.

"I'm glad you asked that," he said. "It's a very legitimate question. The Founding Fathers in their wisdom established a definite procedure for removing a duly elected president. It is called impeachment. I realize now that while I may have served the country by stepping aside last time, it would have been better in the long run to have allowed that procedure to go forward."

"Here comes the civics lesson," Barney growled.

"Instead, the press, having trumped up the charges against me and magnified them out of all proportion, proceeded to hound me. They contended that my pursuit of my constitutional rights was paralyzing the conduct of the government. I could see for myself that there was a lot of truth to the contention. I was inundated with extraneous issues, to a point where my official responsibilities were being crowded out. And so, with the greatest misgivings, I agreed to resign."

A man in the crowd rose, cupped his hands to his mouth, and shouted: "What do they know?" Others turned to look at him, then cheered and applauded. Hacker acknowledged them with a wave of his hand and then, quieting them, went on:

"But I realize now, my good friends, that I served neither myself nor the national interest in doing so. What I did when I listened to those people was to become their accomplice in undermining our great system. I came to realize, too late, that it was my *obligation* to stand and fight—and many, many thousands of you wrote to tell me so then—against this undermining of the American Constitution itself."

There was more applause, but he talked over it. "It was my *obligation* to defend myself through the constitutional procedure of House impeachment and Senate trial, and to win vindication. Many people have asked me in the last two years, my friends, whether I have any regrets. I'm here today to tell you I deeply regret having permitted my enemies to persuade me to resign the presidency."

"So do we!" somebody called out.

"I'm here today to apologize to you, and to all the many millions of good people like you who did not want me to resign. Sure, there would have been an extended period of confusion and political contention had I stayed and fought. But that is what self-governing is all about. If we wanted the media or a few of their political henchmen to run this country without the inconvenience of public debate and controversy, we would have no need for a Constitution."

"Right!" a voice shouted.

"But we are a government of laws, not of men, no matter how many newspapers and television stations those men—or women—may control. Because I resigned, the media have grown unprecedentedly in power. Today we have a communications dictatorship, elected by no one, controlled by no one, wielding vast influence over every phase of life in America. This communications dictatorship must be brought to heel. It must be brought under the will of the American people, subject to the same laws that govern the rest of us."

The crowd suddenly was on its feet, cheering, fists shaking in the air. He continued:

"And so, as I embark on my campaign to win your primary, I pledge to you two things. First, that if I am re-elected—and I say re-elected because in justice I am still your elected president—and my enemies ever attempt to force me from office a second time, I will never resign!" The audience rose again, yelling and clapping. Hacker nodded, a smile now punctuating what had been a somber mien, and raised both his arms for quiet, so that he might proceed. "I will oblige the usurpers to put our great Constitution to the test. If that is done, both the Constitution and I will be vindicated."

More cheers and applause, and again a signal for quiet. "Second, if I am re-elected—*when* I am re-elected—I pledge that I will take the leadership in a broad-based citizens' effort to bring this unelected communications dictatorship to account to the people." Again the crowd rose, cheering. This time he let the enthusiasm mount and prevail; he stood at the microphone, confident but benign, as he gauged the effect of his words. Finally, he put up his hands again. The noise slowly subsided and he resumed.

"I pledge to you that I will make certain that these powerful communications conglomerates do not abuse the privileges bestowed upon them by the government to use the people's—I repeat, the people's—airwaves. I will make sure that the press does not forget that it too is a servant of the people. Because, my friends, the First Amendment was not written as a right of the rich and powerful to have singular influence in our society through monopolistic ownership of the printing press or television. It was included by the Founding Fathers to assure the rights of the people to know what their government was doing.

"As long as the media serves that responsibility, you will find that I will be their staunchest defender. But when they sink into character assassination and mass thought control, then it is incumbent upon the people's elected leaders to fight them tooth and nail. I pledge to you that when I am your president again, you will be ruled not by an unelected communications dictatorship but by the man you have selected at the ballot box—for four full years!"

The audience rose again, screaming, stamping feet, clapping. Hacker bathed in it; he held his hands over his head, yet toning down his defiant words as always with a broad, engaging smile. At one point he looked down into the press section, and Nora thought she saw him wink quickly at Barney Mulvihill. Reporters at the press tables turned to watch the unfolding phenomenon. As the applause continued, some men and women in the front rows began to call out to Hacker, and to the press tables.

"Give 'em hell, Ed! . . . Stick it to them! . . . How do you like that, you bastards!" Some shook their fists and a few extended what had come to be known as the Nelson Rockefeller finger of contempt.

"It's like the Goldwater convention in San Francisco in sixty-four," Mike said to Nora. "He stands up there, smiles as nicely as you please, and all the while he's tossing them raw steak. This is going to be one hell of a campaign."

"I can't believe it," she said. "Do these people actually believe that crap? Don't they see? It's so transparent it's embarrassing."

"Yeah," Barney put in. "That's what we said about Agnew. We told ourselves nobody would ever buy it, and before we knew it we were spending more time defending ourselves than doing our job. Hacker knows what he's doing. He could talk a dog off a meat wagon."

After the noise had subsided, the questions from the floor continued. They were all carefully planted among Hacker sympathizers, and again and again he returned to the same theme: that his power had been usurped by a runaway media, and that it wouldn't happen the next time.

Once, a young college student, clearly not a Hacker supporter, tried to get one of the microphones.

"Mr. Hacker! Mr. Hacker! What about the contributions? What about the ambassadorships?" he called out. Hacker "staff aides" immediately muscled him aside.

"Wait a minute!" he demanded. "Is this an open forum or not?"

"Boo! Sit down, bum!" voices in the audience yelled. "Get him out of here!"

The bedlam finally intimidated the young man and, "helped" by Hacker's people, he sat down in frustration.

"Goldwater in San Francisco, hell," Barney said. "Hitler in Nuremberg."

"You always get carried away," Mike told him.

"We'll see," Barney said.

When the question-and-answer period was over, Hacker stepped down from the stage and walked into the crowd. Men and women bunched around him at first, shaking his hand. But soon his aides and the Secret Service agents had herded the well-wishers into a long and orderly line stretching back up the center aisle to the rear of the hall. For nearly an hour, Hacker stood and greeted them as they filed by.

"They treat him as if he's still president," Nora remarked to Mike.

"Yeah, and he's playing it for all it's worth."

"But they're his people. They probably were bused in."

"Some, sure, but not all of them. And those cheers you heard when he started to ride us. There was nothing phony about them. We're his whipping boy, and we're a good one."

Nora watched Hacker closely as he greeted his supporters. She noticed that as each one approached, Hacker would immediately establish unshakable eye contact with the individual, seizing onto the eyes as firmly as the proffered hand, holding them fixedly with his own until the individual was past him and had let go of his hand.

"It's as if he's saying to each one, 'I see you. I recognize you as an individual,'" Nora noted to Webb.

"That's Hacker," he said. "He's very good at it. He's had practice."

As the greeters moved off, Nora saw that most wore looks of contentment. That was Hacker, too. It was not simply that he was a former president, although that was part of it. He had the ability to convey pleasure and a sense of fulfillment in others by his presence and his attentive manner. He didn't try to hurry this ritual. He acted as though he had all the time in the world and could think of nothing he would rather do than stand there and shake hands with a bunch of fawning strangers. When the last of the crowd had filed by, the candidate glanced over at the press table, observed his observers, and walked toward them.

"Well, boys and girl, what did you think? Did I get them or didn't I?"

"You got them," Barney acknowledged for the group. "But this is just New Hampshire."

"Just New Hampshire? You know better than that, Barney. If I can do it here, I'm on my way. I'm a winner again. Nobody will be able to lay a glove on me all the way to the convention."

Hacker reached over, took Nora's hand, and kissed it in his most courtly manner. "And now, my friends, I believe I shall retire." And he walked off, his attentive entourage behind him.

"Was I supposed to follow him, or what?" Nora asked.

"No, he'll send a lackey for you when he wants you," Barney said.

"You're not serious, are you?"

"No, I'm not. Ed Hacker seldom mixes business and pleasure."

Nora returned to her room to dress for dinner. She had slipped out of her clothes and was just running the shower when her phone rang. She was surprised, in light of what Barney Mulvihill had just said, when she recognized the voice of Ed Hacker on the other end. Would she care to drop by for a drink? And she was equally surprised to hear herself responding that she would.

9

As Nora Williams approached Edwin Hacker's suite, which was guarded by the ubiquitous Secret Service agents, she drew her notepad and a pen from her purse, a conscious attempt to set the ground rules of her visit. Yet she felt a pang of disappointment when her knock on the door was answered by the former president's wife.

"Good evening," she said smiling, "I'm Mildred Hacker. Please come in."

Nora walked into a large sitting room, where the man she had seen with Hacker at Paul Young's was lounging on a sofa. He rose halfway, reached over, shook her hand, and introduced himself as Leo Manasian, which of course she knew. He gave no sign that he recognized her. Then he introduced Bea Morrison. The woman merely nodded, neither smiling or rising.

"The president will be with us in a minute," Manasian said. "He's on an important phone call."

Mildred Hacker had already made a drink for Manasian and she handed it to him, then took Nora's order. Nora asked for a scotch, though she did not usually drink when she was working. It was part an intentional show of professional confidence, part the need for a bracer. She had never, after all, interviewed a former president before.

"How do you like being a famous columnist so suddenly?" Manasian asked.

Nora was defensive. "Oh, I'm not famous. It's Mike. He's being incredibly good to me."

"Well," Mildred Hacker said, "you must be very good to be given such an opportunity."

A voice called in from the next room. "I don't know how good she is, but she sure looks good," Ed Hacker boomed, strolling in, going directly to Nora, this time bending over and kissing her on the cheek. She smiled, but her hand tensed around her glass.

Hacker went to the bar, poured himself a bourbon and water, and returned to the sofa, sitting next to Nora, with Manasian on her other side. The former president immediately took over the conversation.

"Well, I just thought we ought to get acquainted, since it looks like we're going to be seeing a lot of each other," he said. Casually, he put his free hand on her leg, just above the knee, where the hem of her skirt touched, and he held it there. He did it as if he and the young woman were alone in some dark cocktail lounge. As far as his wife and his personal secretary were concerned, it was an invisible hand that had deposited itself with such familiarity on that desirable extremity. The move simply had not been made. Nora's first reaction was to try to squirm out from under, but she did not want to appear skittish. So she endured it, disappointed with herself at the same time for tolerating a gesture she abhorred.

"Let's face it," Hacker went on, "it's going to be difficult for you, what with your partner's demonstrated dislike for me and your boyfriend working for the other side. But I just want you to know that I think you'll try to give me a fair shake, and I intend to do the same for you."

"Mr. Hacker," she said, purposely not using his former title as a means of evening the odds, "I don't want you to be under any delusions. Mike Webb is a fair-minded, responsible journalist and you can expect a fair shake, as you put it, from both of us. And as for my 'boyfriend,' as you call him—God, I haven't heard that expression since my father used it when I was in high school—he's another news source, like yourself, as far as my job is concerned."

The Hand was still there, like an amputee's mechanical hook that everybody in the room is overly conscious of but studiously avoids staring at. Suddenly, Nora rose and took a step toward the bar.

"Could I have a little water in this?" she asked no one in particular. The Hand fell like a stone as her lap disappeared, and Hacker nearly lost his balance. Mildred Hacker got up at once. "Oh, I'm sorry, I'll get it for you," she said. "I always make the drinks strong for these men." She said it as if Bea Morrison were not also in the room, or so it seemed to the visitor.

Nora remained standing. It made her feel less of a captive. Manasian glanced quickly at Hacker, who for once was plainly embarrassed, then quickly away.

"Yes, of course. Young Sturdivant is just a news source now," Hacker said, easing off. "I didn't mean to suggest otherwise. What I mean to say is that I hope we can start with a clean slate, you and I. I want you to feel free in the weeks ahead to come and see me or Leo, or Bea, or even Mildred, about anything you want to know. Anything."

Nora glanced around the room and spied a copy of the local newspaper on an empty chair. She walked over, picked it up, folded it to show the front-page editorial, and handed it to Hacker.

"Okay," she said. "For openers, I'd like to know what this is all about."

Hacker took the paper, put on his reading glasses as if he did not know its contents, and began to peruse it. As he did, a grin came across his face, and then he gave way to open laughter.

"That Cormier! Isn't he a riot?" He looked up at her, mischievously. "The man will do anything to sell papers."

The color began to rise in Nora's face. "Is that what you call a fair shake?" she asked.

"My dear girl. It's a free press, isn't it? I can't tell him what to write and what not to write, just because he supports me. You're being too thin-skinned, if you ask me. Politics is a tough game to be in."

"But I'm not *in* politics. You are. I'm just trying to write about it."

Hacker smiled and turned to Manasian. "She's 'not *in* politics.' Did you hear that, Leo? Young lady, either you're pulling my leg or you've got a lot to learn. Given the circumstances, you're not just covering the story. You're part of the story. You can't avoid that. You may want to. But you can't."

"I'm part of the story only because he's writing that I am."

Bea Morrison, seeing that Nora was becoming agitated, spoke for the first time. "Look, Miss Williams," she said. "You have to know Amos Cormier. Nobody tells him what to do. Not even a former president. All we can do is give you our assurance that we've had nothing to do with it." It was not the sort of authoritative statement a mere secretary would make, and Nora made mental note of it.

"Exactly," Hacker interjected. "And we *will* have nothing to do with it. I can promise you that you'll never hear *me* raise the peculiar situation you're in. As far as I'm concerned, it's your business."

"'Peculiar situation'?" Nora repeated. "It's not a peculiar situation. Would you be saying that if I weren't a woman?" She hated to fall back on that crutch, but there it was. Manasian shot another look at Hacker, and Nora caught it, but said nothing.

"If you weren't a woman, and such a beautiful woman, I wouldn't have asked you here," Hacker said, playing the gallant again.

Nora was growing exasperated, yet intimidated by the Hacker charm.

"Mr. Hacker, you know what I mean."

"Yes, of course, and there may be something to what you say. But let's face it, Nora," he said, sliding into the first-name basis casually, "we live in a society that is not yet ready to deal with women on an equal footing with men, as much as you and I may deplore it." He said this as if his wife and Bea Morrison were not present. "If you were a man and had a girlfriend running the campaign of a presidential candidate, I doubt anyone would think much of it, let alone say anything about it. But you're not a man, and we're talking about the world as it is. I didn't make it that way."

"You didn't make it at all, Ed," Mildred Hacker suddenly put in. "In seven days or any other period of time."

Nora and Leo Manasian laughed, but not Hacker and Bea Morrison. Still, the tension eased. Nora was surprised to hear the wisecrack from the former first lady, and liked her for it. Hacker seemed not to have understood, or at least not to have paid attention. Manasian, taking advantage of the laughter, tried his confidential approach. They had asked her to come, he told Nora, partly because they wanted to get along with everybody in the press, and partly because they figured they needed an intermediary with Webb, after all that had happened.

"I'm really not an ogre," Hacker said. Nora was now sitting in an armchair, more confident than she had been when she first walked in and encountered The Hand. "Sure, I say some outlandish things about the press, but that's all part of the game," he told her. "You kick me and I kick you. The voters love it."

"But you really believe the press was responsible for your resignation out of some personal hatred?" Nora asked.

"Well," Hacker said, "you'll have to admit that a case can be made. I know you folks are just doing your job as you see it. I see it from a different perspective, and I think a lot of folks agree with how I see it. I just try to increase the numbers. Can you blame me?"

Nora was growing impatient. "Mr. Hacker," she asked, "what is it you really want from me?"

Bea Morrison coolly answered for him: "Miss Williams, it's probably insulting for us to say this to you, and the wrong thing, but maybe we've got some reason to be concerned. All we want is for you to cover us like the pro we know you are. I don't think you realize the pressures you're going to have on you before this thing is over. No doubt you're going to have plenty of access to the other side. We'd just like for you not to forget that we're here, that we have a point of view, and you can have access to us. All we're interested in is fairness, and we know you are too."

What Nora knew now was that she had to get out of there.

"Fine," she said, placing her drink on a coffee table in front of her.

"I appreciate your concern, and I can assure you I'll bend over backward to be fair. Even with my peculiar situation."

She tried not to put too much bite into this last. It seemed to go over Hacker's head. He was flashing his broadest, most winning smile, and he rose, reached over, and pulled her against him, kissing her again on the cheek. She woodenly shook hands with Manasian and Mildred Hacker, nodded to Bea Morrison, then turned and walked out. Hacker winked at Manasian as Nora reached the door.

"Jesus," she said aloud as soon as she was out in the hallway. "Wait until Mike hears this."

Mike Webb was in the bar when Tom Sturdivant came in. Tom spied his former partner, hesitated for a moment, but when Mike turned his head and saw him, he walked quickly over. Mike took notice that the swagger was back in Tom's step. Clearly he was feeling better about himself and his decision.

"Mike," he said, "can we talk?"

"Why not?"

"Let's take a table."

Mike picked up his drink and the two men went to a corner of the bar, out of earshot of the crowd.

"Well?"

"Look, Mike, what's done is done," Tom said. "We've got to move on. We both have a job to do up here."

"Getting your lines out, are you?" Mike answered, not bothering to veil the sarcasm.

Tom ignored the crack. "George would like to talk to you. He realizes the tension but he wants you to be plugged in to what we're doing, directly from him. He wants you to ride with us tomorrow."

"Does he?"

"Mike, it's not a bad thing to have a candidate offer to let you have a good look inside."

"At what price?"

"At no price. We're on the side of the angels on this one. We don't need to do any selling. But we may come up with some stuff you can use, and it's to our mutual advantage if it comes out in a responsible column."

"You can give it to the AP."

"Come on, Mike, don't be a thickhead. We both know how this business works. You've got ten times as much clout as the wire services on political stuff."

"Why come to me? Why not work through Nora? She's an equal partner now. She's the new Tom Sturdivant."

"Because I know who runs the column. . . . And besides, I wouldn't feel right."

Mike looked at him, then laughed. "You feel you can put it to her only one way at a time, is that it?"

Tom tensed. "Mike, don't be a bastard. It doesn't become you."

Mike took a long drink, then set his glass down carefully in the wet ring it had already made on the table. "Tom," he said, "you have to understand something. The whole world, including Ed Hacker, is just waiting for the first time they can say the column has become George Sturdivant's house organ. You've made this a very dicey situation for me. And the thing with you and Nora makes it that much tougher. But I can't abstain from covering this campaign. You'd better be very careful, and very right, about anything you try to peddle to me."

"I know that," Tom said, earnestly. "What I'm trying to say to you is that George doesn't want you to shut him off just because of what's happened. He admires you and he values your friendship."

Mike looked up to the ceiling and down again. "Don't lay the friendship bit on me," he said. "When a man runs for president, friendship goes on hold until after the election. Don't insult me with such crap, will you?"

Tom smiled. "You know," he said, "I sometimes think your mother was frightened by a high-school journalism teacher. If George got into a real bind and called on you, do you mean to tell me you'd turn your back on him?"

"Tom, you know I'd give George my last buck. For a square meal.

But not as a campaign contribution. As long as he's running, he's got to expect that if I catch him with his hand in the cookie jar, I'm going to blow the whistle as loud as I can."

"Sure, we know that. That's no problem. George is so honest it's pathetic. What we would be more comfortable knowing is that you won't feel compelled to lay off the other guy, for fear it will look like you're doing our work."

"Are you kidding?"

"No. It could happen. Hacker has already started to stick it to you. . . . Was it really wise to take Nora on, under the circumstances?"

Mike leaned back, so he could take Tom in fully. "So that's it," he said. "It makes you uncomfortable, does it? Would you feel better if I bounced her out of a job? Then, I take it, you would haul her in out of the cold and be a big hero. God, you are one sweetheart."

"Don't be ridiculous. Nora would no more work for a politician than you would. I found that out. But you *are* putting her under a lot of pressure."

"I am? Look, buddy, you're the one who's sleeping with her, not me. If anybody is—you'll pardon the old-fashioned expression—compromising her, it's you, not me."

Tom looked squarely at Mike and was about to speak when he saw Nora approaching. He rose as if to embrace her, but she slipped around the table to the opposite side and took a seat. She said nothing but was clearly trying to catch Mike's eye. Tom read the signal and excused himself, throwing some bills on the table for the check as he walked off.

The moment Tom was gone, Nora leaned over confidentially. "You will not believe what just happened to me," she said.

"Try me."

"I got a call from Hacker, asking me over for a drink."

"Oh? He works fast."

"When I got there, his wife, his 'secretary'" (this time with raised eyebrows) "and Leo Manasian were there."

"How disappointing for you."

"Don't be a smart-ass."

Nora recounted the conversation, and Mike nodded as he listened. Only when she told the Saga of The Hand did he permit himself a wan smile. She was disappointed. She thought she had recaptured it in all its comic outrageousness.

"Just your basic intimidation of a young reporter," Mike said when she had concluded. "Don't let it bother you."

"It doesn't. It's just that I'm surprised they could be so heavy-handed about it."

"That's their style. They want to make you nervous. They figure if I have a squirrelly dame on my hands I'll be too busy to go after them."

"A squirrelly dame?"

"Just an expression. But don't let them turn you into one. Ignore them."

"I already have. . . . What did Tom want?"

"A little of the same, from the other side."

"What do you mean?"

"George is afraid I'll pull my punches on Hacker to prove I'm fair."

"Oh, terrific."

"And he suggested you were maybe too much baggage for me to carry."

"Oh, really terrific. Why?"

"Because they could accuse you of being vulnerable to . . . Tom."

"He said that?"

"I didn't make it up."

Nora frowned and began distractedly picking at a bowl of potato chips on the table, fishing out the larger ones, breaking them in half, then in half again, and again, until she had a pile of crumbs in front of her. Mike watched her but said nothing.

"Well," Nora said at last, looking down at the debris and avoiding his eyes, "I don't think you're going to have to worry about that."

"Why?"

"Mike, I feel uncomfortable talking about it to you."

"Okay."

"I care for Tom very much."

"And?"

"I feel I need him . . . when I'm in over my head."

"Well, then?"

"But I know it's impossible."

"Nora, this campaign won't last forever."

"I know, but I can't take any chances. You're giving me the greatest opportunity of my life, and I can't blow it."

"Look, I never asked you to give up Tom, and I'm not asking you now."

"Aren't you?"

"No. Why should I?"

She looked blankly at him. There was an awkward pause, and then she said, "I'm going to do it anyway."

"Just like that? In cold blood?"

"I wish you wouldn't put it like that," she said. "I just know that when the time comes to make a break, you have to do it cleanly."

Mike studied her. "It would jolt Tom, do you know that? He's never been denied anything he's wanted. He's so sure of you."

"I can't help that. I've learned it's the only way."

"Yeah? How does somebody learn a lesson like that?"

She paused again, as if debating with herself whether to go on. She looked off again, avoiding Mike's eyes, and finally continued. "Once, a few years ago, I was driving home late one afternoon and this cat darted into the street. I hit it. I couldn't avoid it. It was all smashed up, but it wasn't dead. A little girl was on the sidewalk and she bent over it. It was howling in agony—"

She stopped abruptly and looked up at Mike, biting her bottom lip.

"And?"

"And so," she said, "I got out of the car, went over and—killed it."

"You killed it? How?"

"With my hands. I broke its neck."

"You what?"

"I twisted its neck until it snapped. . . . It was the only thing I could do."

Mike stared at her. "And what about the little girl?"

"I explained to her that the cat was suffering. . . . And I brought her a new one the next day."

"And that was it?"

"Yes. That was all I could do."

"And now it's going to be Tom's neck?"

"I wouldn't put it that way."

Mike took another drink. He looked at her and felt a coldness moving up his back. "I'm sure glad I'm not in his shoes," he said.

She frowned again. A forlorn look came over her for a moment. Then she took a drink from his glass, set it down, and, nervously, half-smiled at him.

10

A chauffeured maroon Cadillac stopped at a side entrance of the Wayfarer. Ed Hacker, Leo Manasian, and Bea Morrison, all bundled in heavy coats against the bitter early-evening cold, quickly got in, and the car moved out into the clear night. Within twenty minutes, it pulled past a guarded gate and up a long driveway to a huge old house that might have been mistaken for a country inn. A tall, athletic-looking man in his fifties stood on the porch. He wore a red-and-black lumberjack's shirt, and high laced boots with brown corduroy trousers tucked into the tops.

"Mr. President, so good of you to come," Amos Cormier said, extending his hand.

Hacker introduced Manasian and Morrison to the publisher. Cormier led the three into the house, where a butler dressed like a handyman took their coats, and then showed them into a spacious living room. A crackling fire was burning in a marvelous old stone fireplace. Cormier had the handyman-butler serve drinks all around and they all settled into the deep brown leather chairs and sofa.

"Well, you're here," Cormier said, robustly, "and you're on your way."

"I hope so," Hacker said.

"What did you think of my editorial this morning?" the publisher asked.

"Fine, it was fine, Amos," the candidate said, "but there's always a problem of laying it on too thick. We don't want to create any backlash for the opposition."

Cormier laughed. "Backlash? There's no such thing up here," he said. "I've been writing tough pieces here for fifteen years and the readers can't get enough of them. When I get through with Webb and Sturdivant and all that gang, they'll be lucky to get out of the state without being lynched."

Manasian smiled, a bit nervously. "That may not be the best thing for the president, though, Mr. Cormier," he said. "It won't look good, out of the state especially, if it appears he's just parroting your editorials, or that we're writing them for you."

Cormier scowled at Manasian. "The trouble with you professional politicians," he said, "is that you try too hard to figure all the angles. You want to hit the opposition but you want to be safe, too. Well, I never got anywhere in this world pulling my punches."

Bea Morrison tried her luck. "As you know, Mr. Cormier," she began, "the central theme of our campaign is that the press was responsible for President Hacker being forced out of office. We're just a little concerned that if you're out there backing us to the hilt all the time, it could erode that theme. You are, after all, part of the press."

"Young lady," Cormier replied, "I can tell you just don't understand New Hampshire. "I'm not *part* of the press up here, I *am* the press. Nobody pays any attention to any of the other papers. And they don't look upon me as part of the rest of the press. I've worked for years persuading my readers that my loyalty is to them, not to some phony journalistic fraternity. That's why I print so many letters to the editor. I make them feel it's *their* paper. Why do you think I'm able to attack the rest of the press so effectively myself? I'm the best thing you've got going for you up here, and you're telling me to cool it?"

"Of course not, Amos," Hacker said, playing the diplomat. "It's just that we want to coordinate the campaign, to make sure we're all working together, toward the same objective."

"Listen, Mr. President," Cormier said with a touch of sarcasm, "nobody tells me what to put in my newspaper, or how to put it. Because nobody knows my state or my people better than I do. Instead of coming in here and trying to tell me how to write my editorials, you ought to be asking *me* how you should run your campaign."

Hacker backed off. "Certainly, Amos. That's why we're here. We want to go over our battle plan with you. To get your suggestions. You remember I phoned you before I announced I would enter this primary."

"Sure, you touched base."

"But we've got to be honest with each other."

"Here it comes," Cormier said, his eyes shooting to the ceiling.

"You're a very controversial figure up here, you have to acknowledge that," Hacker said.

"I make no apologies for it."

"You shouldn't. But the fact remains that you have your enemies as well as your friends. And the thing is, your friends are my friends. I already have them, Amos."

"And so my editorials won't bring you any new support; is that what you're telling me?"

Hacker simply nodded.

Cormier got up and stoked the fire. He went to the mantelpiece and, to Hacker's and Manasian's surprise and Bea Morrison's consternation, took a pistol down, waving it in front of him.

"I always have one of these close at hand," he said. "Because I know the intensity of feeling I generate. People either love me or they hate me. That's a good part of my power. Every election up here of any significance is a referendum on me, whether you like to face that fact or not. And this one will be no exception. I'm going to see to that."

"Don't you want the president back in the White House?" Manasian asked.

"Of course. But in my state, I know best how to accomplish that. The thing you don't seem to realize is that *my* people vote. The people who can't abide me are fed up by now. Unless there's some compelling cause to stir them, like a war, they stay home. They've given up. Everybody says, 'Why don't *they* do something about Amos Cormier? It's always why don't *they* do something. Well, there is no 'they' anymore. No matter what I say, they don't pay any attention. The name of the game is getting your own people worked up so they turn out. And I know how to do that—better than anybody."

Bea tried again. "But New Hampshire is only the start of the process," she said. "The president is going to have to go on from here, to other primaries in other states. That's why we're concerned about overkill. Just as you don't want to be labeled as anybody's man in your state, the president can't afford to be labeled Amos Cormier's man elsewhere."

Cormier toyed with the pistol. It was part of his act and they all knew it, but it was disconcerting. "That's your problem," he said, pointing the gun at her by way of punctuating his remarks. "If you hope to win in New Hampshire, or even come close, he's going to have to be Amos Cormier's man. It's as simple as that. And you don't have to worry about me getting in the way of your message. God, there's nobody in creation who's more critical of the press than I am. I've known for years how much political mileage there is in that pitch."

Cormier walked over and put the pistol back on the mantelpiece. The gesture signaled that he considered that part of the discussion ended. He clearly had no intention of trimming his sails in any way to accommodate himself to the Hacker campaign, and the others realized there was no sense pursuing the matter further. They knew that in Amos Cormier they had a mixed blessing, and they did not care to diminish the positive part in a futile attempt to diminish the negative. And maybe he was right that there was no such thing as overdoing a good thing in "his" state.

As they talked, the handyman-butler appeared at the door with a squint-eyed little man who had a distinctly furtive look about him, as if he always expected to be attacked from behind.

"Ah, Governor," Cormier said, not rising but merely nodding to Charles Granger. "You know President Hacker. And his associates, Mr. Manasian and Miss Morrison." They shook hands all around.

"You're just in time," Cormier said. "We were about to sit down to dinner."

"Could I have a drink?" the governor of the state of New Hampshire asked, sounding almost as though he expected to have his request turned down.

"Sure, Charlie, but take it to the table," Cormier said, glancing at his watch.

The host led his guests into a long, high-ceilinged dining room with a huge table in the center and an ancient glass chandelier overhead. He gestured for them to take seats at one end and he settled into a thronelike armchair at the head of the table. During dinner, Leo Manasian laid out the detailed planning for the campaign. The target was the heavy blue-collar vote in the cities of Manchester, the state's largest, and Nashua, and in a geographical crescent that ran from just north of Manchester in a southern and southwesterly arc encompassing New Hampshire's recent population growth. Into the crescent had come a steady flow of factory workers from the Boston and Worcester areas, seeking to escape urban sprawl and ever-escalating Massachusetts taxes. Thanks largely to Cormier, and a series of hand-picked conservative governors elected by dint of the Cormier political magic, New Hampshire had neither a sales tax nor a personal income tax. That fact was a magnet for new residents. The current beneficiary of the Cormier anointing, and of the voters' almost single-minded determination to remain free of these taxes, was Charles Granger. In Cormier's presence he was an obedient lackey, but elsewhere he was a cannonball on the deck of a rolling ship. His suggestion for dealing with airplane hijackings, for example, was to hang apprehended offenders on the spot at airport terminals. The feeling among Hacker, Manasian, and Bea

Morrison was that Charlie Granger and his notions were maybe just a little too much of a good thing. They hoped, obviously, to enlist Cormier's help in seeing to it that while the governor of the great State of New Hampshire endorsed Hacker, he could be persuaded to keep a low profile. Hacker had hoped to discuss the matter with Cormier before Granger's arrival, but there had not been time.

During a lull in a Cormier monologue about how politics was played in New Hampshire, Hacker made his move. "Governor," he asked blandly, "what are your own plans for the next several weeks?"

"Mr. President," Granger said eagerly, "I'm at your disposal. Anticipating your arrival, and your campaign here, I've cleared my desk. If you want, I'll be at your side all the way."

Hacker glanced at his two associates. "Well, that would be fine," he said to Granger. "But you're much too busy a man for that. I wouldn't impose on you."

"It's no imposition," Granger said. "It'll be my pleasure."

Cormier quickly recognized the situation. "Charlie," he said abruptly, "I think you need a vacation."

"What?" Granger said, a puzzled look coming over his face. . . .

"You've been working too hard."

"No I haven't, Amos," he said. "The legislature is doing practically nothing this winter."

"All the more reason for you to get away," Cormier said. "Why don't you go down to Jamaica for a few weeks? It'll do you good."

"In the middle of the primary? I can't do that. I can't desert the president here." Granger laughed nervously as he began to feel the squeeze.

"You won't be deserting him, Charlie," Cormier said with naked brutality. "You'll be helping him."

"What do you mean?"

"You know what I mean. He can't afford your runaway mouth, Charlie. I've told you all along it was going to get you into trouble."

"But I'm up for re-election myself in the fall. How would it look?"

"How would it look if I came out for somebody else, Charlie?"

"You wouldn't do that."

"Try me."

Granger was mortified, especially at having this conversation in the presence of "President" Hacker. He looked solicitously at Cormier. "Amos, I don't want to leave the state with all those national reporters here. Roger Mudd was in to see me today, did you know that?"

"Terrific, Charlie," Cormier said. "But there's only one member of the media you have to worry about, and you're having dinner with him."

Granger did not reply, and the others busied themselves with the food before them.

"I don't like Jamaica," he said finally. "Does it have to be Jamaica?"

"No," Cormier said. "You can go to Hoboken, for all I care."

"I don't like Hoboken either," Granger said, smiling, looking around at the others to be sure they understood he had a sense of humor.

"How about if I get you invited to attend some intergovernmental conference in Europe?" Cormier said. "You'd have to go, wouldn't you? An official responsibility?"

"All right," Granger said, weakly.

"Good," Cormier said, winking at Hacker. "Then it's settled. Have some more roast beef, Charlie?"

"Well," Hacker said to his two companions as they drove back to the Wayfarer later, "one out of two ain't bad. We've got Charlie on the shelf for the duration. We'll just have to live with Amos."

"Better with than against," Manasian put in.

"Especially with that gun," Bea Morrison said. "Is he kidding with that thing?"

"It's a helluva prop," Hacker said. "Maybe I should start toting one myself. I could say it's for protection from the press." He laughed at his own joke.

"That's all you need," she said. "You better not get a ticket for jaywalking while you're up here."

"Me?" Hacker said, feigning shock. "Honey, I'm clean. Everybody knows that."

She looked at him and smiled. "Well," she said, "you're careful, anyway."

11

Mike Webb lay on his back in the motel room, his eyes open but able to perceive only shadows and shapes in the dark. Finally, the phone rang. He had been waiting impatiently for it.

"Good morning, sir," the voice of the motel operator said. "It's five o'clock, Saturday, January fifteenth. Senator Sturdivant's party is leaving from the front entrance at five-forty-five."

"Thanks. What's the weather?"

She laughed. "We only have two kinds of weather in Manchester at this time of year, sir," she said. "Clear and cold and wet and cold. It's clear and cold."

Webb swung his legs over the side of the double bed and without bothering to flick on the light made his way to the bathroom. That was one of the utilitarian marvels of American motel architecture. In Manchester, New Hampshire, or in Keokuk, Iowa, the route was nearly always the same; out the right side of the bed, three steps forward, turn right, three more steps, right again into the bath, light switch on the wall just inside, chest-high. Webb liked to see, in the midst of a frenetic campaign, whether he could make it into the bathroom before his mind focused on what city or town he was in. This time, though, the motel operator had spoiled the game with her weather report.

Webb stripped off his shirt of the previous day. By sleeping in it, he did not have to pack sleepwear and thus saved space in his bag—another sign of the experienced traveling man. He turned on the shower and soaped himself under a stream as hot as he could stand, the pelting water reviving him. Then, gradually, he lowered the temperature of the water, to warm, lukewarm, then cool, then icy cold. He stood unyielding against the spray. The old gag, that a man who says he enjoys a cold shower in the morning will lie about anything, did not apply to him. It was, doubtless, part of Mike Webb the morning person, a man who hit the ground running at the start of a day. In that sense, he betrayed the stereotype of the newspaperman as inveterate keeper of late hours, and his early and energetic start was all the more remarkable because, these days at least, he was able to sleep so little.

Webb stepped out of the shower, shivering, toweled himself off quickly and shaved. He walked to his open bag, extracted a pair of thermal underwear, and pulled it on. He slipped a heavy blue turtleneck sweater over his head and found a pair of gray flannel trousers and a black tweed wool jacket to buttress himself against the New Hampshire cold. He put on work boots and a tan, large-buttoned car coat, picked up his portable typewriter, and went out into the motel corridor. He walked to the front desk and then outside. For all his preparations, the biting cold caused him to catch his breath. It was still dark and the sky was starless. Members of the Sturdivant entourage and the press corps stood stamping their feet and clapping their gloved hands together, their breath raising white puffs in the air as they spoke.

Tom Sturdivant spied him and walked over. "Good morning, Mike," he said. "Do you want to ride with us to the first stop?"

"Sure."

George Sturdivant came out, looking a bit hung over.

"You all right?" his brother asked him.

"Yeah," the senator said. "I just stayed up too late last night going over those position papers you unloaded on me. Frankly, I think it's a waste of time and energy to talk about national health insurance. Hacker is what people have on their minds."

"I know," Tom said, "but you can't be a Johnny-one-note. You have to be *for* something."

George Sturdivant shrugged and turned to greet Webb. His handshake was perfunctory compared to the viselike grip of an Ed Hacker. Glad-handing and backslapping did not come naturally or easily to the senator from New York. No aspect of campaigning, for that matter, came easily. As he stood there in the frigid New Hampshire early morning, he grimaced against the wind—a blue blood who would much rather have been warming his blue blood before a blazing fire inside. Embarking on an appeal to strangers in an unfamiliar state to choose him over a disgraced former president plainly did not thrill him. The choice seemed to him to be so obvious that it was demeaning even to have to make the pitch. But George Sturdivant knew it had to be done and so he steeled himself.

"Let's go. I'm freezing," he said to his brother, getting into the rear of the waiting first car of the small motorcade.

Tom nodded to Webb to get in beside the senator, then sat next to the driver. Other reporters streamed out of the motel and into a chartered bus, two cars behind the candidate's.

"Where's Nora this morning?" George Sturdivant asked, first of his brother, then of Webb when Tom did not reply.

"She's going out with Hacker today," Webb said. "He doesn't start as early as you do."

The motorcade pulled away from the Wayfarer and swung onto the Everett Turnpike, south toward Nashua.

"Well, Mike, here we go," the senator said. "What do you think?"

"I think like always," Webb said. "It's always a fair fight up here, so it's up to you."

"I don't know," George Sturdivant said. "It's such a goddamned tiny state. And more conservative than the rest of the country. Look what happened to Muskie up here, and Romney, and Rockefeller."

"Yeah," Webb said. "But what about McCarthy and McGovern? They didn't win here, but they surprised everybody by running strong, and it was just as good."

"Well, I can't afford a strong second. If Hacker wins here, he's back in business, and you know it. It'll be like Nixon in sixty-eight when he won up here. All that about him being a loser after sixty, and sixty-two in California, was wiped out overnight. It would have been better for me to take Hacker on in a bigger, more liberal state. But you can't duck New Hampshire. It puts a whammy on the whole system; if you skip it, you're a coward. It's ridiculous."

"Maybe," Webb said, "but I like it myself. Don't let the picturesque towns and the white church steeples fool you. This state's becoming more industrial every year, especially down this way, with the spillover from Boston. And the people are savvy politically. They've seen and heard everything by now. If I were a candidate, I'd just as soon take my chances here as anywhere else."

"If I could believe you," the senator said, "I'd feel better. But with Cormier propagandizing every day in his paper, it's going to be hard to get at Hacker. I don't want to make a martyr out of the guy. But it's ludicrous on its face. A man forced out of the White House in disgrace with the gall to ask the voters to put him back in."

"Gall he's got," Webb said, "in spades."

"Well, I can't let people forget who he is, what he's done. If I had him to deal with alone, I'd feel a lot better. But with Walter Grafton running here too, it could be trouble. I can't afford to have liberal votes drained off to him."

"Have you made any effort to keep him out?" Webb asked. "Have you talked to him?"

"To Grafton? The original cigar-store Indian? It would be a waste of breath. He's waited a long time for this shot, and he's pissed off at me for getting in. He must know he can't be nominated, with or without me running. But he's bull-headed. He's the Scoop Jackson of the eighties."

"Scoop thought he could win," Webb said. "You guys are like that. All of you. People around you tell you how great you are and you believe it. The thing is, most of you have suspected as much all along."

The senator laughed. "Yeah, I guess you're right. That's why I had to have Tom with me. He won't bullshit me like the others. . . . I hope you understand, Mike. That I need him . . . I wouldn't have asked him if I didn't."

Webb said nothing. He watched Tom Sturdivant's reaction. The younger brother was turned in his seat, listening to the conversation. Tom looked at the senator coldly, as if trying with his gaze to force a shift of subject.

"Sure," Webb said finally. "Forget it. You need him, and I don't."

An awkward silence took over. Tom turned and faced the front again, busying himself studying a road map that he already knew by heart. As the motorcade glided quietly through the approaching dawn, Webb brought the conversation back to the Sturdivant campaign strategy, eliciting the stuff of which the next column would be fashioned. There was a debate going on within the Sturdivant campaign: whether the candidate ought to keep hammering at the old charges against Hacker, or let the familiar record go unmentioned. The senator felt the public needed its memory constantly refreshed; his brother argued that continued attacks would play into Hacker's hands.

When George Sturdivant asked Webb what *he* would do, Webb was curt and adamant. "I'm reporting on this campaign," he said. "Ask your brother. That's what you've got him for."

As Webb took notes, George Sturdivant watched him uneasily. Webb caught the apprehension, the concern of the politician that he might be saying something that, if printed, could cast him in a bad light.

"We're just talking now," the senator said, hoping the words might persuade Webb to cease scribbling. "Just between us."

Webb looked up from his notepad. "What does that mean?"

"Well, I just wanted your advice."

Webb addressed his former partner. "Tom, straighten out your brother, will you? Remind him that you're the one in the advice-giving business now. I'm not along for the ride; I'm working. I'm not here to satisfy my curiosity."

"Don't get excited," Tom said. "George didn't mean anything by it. . . . But how *are* we talking?"

"Listen, you can't have a private conversation with me anymore. Don't you know that? What you say, you can expect to read in the column. You want to talk on background, without attribution, okay. I'll accept that if you feel more comfortable with it. But I'm not on your team."

"Of course we know that," Tom said.

"Tom, it may be impossible for me to cover this campaign, the way things are now. And especially with Hacker trying to make me out as a mouthpiece for you. And I can't put Nora on this campaign, that's for sure."

"Why not?" George asked.

Webb looked at Tom, then shook his head, but said nothing.

The motorcade pulled up to the main gate of a large factory in Nashua that manufactured women's sweaters. It was a four-story red-brick affair with old-fashioned wooden fire escapes, where in summertime the workers often sat and ate their lunch. But now icicles hung from them and they were not good for much of anything, including escape, because they were in dire disrepair, some with no ladders from one floor level to the next. On the ground floor, next to the entrance where the workers punched in, was a thrift shop where seconds and imperfects could be bought retail. George Sturdivant stepped out, turning the collar of his coat up around his neck, and took his place at the narrow entrance. Workers were just coming on for the morning shift and, as each one went by, the candidate extended his hand. Most shook it in a detached, unenthusiastic way; some shyly looked at the ground as they passed; a few muttered some hostile remark about "all politicians" and brushed by; occasionally, one would take George Sturdivant's hand animatedly, commend him for the job he was doing, and pledge support.

Webb watched this political tribal rite he had seen performed by countless candidates in countless earlier campaigns, in New Hampshire and at factory gates across the country. Whether the exercise won many votes or not, no one could tell. But it met certain other campaign criteria; it was "a good visual," providing action that could be captured by the television cameras; it was early, that is, it took place in plenty of time for the film or tape to be shipped to New York for processing and use on the early-evening news shows; it was "genuine," that is, it showed the candidate with real voters, getting out "among the people," without which no candidate could profess to know what was on their minds. The fact that there was no opportunity for an exchange of serious talk did not matter in the scheme of things. The candidate was qualifying himself to report to other voters on how he had met the working people of the country and understood their deepest and most heartfelt concerns.

When the shift was inside the plant, the senator got back into his car.

"Are you coming with us?" Tom Sturdivant asked Webb.

"No, thanks. I've got enough for now," Webb said evenly. "I'll ride the rest of the way with the troops."

"Whatever you want," Tom said.

Webb walked back and got aboard the press bus.

"Aha, the columnist goes slumming," said Ray MacIntosh, the political writer of the *New York News,* sitting up front. A cherub-faced man in his mid-thirties with the chutzpah and ego of a Sammy Glick, he was only half as good as he thought he was, but that, it had to be said, was good enough. "Did you get the straight word coming over here, Mike? Or did you give it?"

Webb ignored him, or did his best at what was an impossible task. He spied Barney Mulvihill sitting toward the rear, walked down the narrow aisle, and took the seat beside him.

"You've got Ray worried," Mulvihill said. "He'll be chewing his knuckles all day, afraid you've got something that'll make him look bad to his desk in New York."

"Yeah," Webb said. "We won't have to bother giving him The Treatment today." The Treatment was a stunt with which Mulvihill and Webb had amused themselves when MacIntosh, insecure for all his brashness, first joined the political beat, two presidential campaigns earlier. When they were certain he was watching them, they would start, in their most surreptitious manner, to "read" a blank sheet of paper, whispering serious asides. MacIntosh's curiosity and nervousness would get the best of him and he would "casually" approach them. But the paper would be whisked quickly and conspicuously into a breast pocket, a maneuver that only intensified his jitters. Sometimes, in a busy pressroom, Webb or Mulvihill would start typing furiously, at the same time trying—without success, of course—to feign an air of normalcy. MacIntosh would immediately tumble, and in short order would stroll "casually" by and read the smoking if ersatz copy over the writer's shoulder as it poured from the typewriter. It took only a few applications of The Treatment, however, before MacIntosh caught on. He was smart and hardworking; his insecurity was as unnecessary as his chutzpah and egoism were unbecoming. Still, he continued to have an inflated opinion of himself, and so Mulvihill and Webb could seldom resist applying the needle.

"How'd it go?" Mulvihill asked Webb of his session with the Sturdivant brothers.

"Oh, I got a piece out of it," he said. "The predictable internal debate about how to handle Hacker. They've done nothing to try to get Grafton out, can you believe it?"

"I'm not surprised," Mulvihill said. "George has always been a procrastinator. . . . Where's Nora this morning?"

"She going to do Hacker today."

Mulvihill seemed about to say something, then hesitated, but finally went on: "Mike, how's that going to work out? I mean, she's a terrific broad, but can she cut it in this league? Hacker's going to try to murder you with that connection."

"I know, Barney."

Mulvihill eyed his old friend carefully. "Why did you do it, Mike? . . . You're not making her, are you?"

Webb smiled. "Barney, if you weren't real, you'd have to be invented, do you know that?"

Mulvihill grinned in return. "Well, now that we're talking about it, nothing else makes sense. . . . Were you *that* pissed off at Tom?"

Webb nodded. "Yeah, that was part of it, I have to admit it. If you would have come in with me, Barney, you would have saved me from myself."

"Mike, I'm no pundit, and I know it."

"Am I a pundit? Is that how you see me?"

"Well, you ain't no Homer Bigart anymore. Doing a column is just a little too fancy for me. I'm happy being a foot soldier, that's all."

The two friends looked at each other awkwardly.

Finally, Webb brought himself to discuss it. "Nora's damn good, but this wasn't the right time," he admitted. "I know that already. George and Tom just tried to do a number on me. It would be much better if I had somebody else, totally unconnected with either of them, to handle this side of the campaign. Nora's useless there, for obvious reasons."

"What are you going to do about it?"

"What can I do? I'm stuck with it. I can't cut her loose now. There's been too much publicity about her coming on with me. It would kill her professionally before she had a chance."

"You can let her handle Hacker, and you cover these guys."

"Hacker's already started to intimidate her, throwing her connection with Tom up to her."

"What about that?"

"Barney, I don't like to get into their personal life."

"Okay, forget it. That's their business. But it's your business too, so be careful you don't get burned."

They saw MacIntosh coming down the aisle. Webb started talking abruptly. "So I said, 'George, you can't quit now, you've just started.'"

"Funny," MacIntosh said, "very funny. Don't you guys ever get tired? That routine's got whiskers. You need somebody new to write your material." MacIntosh tried to keep it light. He always tried to keep it light, especially when he was nervous about being beaten on a story, and he was nervous now.

"Are you going to burn me tomorrow, Mike?" he asked. "You don't have to tell me what it is. I just want to know whether to expect a call from New York in the middle of the night."

Webb smiled. "Ray, not knowing is half the fun. Do you tell me when you beat my ass?"

"It's been so long," Mulvihill offered, "that he can't remember."

MacIntosh changed the subject. "Where's your beautiful partner? Is she staying at the Wayfarer? I think I'll ask her to dinner. I'll offer to throw a story or two her way. That always works with them."

"Forget it," Mulvihill said. "She's got class. She wouldn't tell you if your coat was on fire."

"Yeah? We'll see. The trouble with you guys is that you always underrate me."

"That's a problem you never have."

"True," MacIntosh shot back. "To thine own self be true, I say."

"He quotes the Bard too," Mulvihill said. "What next?"

The bus lurched to a stop. The motorcade was at another plant gate. Inside a small sentry box, a solitary guard in a blue uniform with a bright-red scarf around his neck sat reading a hunting magazine, paying no attention whatever to the new arrivals. MacIntosh broke off the banter and headed toward the door of the bus, with Webb and Mulvihill behind him.

George Sturdivant was already out of his car and walking quickly through the snowdrifts toward the factory. The press corps fell in behind him as he entered and climbed a stairway. Men and women stood at benches assembling and packing women's shoes. They toiled wordlessly, performing their familiar assignments automatically, catching the rhythm of the assembly line, making their limited contribution, fastening a bow or a buckle neither carelessly nor too fastidiously. Most seemed slightly disoriented by the intrusion of the Sturdivant entourage, though the younger women adjusted quickly— seeking out faces they thought they had seen on television, on "Meet the Press" or one of the other Sunday interview shows. The senator stopped at each bench, shook hands, and chatted easily. He was low-key and had an engaging smile, but he generated little excitement. As the party moved through the factory, Webb stopped and interviewed some of the workers to whom George Sturdivant had spoken. Most of them knew who the senator was, having seen him on television, but they had little to volunteer about him.

"It's this fellow or the crook," said one elderly woman as she laced a pair of new work shoes. "The crook deserved to be kicked out. He's got his nerve trying to get back in."

Another older woman told Webb the opposite. She had nothing against Sturdivant, she said, but she still liked Hacker. "He didn't do anything all the others didn't do," she said. "You people didn't like him because he ain't polished, so you got him. But we're gonna put him back."

Other interviews were similar; in this factory at least, the issue was not George Sturdivant but Ed Hacker, as Webb knew it would be.

For the rest of the day it was more of the same; everywhere George Sturdivant went to meet the people, they greeted him courteously but blandly, and what they cared about was not George Sturdivant but Ed Hacker. Either they wanted him disposed of once and for all or they wanted him resurrected. As Webb recorded their views for another column, a feeling of uneasiness came over him. A fascinating political exercise was in the making, a test of the sophistication and dependability of the electorate; a test of whether voters put their faith in the judicial processes or in the protestations of one man—one colorful, charismatic, spellbinding man. If, after all Ed Hacker had done, the American people could seriously consider returning him to the presidency, the country was in worse shape than Webb had imagined.

On the press bus late that night heading back to the Wayfarer, as others slept or sipped beers and quietly talked, and as a few pecked at their portable typewriters, Mulvihill, Webb, and MacIntosh discussed the day.

"That damned resignation," Mulvihill said. "If they had refused to plea-bargain with Hacker to get him to quit, if they had gone through with the impeachment, the guy wouldn't be out here now. This primary is a referendum on his guilt or innocence; that's all it is. It's as if he's taken an appeal to the voters, and they don't care about any other issue."

"I said at the time they should have impeached him," MacIntosh insisted.

"Yeah, sure, we all said that, Ray," Webb told him, "but we also said the most important thing was to get him out of the White House, and fast."

"I didn't," MacIntosh said.

"Okay, you didn't. I won't go to the bother of pulling the clips on your stories at the time, and embarrassing you."

"Well, he wasn't impeached, and he's taking his case to the highest court in the country," Mulvihill said. "And it's not Warren Burger and Company. It's the people we talked to in those textile and shoe mills today. If they say Ed Hacker wasn't guilty, that will be the verdict that counts. If he can come out of New Hampshire running even a decent second, he'll be alive again. None of us may like it, but that's the way it'll be."

"I think he has to win here," MacIntosh said.

"It's the perception that counts," Webb said. "McCarthy lost to Johnson here, and McGovern lost to Muskie, but they were perceived as winners because they ran so much better than they were expected to. Reagan lost by an eyelash to Ford, a sitting president. That should have been close enough for him to have been perceived as the winner. But his people were so sure he was going to win, and didn't bother to hide it, that they succeeded in having him perceived as the favorite. So when he lost, he really lost. If Hacker gets away with poor-mouthing his chances, and he even comes close, he'll still be in it. That's the way it looks to me anyway."

They were still debating the point when the bus pulled up to the Wayfarer. The three veteran reporters went into the bar for one drink, then two, then returned to their rooms. When Webb turned the key and walked in, he was surprised to find a small lamp lit on the nightstand. And he was surprised to see someone, a woman, lying motionless in his bed, her back to him.

Oh God, he thought. I'm too tired for this.

12

Webb walked to the bed and leaned over the woman. He touched her shoulder, and was startled. Ruth Webb turned, red-eyed, and looked up at him. He sat on the edge of the bed, beside her, saying nothing.

"I'm sorry to burst in on you," she said in a wavering voice. "In all the years, I've never done this before. But I needed to talk to you."

"What's wrong? Why didn't you just phone?"

"I didn't have a telephone conversation in mind."

He got up, fearful of what was coming next, and walked over to his bag, taking out a bottle. "Want a drink?" he asked.

"No, thanks."

"Come on, have one," he said. He poured an inch or so for each of them, went into the bathroom, and put some tap water in each glass, then came out and handed her one. "All right. What's this all about?"

She sat up in bed, sipping the drink.

"I . . . want out, Mike. . . . I can't face another year's campaign at home alone."

"What do you mean, you 'want out'?"

"I'm going to leave you. I just can't take this life anymore. And you have no intention of quitting."

"I can't quit, Ruth. What would I do?"

"Other men get out of it. Other men . . . grow up."

Webb took a long drink and started to pace.

"That's the problem," he said. "You still think this is all a boy's game with me."

"It's not real life, Mike. You live through other people's lives. All these years you've been an observer, and that's forced me to be an observer too. Well, I'm not satisfied leading my life vicariously. It may be enough for you to trail all these ambitious politicians around the country, being some kind of referee in their lives. It's not for me."

Webb refilled his glass.

"What brought all this up suddenly?" he asked.

She laughed, nervously. "It's funny," she said. "It started with Tom."

"Tom Sturdivant?"

"Yes. When you told me what he had done, I know you expected that I would share your disappointment, your outrage. But do you know what? I found myself agreeing with him. He was committing himself to something in his own life. I know you thought that made him some kind of Benedict Arnold to the cause. What cause? The lofty 'profession' of journalism? The religion of truth, as revealed only to you apostles of the portable typewriter? What nonsense!"

Webb sat down on the bed again. "I just believe in what I do, that's all, Ruth. I don't try to make a big deal out of it."

"No, all you do is eat, breathe, and sleep it. I don't think you realize how it has rubbed off on you. You're so determined to stand off at a distance and observe others that it's as if you stand off from yourself and observe. . . . You stand off from me and observe. Or maybe you don't even observe anymore. I don't know."

"Is that it? Is it that we don't have much of a . . . personal life together anymore?"

She fell back onto her pillow, sighing.

"Don't you see?" she said. "You can hardly bring yourself to talk about it."

He said nothing.

She looked at him, wearily, then sat up and said: "If we had had children, it might have been different. I might have been able to accept what has happened as inevitable. At least I would have had *them*."

"Ruth, are we going to go gack to that again?"

"Why not? Maybe they could have brought you out of yourself. Maybe they would have done what I couldn't."

She looked long at him, almost apologetically, waiting for him to say something.

"What is it?" he finally asked, without anger. "Do you have someone else?"

"No, no," she said, brushing the question aside. "The fact is, I have no one, not even you. I've been by myself for so long now, Mike, I might as well make it official. You don't need me, and you never have."

He looked at her, trying to glean whether she wanted him to talk her out of it. But there was no sign of that—none at least that he could read from her face. It was all resolution—no tears, eyes unblinking, lips tight, jaw set. He had always told himself he knew exactly what she was thinking: that her face was as transparent as clear glass. If it were so now, what it told him was that she meant all she said; she was not bluffing, not playing a game.

"What will you do?" he asked. The tense he used seemed to catch her unprepared, to unnerve her, conveying as it did his acceptance of her decision.

"Well," she said, "that's why I had to come right up and tell you. I've been offered a part off-Broadway. After all these years. One of my old directors. I wrote to him last week and he phoned me today. Somebody quit on him. I have to let him know right away, tomorrow, one way or the other." The words poured out, like a dam had broken. She reached out and touched his arm. "It's what I really want, Mike," she said, evenly. "It's what I need. I'm going to pick up my old life again. My old friends are still in New York. My old interests are still there."

Webb had trouble grasping the reality, and the finality, of what she was saying.

"Why don't you go up there for a few months?" he asked. "Until the conventions. Then I'll have a couple of weeks off. We can take a trip somewhere."

"Mike, I can't do that. Anyway, what would it prove? This is a serious offer, and I'm serious about getting back into the the theater. Don't you see?" She was not angry. She spoke to him impatiently, as if he were a small boy who did not quite comprehend. "Afterward, you'd be off again for the fall campaign, and after that it would be something else. It always has been and it always will be. And I'd be left in Washington. No, I made a mistake cutting myself off from my real interests for so long. Did you ever stop to realize that you haven't gotten off the campaign merry-go-round in years? At least politicians run toward an election night. After it's over, they've either won and they settle into the office for a few years or they've lost and they go on to something else. You just keep running and running. You start out a couple of years before a presidential election and you nurse a few hopefuls along until the campaign starts in earnest. You go along with them all year and when you finally deposit the winner at the White House for four years, you just turn around and start looking for another horse to ride for the next time. It's madness, Mike."

He absently rolled the empty glass between the palms of his hands and nodded his assent. "Yes, I suppose it is."

"Wouldn't you ever like to do something yourself—run for some office, run somebody else's campaign—the way Tom is doing? Take a job in which you can make things happen, instead of simply being the scorekeeper all the time? . . . No, you wouldn't. I can see by your face. You don't know what the hell I'm talking about. That's the trouble."

Again he said nothing, just looked at her.

"I'm exhausted," she said, finally. "You are too. Get some sleep. I have to catch the plane back in the morning." She set her glass down carefully on the nightstand, reached up, turned off the light, rolled

133

over on her side, her back to him again, and said no more.

He got up, took off his workboots and heavy socks, stripped off his coat and pants, and his shirt, and stood wearily in his thermal underwear. He took top and bottom off, hesitated, then climbed into the bed behind her, pulling the covers over his naked shoulders.

The room was quiet. He could hear the wind whistling outside. He lay there listening for her breathing, but could not hear it. He reached out to her.

"Please don't," Ruth Webb said, simply, not unkindly. "It's too late for that."

He knew now that although he was exhausted, once again he would not sleep. He lay next to his wife, the physical gulf between them only inches, but miles in another sense, and he listened for sleep to take her. Half an hour passed before he heard the heavy, methodical breathing that told him she at last had gone off. The shock of her sudden appearance, and the irrevocability of her message, were still with him. He seemed to himself curiously passive in accepting it. Perhaps because the case she made was so irrefutably valid, he had been unable to offer a persuasive rejoinder. He was, without question, an observer of life. That was his training, his discipline. Stay out of it; just tell it. That was the gospel of what he did. Still, something *was* missing. A few nights earlier in Washington, driving home late, the old Peggy Lee song "Is That All There Is?" had come over the car radio. For a reason that was inexplicable to him then, the song brought on his depression in a rush. Far into the night the tune and the lyrics plagued him. He had not slept much that night, either. Now in his mind he reviewed the conversation with Ruth, especially about the ceaseless running. She was right; he was one of those frantic ferrets scampering endlessly on a spinning wheel, round and round and round. And it was, as Ruth had said, madness.

But what was there that he would rather do? With a silent desperation, he tried to think of something. The obvious ideas he immediately dismissed, the ideas she had thrown out—running for office himself, running a political campaign for someone else. Even she

134

realized how boxed in he was, how limited the possiblilities were, because he had so completely immersed himself in political life. Maybe he could write a book. He smiled at the thought; he would no more be satisfied shutting himself off, putting himself through that kind of social celibacy, than he would be entering the priesthood. The solitude of the long sleepless nights was bad enough. No, he had to be part of the race, whatever race it was—even if only on the outside looking in. And if that made him a Peeping Tom of life, he would have to live with it. And if he had to live with it without Ruth, he would have to do that too. He was too old to change.

Too old? At forty-seven? The idea was preposterous. He let his hands run easily over his body; over the strong, broad chest, the flat stomach, the sturdy thighs. He was not old. He never ceased to be amazed at pictures of his contemporaries in the newspapers, men who had lost their hair, men who had turned paunchy and jowly of cheek, most important, men who had lost that certain look of life yet to be fulfilled, and hence stripped of youthfulness. Some men were old at thirty-five. He had seen so many of them in the government bureaucracy. They dressed in a uniform of tired drabness; dull brown or gray suits and dime-store ties over white synthetic-fabric shirts, wearing shoes run down at the heels and never shined; an army of bookkeepers, clerks, accountants. He looked down on them in their deadly lives, a bloodless lot who permitted themselves to be tied into a weary drill of catching buses to and from the cardboard suburbs monotonous in their sameness; lashed to the same desks for the same predictable hours in the same predictable routine for year after tepid year; enduring all this for a secure retirement, secure in the continuing drabness of another, slower, pressure-free routine. He despised them in their surrender to such a life, despised them in their total surrender, even to dressing the part. In their way, they were just as bad as the middle-aged peacocks who labored incessantly to keep the advance of the years at bay with their ridiculous, garish wardrobes and hair styles and embarrassingly transparent efforts to embrace a generation that was not theirs. For himself, he wanted a comfortable accommodation, neither giving in to his age nor denying it. He knew who he was, and he ran with no pack. Of that he had thoroughly convinced himself.

Yet, for all that, was he any different from those gray ghosts of bureaucratic conformity who willingly collaborated in the draining away of their own lives? By committing himself to the sidelines, by limiting himself to watching and commenting on how others wrestled with life, was he any better?

Even this endless debating with himself night after sleepless night. This, too, was madness. It got him nowhere. What did it matter to anyone if he was satisfied being the scorekeeper? It gave him a front-row seat; he did not have to be in the game.

He closed his eyes and tried to get off to sleep, without confidence that even his exhaustion would induce it. His wife, who had waited so long for him to find himself and at last was giving up, did not stir as he tossed restlessly; not until daylight approached did he finally doze off.

13

It was nearly midnight when Ed Hacker, Leo Manasian, and Bea Morrison returned from dinner at Amos Cormier's—and the satisfying, surgical dispatch of Governor Granger from the campaign.

"I hated to waste the night on that," Hacker said to his companions as they headed for his suite.

"Well, if you have to waste one, Saturday is the one to throw away," Manasian observed. "Nothing else you could have done would have gotten any press. The Sunday papers all have early deadlines and there's no 'Today' show on Sunday."

"What time is it?" Hacker asked as they entered the suite.

"Ten of twelve," Bea told him.

"Leo," Hacker said, "why don't you get some of the boys in? It's too early to go to bed. We can have a few pops and talk."

Manasian nodded his assent and then looked at Bea, who smiled and shrugged. As they talked, Mildred Hacker came out of the bedroom, fully clothed.

"I thought you'd be asleep," her husband said, surprised.

"I was reading," she answered. She did not ask what had happened at Cormier's.

"Some of the boys are coming over," he said.

"I heard."

"You don't have to stay up."

Mildred Hacker studiously avoided looking at Bea Morrison.

"It's all right. I'll stay for a while," she said.

Hacker's cronies, like firemen always ready to respond to the bell, quickly trooped into the suite on receiving the command appearance from Manasian. They had been drinking and playing cards in another room when the call came. For most of them, moments like these, of close-in association with the former president, were what sustained their enthusiasm and loyalty.

For the first half hour or so, Mildred Hacker dutifully waited on the guests, until they got down to serious drinking, pouring their own, and generally acting as though she were not in the room. Bea Morrison joined in with them, saying not a word to her hostess, discussing with the men the details of the day's campaigning and the progress of the effort. The men were extremely deferential to both women, but in different ways. Toward Mildred Hacker, they behaved in the manner of men who knew they were intruders and sought to do and say whatever they could to minimize the intrusion. Toward Bea Morrison, they comported themselves more in the nature of admirers who would have liked to know her better but were obliged by the circumstances to rein themselves in. The difference, noticed by both women, was abhorred by the one and appreciated by the other. Hacker, for his part, said little to either woman and immersed himself in the political talk.

"The press is getting bugged," Greg Commager reported happily to his leader. "They don't like writing all the antipress stuff you're saying, but they have to report it whether they like it or not. It's one thing we have going for us with those bastards. They take their responsibility seriously."

"That's what's so much fun about it," Hacker said. "I kick their asses all day long and then they have to come back here and write about it. I keep reminding them about how unfair they've been to me in the past. It brings out the nobility in them. They bend over backwards and become conduits for me. It's beautiful."

"What about our old friend Mike Webb?" somebody asked.

Hacker smiled. "He's painted himself into a corner," the former president said. "Anytime he writes anything against me, I just say he's caving in to his old partner and George Sturdivant. I couldn't have set it up better myself."

"What about the girl?" That was how they all referred to Nora Williams. The feminist movement had never happened so far as the Hacker bunch was concerned. They all treated Mildred Hacker just the way her husband did—as a necessary appendage who had to be around, but never listened to. And Bea Morrison's acceptance had not the slightest thing to do with feminism; she was beautiful; she was Hacker's; she was smart and efficient.

"The girl's a pushover," Commager offered. "She's in over her head. She wouldn't know a story if it bit her on the ass. And Webb knows he can't really trust her, because she's Tom Sturdivant's girlfriend. I can't figure how Webb let himself get into such a spot. We don't have to worry about him."

"I wouldn't be too sure," Bea Morrison said. "We ought to keep an eye on him."

Hacker turned to her. "Why don't you just put the make on him, Bea?" he said. "You like older men."

They all laughed a bit uncomfortably. She laughed too; it was the easiest way to slough off the crack. Mildred Hacker said nothing, but in a few minutes she slipped out of the living room, into the bedroom, and closed the door. Nobody noticed for some time that she had gone, and then nobody said anything about it. They were used to such exits.

In the midst of the noisy joviality, the phone rang. Leo Manasian picked it up, then went over and whispered something to Hacker. The candidate nodded and Manasian went back to the phone, glanced at his watch, talked to the caller very briefly, then hung up. "Something's come up, men," he announced. "You're going to have to take the party elsewhere. Go down to my room if you want, and take a couple of bottles with you."

When Manasian issued such orders, which was seldom, the

disciplined forces of Ed Hacker never questioned them. They set down half-finished drinks, shook the leader's hand as he stood by the door, and trooped out obediently. Only Manasian and Bea Morrison remained with the candidate, as was always the case.

"What's going on?" she asked after the last of the revelers had left.

"That was Walter Grafton on the phone," Manasian said. "He asked if he could come by. Sounds like he's got an offer to make."

"Yeah, an offer," Hacker said sarcastically. "The bastard wants to hold us up, mark my words."

"Well," she said, "we ought to listen to him. We don't want him folding his tent right now and leaving us with George Sturdivant to deal with alone."

In a few minutes Senator Grafton rapped on the door and was admitted. He was a rumpled, tweedy Ohioan of sixty-four who seemed to have been around national politics forever. There was still much of the small-college political-science professor in him, which meant that he tended to be pompous and a terrible bore, always talking loftily about the great calling of politics while getting his own hands as dirty as the common hack. But he had his loyal followers and he kept them by mouthing the expected liberal slogans. He gave the purists a place to go.

"Mr. President," Grafton said solemnly, with the manner of a revered elder statesman entering the Oval Office rather than a commonplace motel room.

"Hello, Walter," Hacker said, rising and extending his hand. "What in the world brings you here? You know Bea Morrison, don't you?"

Grafton nodded pleasantly to her.

"May I get you a drink, Senator?" she asked.

"Yes, I'd like a bourbon on the rocks if you have it," he said.

"Of course," she said, and went to fetch it. She didn't mind playing the role of waitress when it helped the cause.

"Well, Walter, what can I do for you?" Hacker asked.

"Mr. President," he said, "I want you to know first of all that I want the nomination, and I intend to do all that's in my power to get it."

Hacker glanced at Manasian. "Of course, Walter," he said. "I never doubted that for a moment."

Grafton nervously took a swallow of his drink. "Good," he said. "It's important to me that you understand that."

"Go on."

"But the fact is, my money situation is not what it ought to be."

"Whose is?" Hacker said, giving Grafton no help at all.

"Well, what I'm trying to say is that unless I get some campaign money very soon, I'm going to have to get out of the race."

Hacker responded with mock surprise: "You don't say! Walter, say it ain't so."

Grafton was now so intent on delivering his message that the sarcasm went right by him. "Yes, I'm afraid it's so," he said.

"Well," Hacker said, with instant solemnity, "I'm sure sorry to hear that. I certainly am."

Manasian joined in. "Why are you telling the president this?" he asked innocently. "He's running against you."

They were determined, clearly, to make their victim squirm, and they were succeeding.

"Yes, of course," Grafton said. "But I'm sure you appreciate that it's in your interest to have me stay in the race right now."

Hacker registered an expression that suggested the idea had never crossed his mind. That was the thing with Grafton. He was so full of himself that he was capable of believing that this kind of nakedly embarrassing and self-serving gambit could be brought off, and Hacker was more than willing to play straight man. "How's that, Walter?" he asked. Manasian and Bea exchanged quick glances, then looked away.

"My vote and George Sturdivant's vote are pretty much the same. From the same kind of people, I mean. My candidacy cuts into him, not you. Everybody knows that."

"Oh, sure," Hacker said. He volunteered nothing more and waited for Grafton to go on.

"As I said, it's in your interest that I stay in."

"But, Walter, you just got finished telling me you intend to win the nomination."

"Yes, but farther on down the road. I know I can't finish first up here, and probably not second either. But I could take enough away from George to at least make it close for you."

"Yes," Hacker said, as if the thought had not previously occurred to him, "I guess you could do that. But why would you want to?"

"Because," Grafton said in his most professorial manner, "I'm convinced that I would be the stronger candidate against you. If it just comes down to me and you, I think I can beat you."

"What makes you think so?"

"Well," Grafton said, "I feel uncomfortable reminding you of this, but I was the first man in the Senate to call for your resignation, two and a half years ago."

"That's right," Hacker said. "A helluva recommendation."

Grafton never saw that remark go by him either. "In a two-man contest with you, I'd stand a good chance."

"Yes, Walter, I think you would," Hacker said, "And so?"

"But if George wins impressively up here, neither of us is likely to be the nominee," Grafton said.

"Walter, if I were you," Hacker said, "for openers I'd stop saying all those nasty things you've been saying about me and concentrate your fire on George."

"I can't do that. I'm a liberal and George is a liberal, and you're the issue in this campaign."

Hacker pondered the situation, taking a sip of his drink, rolling it around in his mouth before swallowing. "Walter, I'd say you're in a tough spot. I wish I could help you, but I want to be nominated myself."

Leo Manasian moved in. "Maybe Senator Grafton has some kind of interim solution in mind, Mr. President," he said. "Maybe he thinks something could be worked out that would be in your and his mutual interest."

Grafton focused on Manasian as if the man had just tossed him a lifeline and hauled him from the roaring sea. "That's really what I've been driving at," the senator said, eagerly nodding his head.

Hacker and his two associates sat there, waiting for Grafton to finally get down to it. He in turn stared at them, hoping the light would flash on for them without further illumination from him. Hacker glanced at Bea Morrison, inviting her with his eyes to join in.

She caught the signal at once. "Mr. President," she offered, "obviously you can't do anything for the senator. But I have a lot of friends in the party who I'm sure would want to see him stay in the race. I could talk to them."

"Would that help?" Hacker asked Grafton.

"Well, Mr. President," he said, "I suppose it would, but it would of course be much better if you could talk to them."

Hacker smiled. "Walter, you know I can't do that. But if Bea here would go to them, they'd understand all right. Walter, you have to appreciate my position. These things have to be done with a certain amount of finesse."

"Yes, of course."

Manasian moved in again. "Assuming that something could be done for you, Senator," he asked, "what would you be prepared to do for us?"

Grafton responded as if *that* idea had never occurred to *him*. "I'd be staying in the race, as I said. That would be to your advantage."

"I suppose," Hacker said, "that if this thing happened, you wouldn't be inclined to keep saying all those nasty things about me, would you, Walter?"

Grafton fell silent. Then he said plaintively, "Mr. President, you *are* the issue."

"Yes," Hacker said, "but you can talk about me with a little more restraint than you've been showing, can't you?"

Grafton did not answer.

"Walter," Hacker said, finally, "I trust you to do the fair thing. If

Bea wants to try to help you—strictly on her own, of course—I have no objection. As you say, it is in our mutual interest that you stay in the race."

"I'll get back to you in a few days, Senator," Bea said, standing up and beginning to pick up the empty glasses. The visit was over.

"Yes, yes, that'll be fine," Grafton said, rising, shaking hands all around, and, numbed, heading for the door.

"And, Walter," Hacker said, "we didn't talk, okay?"

"Yes, right," Grafton said. He seemed to want to add something more but was at a loss. As he took hold of the doorknob, he turned again to the others, paused, and said, simply, "Well, good-bye, then."

The moment Grafton was out of the room, Hacker doubled over with laughter. "Can you beat that guy?" he asked. "With opposition like that, who needs friends?"

"What do we do about it?" Manasian asked, shaking his head in disbelief.

"Call up some of our friends who've already given us the legal maximum," Hacker said. "You take some names and give some to Bea. Tell them it's in our interest that Grafton stay in. You don't have to spell it out. They'll get the picture."

"How much should we try for?" Bea asked.

"Let's see, the contribution limit is a thousand a giver. If you can round up fifty between the two of you in the next day or so, it should be enough to get him through New Hampshire. Then we can decide what to do about him after that. We want to make it enough so he knows he needs us, but not enough that he forgets."

Manasian said he would get on the project the first thing in the morning. He said good night and left Hacker and Bea Morrison in the suite.

As soon as the door closed behind Manasian, Hacker loosened his tie and leered at Bea. She smiled at the overtness of the man, turned her back on him, and walked casually to the sofa at the far end of the room, away from the bedroom. She lit a cigarette and began thumbing through a newsmagazine on the coffee table in front of her, as if he were not there. He took due note of her comportment, sauntered over, and sat on the sofa, some distance away.

"Ain't that Walter Grafton too much?" he said, laughing again.

"That Walter Grafton's too much," she repeated. "And you're a bit much yourself. I was ready to give you the Academy Award for your own performance."

"And speaking of my performance," he said, suddenly grabbing her and pulling her closer to him.

"Ed," she said, shifting to a whisper. "Mildred's in the next room."

"Aw, she's sound asleep by now."

"How do you know that?"

"I don't really care whether she is or not."

"Well, I care," she said. "Go check."

"Okay, if you insist." Hacker pulled himself up from the sofa and exaggeratedly tiptoed over to the bedroom. He opened the door a crack and the light of the living room behind him sent a narrow ray across the bed, catching his wife's face, eyes open, staring back at him. He registered no expression at all, but simply closed the door and tiptoed back to the sofa. He pulled Bea Morrison to him and whispered: "Sound asleep."

In the opposite wing of the Wayfarer, in Tom Sturdivant's room, his brother George sat glass in hand with members of his own entourage. The contrast with the Hacker postmidnight gathering was striking. The senator's aides sat in small groups and spoke quietly to each other, like guests at a proper Georgetown dinner party. The senator was bored and made little effort to disguise the fact.

"Well," he said after what he had judged to be a decent time, "I've got to get some sleep."

The others broke off their conversations to say good night, but without rising or bothering to shake his hand. Before he had left the room, most had returned to the talk that had been engaging them. As the easy sociability went on, Tom Sturdivant began to empty ashtrays and collect glasses, glancing surreptitiously at his watch from time to time. "What do you say, men?" he said at last. "I'm tired too."

They looked up from their conversations, a bit surprised that so notorious a late-night drinker as Tom Sturdivant would evict them so unceremoniously. There was more glancing at watches, and general agreement that it was time to quit. One after another, they finished their drinks and made for the door, with only a parting word or two to the campaign manager.

"What's bugging Tom?" one aide said to another as they left.

As soon as the door closed, Tom went to the phone and dialed Nora's room. She answered on the first ring.

"Hello."

"Did I wake you?" he asked.

She said nothing.

"Nora?"

"No, it's all right. I was working."

Another awkward pause.

"I'd like to come over," he said tentatively.

"No," she said. Then, "Mike might call. I left a column for him. Or he might come by."

"So what? He knows about us."

"Tom . . ."

"What is it?"

Another long pause. Then she spoke, an edge of wariness in her voice. "I'll . . . come over there."

He was surprised but relieved.

"Fine. I'll pour you a drink in the meantime."

"Okay," she said, and she hung up without saying good-bye.

In a few minutes there was a light tap on his door. He opened it and let Nora in. She wore no makeup and looked drawn. He closed the door, turned the latch, and embraced her. She accepted his arms but did not respond. He stepped back.

"Did you have a hard day?" he asked, for something to say.

She sat in a chair by the curtained window and searched her purse for a cigarette. "Yes," she said. "That Hacker is a whirlwind. He campaigns like a young kid going after his first office." She did not ask him what kind of day he had.

"We had a rough one, too," he volunteered. "I'm sure Mike got a column out of it. He rode with George and me for a while."

Tom walked to a small table and poured drinks for the two of them. Nora took hers without comment and quickly drank nearly half of it. It was unlike her; he knew for sure something was amiss.

"Okay," he said, sitting on the edge of the bed. "Let's have it."

She drew nervously on her cigarette. "It's just that I don't feel comfortable like this. I don't think it's a very good idea now. It's . . . unprofessional."

He nodded. "'It's unprofessional.' I've been reduced to a source already, is that it?"

"I didn't say that."

"Well, what are you saying, then?"

"Tom, don't make it any more difficult. Please." She got up and poured herself another drink. As she did so, he rose quickly from the bed and came up behind her, putting his arms around her, drawing her to him.

"Tom, don't," she said.

He held her and she did not resist. He turned her around, still holding her close to him, and kissed her. She turned her face up and accepted him, reaching up and putting her arms around his neck. He held her fast, as if he were holding desperately on to their life together, and she gave herself to the same desperation, drawing him to her, taking the lead in it. She was shaking visibly, and abruptly she let go and pulled away. Without speaking, without looking at him, she turned to the bed, switched off the lamp, and began to undress. She let her clothing fall to the floor as she stepped out of it, and, as if he were not in the room, lifted the sheet and blanket of the bed and moved in beneath them, facing the center, away from him. He stood stunned for a moment, then walked over and flicked off the wall switch, stripped hurriedly, and joined her. She reached out for him at once, hungrily, yet in a strangely impersonal way. She searched out his lips and mouth

147

and pressed herself against him, demanding him without speaking. He tried to slow her, but she commanded his participation with her moving body, until it became too much for him. He entered the tide and rode it with her, letting her dictate the pace, and in a moment it was accomplished and it was over, as it always was with them. Her breathing came hard in the stillness, and then, catching her breath, she began to sob, releasing him for the first time. He lay there holding her, saying nothing.

In a few minutes, she was quiet, and in the darkness he felt a new tension between them.

"Nora," he said at last. "Is there something I can do?"

"No," she said, with a coolness that denied her ardor of moments before. "No. You can't do anything. And I can't do anything."

"What does that mean?"

She did not answer.

"I said, what does that mean?"

"Please, Tom. I don't want to talk about it."

He reached over her and turned on the lamp. She drew her arm up over her eyes, tearful and red.

"Please put that out," she said.

"No. I want to know what's going on."

"I'm so tired, Tom. We'll talk about it in the morning."

"In the morning? You come in here and stand me on my head, and then you say we'll talk about it in the morning? I don't believe this is happening."

She sighed. "All right, then," she said, her voice full of resignation. "Tom, this is the end of it for us. Surely you knew that. You knew it was coming."

"And what was this just now? One for the road?"

"I didn't plan it that way."

"Oh? How did you plan it? A singing telegram?"

"I had hoped we could have been . . . civilized about it."

"But you're here with me now," he said, a trace of pleading in his voice. "Doesn't that mean anything?"

She did not reply.

"Well, doesn't it?"

She looked directly at him for the first time. "It means that I care for you very much, and this may be the hardest thing I've ever had to do in my life."

"Then why do it?" There was a slight belligerence in his voice. He reached out to draw her to him, but this time she pulled away.

"Because I have to," she said. "As long as we're together, the column is going to be compromised. All day today, Hacker kept making cute little remarks, little digs about it. I can't deal with that kind of needling, that kind of ridicule in front of the other reporters. I'm on a tough enough spot as it is."

His anger was rising. "I see," he said. "The hard career woman. And if I get in the way, I get thrown over the side. . . . If I had a knife right now, I'd be tempted to cut you, to see if you'd bleed."

"Tom, please don't make it any harder for me."

"What do you expect after four years? I suppose if I hadn't come with George, if I had stayed with the column, this wouldn't have happened."

"No, I suppose it wouldn't," she said. "But it did happen. I tried to tell you, but you wouldn't listen to me."

He tried to hold her again, but she moved away.

"Please, Tom, I'm exhausted. Maybe I should go back to my room."

"Why not?" he said, bitterly. "One quick roll and out. I'm surprised though. That never was your style."

"Tom, don't be crass at a time like this. . . . I'd like to stay here with you. It's always been better with us in the morning. I'd like to leave on good terms."

"Good terms? What are we, business partners?"

She smiled nervously at him, then reached over with both hands and pulled his face to hers. She kissed him lightly then put her arms around his neck.

"I'm sorry," she said simply. She held him there, not speaking, and soon he could hear her steady breathing in sleep. He lay with his eyes open, unbelieving—not that it had happened, but at the way it had happened, and at the way she was able, so matter-of-factly, to smother it in sleep. It was nearly an hour before he himself was able to fall off.

He was still asleep when first light came and Nora awakened, gathered her things, went quietly into the bathroom, washed her face, dressed, and slipped out. As she walked down the corridor toward her room, she saw a woman coming from Mike Webb's room ahead. Instinctively she drew back and slowed her pace until the woman—she could see now from the graceful walk that it was Ruth Webb—had turned the corner and was out of sight. Nora walked past Mike Webb's door, turned, and went down the corridor to her own room. She let herself in with her key, closed the door, and locked it behind her, then went into the bath. Soon the warm shower was beating down on her. As she soaped herself she shook her head from side to side, as if she were in the midst of some torturous, soundless conversation. Then at once the calm mask of her face broke and she began to sob again, hugging herself with her arms crisscrossed against her chest, her face lifted to take the spray full force, tears awash in the water cascading over it.

14

It was nearly noon on Sunday when Mike Webb at last awoke. He looked around the room to orient himself, saw the empty place next to him and remembered. He lay there thinking of what Ruth had said to him and felt strangely unmoved, as if it all had happened to someone else. She was right, of course. He *had* become a mere observer, even in the painful scene of the night before. He rose and, rubbing his heavy growth of beard, walked toward the bath. As he did, his bare foot kicked something and, looking down, he saw an envelope that must have been slipped under the door earlier.

It was a column from Nora about Hacker. He sat by his window and perused it, then read it through again. He got up, tossed the sheets of paper on his bed, went in and filled the tub. For a long time he soaked in it. Afterward he shaved, dressed leisurely, then walked over, picked up the column, and stood reading it a third time. Then he folded it and went to the phone.

"Nora? Are you up? Come over to my room, will you?" There was the slightest edge in his voice. He walked to the window and watched a light snow come down on the roof of the opposite wing of the motel. Presently, there was a tap on the door. He let Nora in. She was dressed in blue jeans tucked in calf-length Frye boots, and a dark-blue turtleneck sweater. Her hair was pulled back and she wore no makeup. It made her look like a kid. She was apprehensive, and it showed.

"Sit down," he said. "Want a drink?"

"At noon? No, thank you."

He went to the window and watched the snow again, saying nothing.

"What is it, Mike? You don't like the column."

This last was a statement, not a question, and he was relieved to hear it. "No, Nora," he said simply. "It doesn't do it."

He said nothing more at first, trying to find the right words.

She broke the silence. " 'It doesn't do it.' Terrific. Well, tell me the problem. I'll fix it."

"I'm afraid it's not that easy. The whole approach is wrong. It reads like a travelogue. 'A Day in the Life of Edwin Hacker.' It has no bite. Doesn't make any assessment. Doesn't illustrate anything special about the campaign."

"It just wasn't a very good day, Mike."

"Then you shouldn't have written anything. We've got three columns in the bank already."

"Yes," she said. "All written by you."

He turned to her. "What difference does that make?" he asked. "Who's counting?"

"I am," she said. "I want to carry my share of the load. I have to, or I should quit and let you get somebody else."

He did not reply.

"Is that what you want?" she asked. "Is it that bad?"

Webb reached over and put a hand on her shoulder. "No, of course not," he said, sorry at once that he had said it, knowing that with the words he had closed a door, at least for a time. He went back to the window.

"Well, then, what do you want me to do?"

"Nora, you haven't caught on to the style. I just assumed that after reading Tom and me these past years, it would come to you."

"You want me to write just as Tom did?" There was the first hint of anger.

"Not as Tom did, Nora. As *we* did. Both of us. The tone we set for the column, so the reader would have a sense of sameness from day to day, no matter which of us wrote it."

"I've been trying to do that. I'll get the knack of it. I don't say things the same way you do."

Neither of them spoke. He stood at the window watching her. She seemed incredibly vulnerable to him, in a way he had never seen her before.

She searched out his eyes for some signal that it was not a crisis between them. "Say something," she said, "Don't make me sit here like I'm being kept after school."

He came over to her again and this time he put his hand on her head. She did not like to be petted that way, but she endured it, accepting his concern for her feelings. "For a while, Nora," he said, "I think I'd better do all the writing."

She frowned. "Six columns a week? You can't keep up that pace."

"Sure I can. If you help me."

"How can I help? You've told me straight out what a lousy writer I am, what a drag I am on you."

"You're not a drag. You're as good at drawing people out as anyone I know, and you're resourceful as hell."

"I just can't write."

"Don't keep saying that. It's a matter of style. I guess I pushed you into it too soon."

She got up and walked past him to the window.

"So, what happens? Do I go back to being your invisible researcher? At least I'll have the distinction of being part of the fastest-vanishing double byline in journalistic history."

"The byline will stay the same, of course. This will only be until you get a better handle on it."

"No," she said. "I don't want charity. I just wish you would have told me a little sooner."

He looked at her quizzically.

"I . . . gave up Tom," she said.

"I told you, you didn't have to do that."

"Well, I did."

"Is that what the choice was? The column or Tom?"

"I thought it was."

"Well, call him. Patch it up."

"No. Too many things have been said. I can't." She headed for the door.

"Where are you going?" he asked, surprised.

"I don't know. To look for another job."

"I don't want you to do that."

She stood by the door, looking at him, her jaw set, eyes brimming.

He walked over and put one arm around her. "Don't do that," he said. "Forget what I said. We'll work something out. I guess I haven't spent enough time with you. I expected too much from you." He kissed her lightly on her forehead and let her go. "I just let things get to me, and I was taking them out on you."

"What things?"

"I was angry and disappointed at Tom, for openers. I think he did a stupid thing and he left me holding the bag. In a way, what he did put unfair pressure on you."

"Is that all?" she asked again, watching his eyes, which were avoiding hers.

"What do you mean?"

She hesitated, uncertain whether she was intruding too much, then went ahead. "I saw Ruth leaving here early this morning," she said.

He looked at her squarely now. "Well, that too . . . She's leaving me."

"Why?"

"Because she's fed up with me being married to my job, and she's got something she wants to do in New York."

They stood awkwardly some feet from each other. The whole encounter suddenly was turning around.

"What are you going to do?" she asked him solicitously.

"I don't know. Nothing, I suppose. Keep plugging, like always."

She sat down on the edge of the bed and lit a cigarette. She stared at him for a moment, as if reading his thoughts.

"Mike, you're not very happy, are you?"

"I guess not."

"You guess? You don't know?"

He sat in the chair across from her. "I haven't been sleeping very well. Basic male menopause, no doubt. I keep asking myself what the hell I'm doing with my life."

"You're doing important work."

"I am? Important to whom? Ruth says I only live through other people. She's right. I've spent so many years trying to be neutral, uninvolved, that I don't think I have any feelings of my own anymore."

"Do you really believe that?"

"Yes."

"Or do you hold your feelings in, because you think that's what's expected of you?"

"What's the difference? Either way I'm just an onlooker."

"Is that what you want to be?"

"I'm too old to change now."

She began to laugh.

He looked at her in surprise. "What's so funny?"

"You're too old. Compared to what? The pyramids?"

"With a few more years I could be your father."

"Well, you're not."

She held him with a fixed stare again. Then the slightest smile crept onto her face. She got up from the bed and walked over to him.

"Stand up," she said. It was an order. He obeyed. "I don't think of you in any way as my father," she said. She put her arms around his neck and drew his face down to hers. She kissed him easily, then nestled against him and held on.

"Nora, what are you doing?" he asked. He put his hands on her waist and eased her away so he could look into her face. She was relaxed and smiling.

"I'm out to prove you do have feelings of your own," she said.

She brushed her lips against his cheek and pulled him to her again. She kissed him more earnestly this time. There was a fluidness, a wetness, about her that aroused him. He found himself responding and she let go of his neck and put her arms around his waist, bringing him still closer. She searched out his mouth and drew him in toward her. Then, she broke away, and stepped back, grinning.

"See?" she said impishly. "You're alive, and well, and breathing hard, in Manchester, New Hampshire."

She went to draw the curtain on the window, then moved over to the bed and sat down. "Here," she said, laughing, "help me off with these damned boots." She leaned back on the bed and thrust one leg in the air. He stood immobile. "No?" she said. "Rigor mortis set in?" She reached up and tugged one boot off, and then the other. Then she pulled her sweater over her head, stood up, zipped down her jeans and tossed them aside. That was all she was wearing. "Come on, don't just stand there gaping," she said, turning back the bedsheet and climbing in.

"Nora, this is crazy," he said, looking at her openmouthed.

"Sure it is. Haven't you ever done anything crazy? Maybe that's what's wrong with you." She smiled at him mischievously. He just stood there. Suddenly, she was up, out of the bed, and upon him, playfully trying to pull his own sweater over his head, yanking on one sleeve and falling backward until she was on the bed and he on top of her. Her arms were around him again and, laughing, she kissed him hard. She was like a frisky puppy nipping at a large dog reluctant to enter into the frolic. But in a few moments he abandoned his aloofness. He took her in his arms and poured out all the need to make contact that had been welling up in him. He was all at once supremely sensitive to her touch, and the taste and scent of her, and he lost himself in the dizzying exchange. They held and experienced each other and, after the first shock of her initiative, he took control. He carefully and methodically gauged the response of her body and emotions, until it was she, unaccustomed to being indulged in that way, who was responding to him. He made love to her roughly and gently in turn, and now she clung mindlessly to him, emitting low, staccato sounds of anticipation and pleasure, ever more rapidly in succession, until at last it became a steady moan, her voice trailing off. Now he would not let her relax, and he played her to another pitch, and another, until at last she was sobbing quietly, warmly, in his arms.

"Well," he said.

"Well what?" she asked, softly.

"Well, you asked for it."

"Yes, I did, didn't I?"

She moved closer to him, burying her face in his neck. "You are not," she said, "older than the pyramids."

He laughed, brushing his lips across her face. They lay quietly for a long time. Then Nora spoke, very tentatively. "Mike, can I tell you something? Something personal?"

"Sure."

"It's embarrassing."

"To whom? You or Me?"

"Me."

"Then go ahead, by all means."

"You know that ghastly Hemingway line about making the earth move?"

"Yeah."

"Well, the earth just moved for me. It was the very first time with a man. I didn't even know it really happened like that."

"What are you saying?"

"I never got there with anybody. Nobody ever took the trouble before. The Big O."

" 'The Big O'?"

"That's what it's called in a how-to book I just read."

Webb's mouth fell open with astonishment. "A how-to book? You were reading that? I thought they were just for nervous sixteen-year-old boys. Where did you get it?"

"In a bookstore. Where did you think?"

"You mean you just walked in and bought it?"

"Mike, it's not illegal."

"Well, I've never done it. I've never read one. I'm surprised you walked right in and bought it."

Now it was she who was laughing. A look of some embarrassment crept across his face.

"I don't act as if I think you're my father," she said. "But you're acting as if I'm your daughter."

"It's just that some of the things you say, and do, surprise the hell out of me."

"Yes," she said, "I get a big kick out of shocking you. It's so easy. It's your generation. It's okay to do anything so long as you don't talk about it."

"I don't see what's wrong with that," he said. "Why does everything have to be said? Some things are better left unsaid. . . .'The Big O'. . . My God, I can't believe it."

As they talked, she began to move all over him, touching him easily and naturally. He felt a glow come over him and he relaxed. He lay quietly, watching and feeling her touch him with her thin fingers and her lips, and in a short time they were making love again. He was oblivious to who they were to each other, and who they had been to each other before all this had happened. All he knew was that the heavy weight he had felt pressing down on him for the previous months was lifted, and he was alive with this young woman who had so precipitously unveiled a new side of herself to him in this nondescript motel room, in this old New Hampshire town where he had worked so often and so uneventfully, until now. The column and the campaign were far from his mind as the afternoon slipped into early evening and then night, with the two of them now partners in a way he would not have dreamed of before.

15

Tom Sturdivant was up early; he pushed the window curtain aside
and saw, as he had expected, that it was still dark outside the
Wayfarer. Ever since he had quit the column, and especially since the
last abrupt night with Nora Williams, he had slept only fitfully. He
found himself constantly trying to fill time, to keep his mind from
playing over and over what had happened. The most routine
matters—showering, shaving, dressing—he seized on as something to
do, something to make the time pass. He told himself repeatedly that
in joining his brother he had done what he had had to do, but he was
not convinced. He had not been prepared for the pain of Nora's
rejection, a pain that left him reluctantly each night as he fought for
sleep, and that recaptured him instantly on the first moment of
awakening; his constant companion through interminable hours of
daylight and dark.

He let the curtain go and walked in the dark to the television set. He
switched it on and got nothing but snow on two channels and a static
test pattern on a third. He switched it off again. There was nothing in
his experience that had prepared him for rejection of any kind.
Everything he wanted had always come so easily to him, as far back as
he could remember. The prominence of his father and family, more

than the money, had been his entrée to the people who made a difference, and to the places they could be found: as a young student in New York, on summer vacations on Cape Cod and Fire Island, and in Europe. His early success as a reporter was taken by Tom Sturdivant himself, and by his family, as no more than his due. His mind went back over all of it as he readied himself for a day that most others would not begin for hours.

When he had launched the column with Mike Webb, he remembered as he walked into the bathroom, his father and family saw its success as quite natural, with Webb as mere window dressing. They had congratulated Tom on taking the older man along for the ride. If others saw it the other way around, that fact never infiltrated the pervasive self-confidence that set the family of Schuyler Sturdivant apart, and Tom would certainly not be the one to dispute its judgment.

He stepped under the shower, making the water hotter. Showers always made him think of Nora. When they had met four years earlier, they had drifted so easily into a pattern, so comfortably, that he assumed for a long time that she wanted no more than to share what he had. Of course he knew she had ambitions for herself. But she seemed to put so much stock in the quality of the life she led day-to-day, of enjoying the given moment, that he somehow had failed to gauge the side of her that strove upward. In his own case, it was second nature; that was how he was, and there was no question he would achieve what he wanted. He always had, after all.

Perhaps it was unrealistic, but Tom had seen her going on indefinitely as she had through those first years—a reliable helper, a witty and warm companion. He had put no time limit on it because none seemed to be required. Talk of marriage had come up only occasionally. It was not that he didn't want it, or feared it; it was just that he had not sensed it was time, or that Nora was ready, for such a commitment. Not until their personal lives had begun to unravel in the last weeks had he seized on the idea, and he had not been altogether surprised when she balked.

Tom turned off the shower and stepped out into the heavily misted bathroom. The mirror over the sink was steamed up and he absentmindedly printed Nora's name on the glass, then caught himself. Quickly, with some self-embarrassment, he rubbed it out and cleared a wide circle so he could shave. He lathered his face, unable to keep his mind from going back again. What he had not been prepared for was the near hysteria that gripped Nora when he finally had broached marraige, and he sensed that they had by then already gone past a point of no return. Still, the calculating brutality with which she had finally dispatched him—making love a last time, then coldly informing him, then shutting off with sleep all that had happened— left him numb, emotionally paralyzed.

He shaved quickly, almost carelessly, nicking himself once but not flinching. He was like a sleepwalker going mindlessly through all the motions required of him. He forced himself to abandon the reveries and think about the campaign, about what had to be done on this day; what he might do in the few hours before others were up and about, in the few hours that would torment him if he were unable to engage himself in some distracting chore that would carry him into the dawn. He dressed, fiddled with the television screen again—with the same result—then left his room, walking silently down the corridor to the front desk. A young man sat at the telephone switchboard, his chin on his chest, asleep. Tom walked past him to a small office the Sturdivant campaign maintained in the motel. He switched on the lights, sat behind a cluttered desk, and busied himself with paperwork.

He did not know how much time had passed when he heard somebody at the front desk. He got up and went out. It was just getting light outside. As he had expected, the newsboy had brought the motel's copies of the *State News*. The boy cut the string that bound three large packages of newspapers. Tom took one copy and put fifteen cents on the opened pile. He turned to the front-page editorial. It was the usual daily diatribe against his brother, but it did pinpoint the tactical problem both George Sturdivant and Walter Grafton seemed unable to solve: how to call Edwin Hacker to account for his past sins without feeding the theme of political and press persecution, which Hacker was pounding like a steady tattoo into the consciousness of the New Hampshire electorate. Tom had long since stopped being amused by Cormier, and he was not amused as he read this morning. The editorial was labeled "Georgie One-Note":

We are now less than two weeks away from primary day. At this late hour, certainly, all the candidates should be raising the vital issues of war and peace, of foreign and domestic survival that face the country. In past years, many candidates have done so. But, lamentably, not this year.

This year, a supposedly responsible member of the United States Senate, George Sturdivant of New York, has used the forums of our state for one purpose only—to resurrect the same tired charges that Sturdivant and his ilk, and the Draculas of the American press corps, used so recklessly but effectively to turn a great American, President Edwin Hacker, out of the White House.

For weeks the people of New Hampshire have waited in vain for Sturdivant to raise new issues worthy of a campaign for the presidency. Instead, they have been treated to more and more ancient history, or more accurately ancient fiction, from this sorry excuse for a candidate. Hacker, for his part, has been obliged as is any man under attack to defend himself. It is to the former president's credit that he has declined to descend into the gutter with Sturdivant and his confederates in the press. Instead, he has repeatedly called to the voters' attention the irrefutable fact that the same unholy alliance that got Hacker two years ago is at work here to get him again.

Nobody claims that Ed Hacker is perfect, certainly not this newspaper. We understand there are those who for one reason or another will not be able to bring themselves to vote for him. There are always those knee-jerk liberals who cannot bear to cast a ballot for anyone who, like Edwin Hacker, has a harsh word to say about the Communists, or abortion, or marijuana.

But even knee-jerk liberals can be fair-minded. In the face of the disgraceful one-issue campaign of George Sturdivant, they should think seriously about the other alternative facing them—Sen. Walter Grafton of Ohio. We have no love for Grafton. We think he is a mealymouthed toad who should be in an old-folks' home, not the U.S. Senate. But at least he has had the good judgment to mute his remarks about former President Hacker and try to raise some other issues. If you have to throw your vote away, throw it away on Grafton.

Tom Sturdivant smiled weakly as he read the long editorial. It was, of course, ludicrous, as all of Cormier's rantings were. But he couldn't argue with the premise. No matter how the Sturdivant campaign tried, it did not seem able to move the discourse away from the issue of Hacker. It was true that George Sturdivant was beginning to sound like a broken record. The notion that Hacker could even attempt a comeback after all that had happened so outraged George that he seemed unable to talk about anything else.

Tom was absorbed in his thoughts and he did not see an elderly man in shorts and jogging shoes—and in tremendous shape—burst red-faced into the lobby.

"Reading more but enjoying it less?" the man asked. Tom looked up from the editorial and saw at once that it was Amos Cormier.

"Yes," Tom said, "you could say that."

"I'm right and you know I'm right," Cormier said. "You clowns are playing right into our hands."

"*Our* hands?" Tom repeated. "Are you on the Hacker payroll now?"

"Don't be funny, Sturdivant," Cormier said. "But why should I pretend I'm neutral? People don't read my paper because they want me to be neutral."

"What about fair?"

"Fair is for love and war. Not politics. Winning is for politics."

Tom gestured toward the end of the editorial. "What is this sudden affection for Grafton?"

"Not affection," Cormier said. "Arithmetic. We've taken some polls and they suggest that our vote and yours have plateaued about even. We may not be able to pick up much more for Hacker, so we need to start nibbling at you. And from Sturdivant to Grafton is a much shorter leap than from you to us."

"How does Grafton feel about that?" Tom asked.

"Who knows? I've never in my life talked to the man. What's he got to do with it? He's there. That's all that counts."

As they talked, Ed Hacker came down the corridor from his room, with Bea Morrison and the ever-present Secret Service agents behind.

"Ah," he said as he spied Sturdivant and Cormier, "am I interrupting an important interview?"

"No," Cormier said. "Your opponent's campaign manager was just giving me a lecture about fairness in the press."

Hacker laughed. "Sorry I missed it. But fairness isn't the problem. It's boredom. Your brother keeps taking the same old shots at me," he told Sturdivant. "People are tired of it."

"I don't think so," Tom said.

"Well, I don't want to debate the point with you."

"You don't want to debate any point with anybody. You want to float through this thing without saying a word more than you have to."

Tom saw an opening and seized it. "The League of Women Voters wants to schedule a debate," he said. "What do you say?"

Hacker thought for a minute. "The three of us? Grafton too?"

"Yes."

"Televised statewide?"

"Yes."

"Well, why not? Two against one. I've always liked those odds. And old Walter sure could use the exposure." Hacker laughed again, put his arm around Cormier's shoulder, and led him into the dining room. Bea Morrison, at his side, smiled smugly.

Tom went to George's room and woke him.

"I just ran into Hacker," he said. "He agreed to a debate."

"How did that happen?" George asked.

"It just came up. Cormier has a long editorial this morning urging voters to switch to Grafton if they can't buy Hacker. Obviously trying to cut into us with liberals and moderates. Cormier's here having breakfast with Hacker and his girlfriend and he told me they have a poll showing it's close."

"Is a debate such a good idea, Tom?" his brother asked.

"Why isn't it?" Tom countered. "Maybe a confrontation will make Hacker squirm. And maybe it can get the campaign onto a new track in the last days. God knows, we need something. Everybody's sick of hearing what a crook Hacker is."

"I'm not," George Sturdivant said. "I could listen to myself saying it forever."

"Yeah, you could, but you don't vote in New Hampshire."

Tom watched the morning television news while his brother showered and got dressed. Then the two of them, with the unmistakably jaunty Sturdivant stride, headed for the Wayfarer dining room and breakfast.

"Tom," George asked as they walked along, "are you okay?" It was not the kind of personal question he was accustomed to getting from his older brother.

"What do you mean?"

"Something's been bothering the hell out of you."

"It's nothing," Tom said, preferring not to discuss it. "I've just got a lot on my mind."

As they entered the dining room, they saw Hacker, Bea Morrison, and Cormier sitting off in a corner, deep in conversation. They naturally turned in the opposite direction, but Tom stopped abruptly when he saw Nora and Mike sitting in a booth, equally engrossed in each other. He grabbed his brother's arm and quickly steered him to the nearest table. George inquiringly looked at Tom, but said nothing. They sat in silence, studying the menu as if they had never seen one before.

"When will it be scheduled for?" George asked at last.

"What?"

"The debate. When will it be?"

"Oh, yeah, the debate," Tom said.

16

The campaign moved swiftly by, and after nearly a month the issue remained Ed Hacker. Neither Sturdivant nor Grafton seemed able to strike any chord with the voters on any of the standard liberal proposals they espoused, and Sturdivant, for his part, was psychologically unable to shift his campaign focus. On a rainy night one week before the primary vote, buses and cars streamed into the town of Hanover. They crammed the main street of Dartmouth College, which dominates the town at the state's western border with Vermont across the Connecticut River. It is just southwest of ski country, and the shops were full of expensive boots, jackets, pants, heavy gloves, wool face masks, and all the other necessary paraphernalia. Snowdrifts covered cars on most of the side streets; many who came for the debate among the three Democratic candidates simply abandoned their vehicles when they could drive no farther, proceeding on foot to a large hall on the campus.

Dartmouth is one of the more picturesque of the Ivy League schools, especially in winter. For Winter Carnival, imaginative snow sculptures decorate the lawns of the largest fraternities. The school shares the high academic reputation of the Ivy League but its relative remoteness makes it an outpost of hard playing and hard drinking. Fraternity life is robust and, from time to time, a cause of friction with the townspeople.

Fifteen minutes before the debate was to begin over a statewide educational-television hookup, Hacker, Sturdivant, and Grafton were in place at a long table on one side of the stage. Four reporters sat at a second table on the other side, from which they would pose questions. The event was billed as a debate, but that was erroneous. Hacker would not accept any format in which the candidates asked questions directly of each other. On the floor just below the stage were the television cameras, and behind them several rows of seats reserved for the press. The hall was packed, with standees lined along both side walls.

Nora Williams, sitting in the front row of the press section with Mike Webb and Barney Mulvihill, took copious notes on everything: how the candidates looked, what they wore, which hangers-on spoke to them, all the minutia she could see and hear.

"Are you getting ready to write a book, or what?" Mulvihill asked her.

"This is exciting," she said, bubbling. "Don't you find this exciting? If one of them flubs, the whole election could go down the drain. I can feel the electricity in here. I can feel the tension mounting. Can't you?"

Webb and Mulvihill smiled. "Where did you find Little Orphan Annie?" Mulvihill asked his old friend.

As a clock on the stage approached the nine-o'clock air time, however, even Mulvihill put aside his casualness and watched the candidates closely. These "debates" seldom were decisive, but they had in them the ingredients for disaster; that potential did create an infectious tension.

At the candidates' table, Hacker impatiently drummed his fingers on a yellow pad in front of him. George Sturdivant, in the center, huddled over briefing papers, his brother talking animatedly into his ear. Grafton, to Sturdivant's right, sat immobile, like the unwanted guest at dinner, which of course was precisely what he was, as far as Sturdivant was concerned.

Each candidate made an opening statement and then the questioning began, first with the former president.

"Mr. Hacker," the reporter said, "ever since your resignation two years ago, you have professed your innocence. You have charged that your political enemies and the press were involved in a conspiracy against you. Whenever you have been asked to be specific, however, you have simply repeated the same allegations. I want to ask you, sir, what specific evidence do you have of such a conspiracy?"

Hacker smiled indulgently at his interrogator. "Mr. Dickenson," he said, "I'm surprised you ask a question like that, because I know you read the newspapers and watch what's going on." Hacker looked directly into the camera, the polished television performer. "As I said at the time of my resignation," he intoned, "I left the White House because I was convinced that the atmosphere in Washington had been so poisoned against me that I could no longer function effectively. That was the truth. A state of paralysis had set in, just as severe as in the last days of Nixon. I made the mistake then of listening to my enemies, who wanted me out, rather than listening to my friends. Since that time I have stopped listening to them and have begun to listen to my millions of friends. They know that the issue is whether the people or the press should be empowered to pass judgment on the individual the people have elected to be their president. That is the overriding issue of this campaign, and I make no apology for making it the cornerstone of my own candidacy."

The audience, as if on cue, burst into applause. The moderator asked for quiet, but the crowd ignored him. Hacker from his perch grinned broadly and waved, while Sturdivant fumed.

"He's shameless," Mike said soberly, like a teacher, to Nora sitting next to him, "but he knows what he's doing." She smiled at him, as if he had said something brilliant. Barney caught the exchange, but said nothing.

On the stage, George Sturdivant was asked by the moderator to comment.

"Mr. Hacker's response is the best illustration of his campaign style," Sturdivant said. "He never answers the question. He simply brushes it aside and makes the same speech over and over. His abuse of his office and of campaign-spending procedures are a matter of record. His political foes and the press did not invent them. Mr. Hacker has said he made a mistake in resigning. For once I will have to agree with him. It was wrong to let him leave office without a court's finding of his guilt or innocence of illegal influence-peddling in the White House. If he had gone through impeachment, I have not the slightest doubt that he would have been found guilty. Then he would not have been able to come back here complaining that he had been wronged. But that did not happen. As long as he proclaims his innocence in the face of overwhelming evidence to the contrary, it is legitimate to remind the American public of Mr. Hacker's record."

Only a smattering of applause greeted Sturdivant's remarks, and the same was the case when Grafton offered a similar observation, though in much more restrained terms. The panel went on to other questions, but in nearly every instance Hacker merely used them as a vehicle to get back to his basic theme—that he had been unjustly hounded from office against the public's will. As the hour wore on, and the exasperation and tempers of the two other candidates and the panelists increased, Hacker became more confident and jovial.

"You're seeing the master," Mike said to his partner. "It's perfectly obvious what he's doing, yet they can't do a thing about it. They can't lay a glove on him."

"I don't understand it," Nora said.

"Look around," Mike said. "All these people hate us. They agree with him that we're a bunch of bastards out to get him, no matter what."

By the time the closing statements were made, Hacker had reduced the exercise to a shambles. Sturdivant and Grafton, again less forcefully, protested his refusal to come to grips with the real issues facing the country. But in so doing they somehow sounded as if they were the ones who were being evasive, who were trying to avoid facing straightforwardly *his* charges against *them*. Sturdivant actually began to stutter at one point, so frustrated was he. Hacker sat back and smiled affably through it all.

After the moderator ended the debate and a technician removed the tiny microphone clipped to his tie, Hacker came down and milled with the crowd. Well-wishers, with Bea Morrison foremost, pressed around him, while Sturdivant stood on the stage, boiling mad. Mike and Nora observed Hacker for a moment, then repaired to the press room, where the clacking of typewriters and telegraph machines had already begun. Mike sat down and started typing the column; it was an easy, straight-analysis piece. Nora sat next to him, nervously. He did not seem to notice.

"Mike," she said. "I thought I might write this one. You wrote the last two days."

He did not look at her, but instead kept his eyes fixed on the copy paper in front of him. "It's just a simple piece," he said. "I'll run it through fast and you can look it over." He continued without saying more, and after a few minutes she got up and walked dejectedly to the other side of the press room. He seemed not to notice that either.

Webb was nearly finished when Tom Sturdivant came into the room. He spied Nora and at the sight of her was gripped by a feeling of apprehension. She saw him out of the corner of her eye and immediately engaged herself in conversation with a colleague. Tom turned, forlornly, and walked over to Mike.

"What do you think?"

"I think he killed you."

"He didn't say anything. He just repeated the same old bullshit."

"But he made George and Grafton seem like they were the bad guys instead of him."

"Do you think people still buy that crap?"

"You heard them in the hall, Tom. You saw them."

"They were his people. A few busloads of supporters brought in aren't the whole state."

"Okay, if that makes you feel better."

Tom moved down to another reporter and another, sampling their views, then turned and walked out briskly, down the front steps of the hall and to the curb, where George Sturdivant was shaking the last few hands of the night. Tom signaled for the senator's car and he engineered his brother into the rear seat. One minute, there had been a mad swirling around the candidate, a constant din; the next, inside the car, it was like a tomb, with not a word spoken.

"Well?" George asked as they moved off through the dispersing crowd.

"Mike thinks the old fraud got away with it," his brother said.

"And what do you think?"

"I think he's right, George."

"Okay, what do we do about it? You're the campaign manager."

"The first thing, we don't panic. The television station is doing a telephone poll right now. They promised to get the results to us in a couple of hours. How it looked in the hall, with Hacker's cheering section there, is one thing. How it looked on the tube is another."

They drove back to the Wayfarer in gloomy quiet, broken only occasionally by halfhearted conversation. Tom flicked on the radio at one point to hear the news and try to pick up some comment on the debate, but it was too early for anything but a rehash.

On arrival, the brothers went to the senator's room for a drink, and to await the poll report. They each had had two scotches when the phone rang. Tom answered, reached for a pad and pencil, and began scribbling.

"Yeah . . . yeah, okay. . . . The senator appreciates it. Thanks. Good night."

"Let's have it," George said.

"Good news and bad news," his brother told him. "On who won: Hacker fifty-eight percent; Sturdivant thirty-two percent; Grafton ten percent. But on who the same people favor in the primary: Sturdivant twenty-eight percent, Hacker twenty-four, Grafton twelve, thirty-six undecided."

George slammed his fist into his palm. "You call that good news and bad news? What's the good news?"

"Well, you're ahead in the primary."

"What? Four points against a man who was thrown out of the White House?"

"It's enough at this stage. After all, he was the president. People know him. Name-recognition is half of it."

"What kind of thinking is that, Tom? If that was valid, the Boston Strangler would be a contender up here."

Tom laughed for the first time since the debate ended. "He's not on the ballot—I don't think," he said.

"Not funny," the senator shot back. "Not funny at all." He got up and poured himself another, stiffer drink. "Well, the hell with it," he said. "I'm going to bed." He started to strip off his tie.

Tom was about to reply when his brother abruptly walked past him into his bedroom. Tom stormed in behind him. "Listen, George," he shouted, "I didn't want this goddamned job in the first place, and you know that!"

The senator, standing at the window, wheeled around. "No, you didn't want to run the campaign, but you want what comes after it!"

Tom turned and marched out through the sitting room, slamming the door behind him. He continued down the corridor in a beeline for the bar. He was only a step or two away when a very heavy older man came up behind him and seized him by the arm. Tom, not seeing the man, spun around, furious.

"Tom, take it easy," the man said benignly. "Do you remember me?"

Tom backed off. "I know your face," he said, regaining control. "I'm sorry. Your name escapes me."

"Al Hemmings. I was with Hacker in his first campaign."

"Oh, yeah. The dirty-tricks artist." Tom said it matter-of-factly, in the sense of a professional identification, not a condemnation. "How are you?"

"Fine. Got a minute?"

"I was just going to bed," he lied. "It's been a very long day."

"Yeah, sure. But it might be worth your while."

"Why?"

The man smiled at him conspiratorially. "Did you hear me when I said I *used* to be with Hacker? The son of a bitch cut me off after he got in. He said I was too blatant for the White House. Can you imagine that—coming from him?"

Tom studied the man. He was a caricature of the slimy politician: short and fat, approaching obesity in fact, with a red face and bulbous nose. Hemmings stood there, smiling, like a cheap hooker suffering being looked over by an uncertain customer.

"We can go to my room for a minute," Tom said.

Inside, Tom took off his jacket and tossed it on the bed. He did not offer to take Hemmings'.

"Is that a bottle over there?" his visitor asked, looking around quickly.

"Help yourself."

Tom did not waste any more time. "Well, what is it?" he asked, even before Hemmings had picked up the bottle.

Hemmings half-filled a glass, taking it neat, and settled into a chair.

"What would you say," he asked, watching his host's face, "if I told you that Edwin Hacker is up to his ass in the casino rackets in Vegas and Jersey?"

Tom sat on the edge of his bed, eyeing Hemmings cautiously.

"I'd ask you if you could prove it, of course," he said.

"I can prove it."

"How?"

"I have papers—memos, business documents, taped conversations, the works."

"Yeah. How did you get them?"

Hemmings grinned. "I ain't called the dirty-tricks artist for nothing," he said.

"When can I see them?"

"That depends. If we can come to a satisfactory arrangement, I could have them here in a day or two."

Sturdivant watched him suspiciously. "Where are they now?" he asked.

Hemmings laughed. "Come on, Tom. Don't treat me like a nickel-and-dimer. If I say I got 'em, I got 'em."

"What do you have in mind?"

"Money, what else? That—and of course I won't mind seeing Hacker get his. A little revenge is always good for the soul."

Tom watched the man, saying nothing. Then he sighed and shook his head. "I'm not buying any information," he said. "I never did it as a reporter, and I'm not starting now."

Hemmings filled his glass again.

"You're not a reporter anymore, Tom. This is politics. Hard-nosed politics. I'm not suggesting anything that hasn't been done a million times, that isn't still done all the time, for all the so-called post-Watergate reforms."

"No, I'm not interested. I didn't get into this thing to become a crook."

"Hey, Tom, that's a strong word. I have certain information that you can use. You're not stealing it, you're just buying it. . . . Don't you even want to know for how much?"

"How much?" Tom asked, almost before he realized he had said the words.

"Fifty thousand. When you see what I've got, I think you'll agree it's reasonable."

"Only fifty?" Tom repeated, incredulously. "Why not a hundred while you're at it?"

"Because I need fifty for some property I want to buy. I'm not a greedy man."

"I see. Well, the answer is still no."

"Why don't you talk to your brother about it? He's a pol. He understands these things."

"I don't want to clutter up his mind with it. Why don't you take it over to Grafton?"

"That tinhorn? He wouldn't know what to do with it. He could screw up a two-car funeral."

"Well, thanks, but no thanks."

Hemmings finished off his drink. "Look, Tom," he said. "This is a free country. There's nothing to stop me from going directly to your brother. I just prefer going through channels. Why don't you talk to him? I'll be around for a few days."

Tom said nothing.

Hemmings got up and extended his hand, but Tom looked at it as if it were infected with some highly contagious tropical malady. The man shrugged, opened the door, and went out. As soon as he was gone, Tom picked up the phone and dialed. He knew he could not sleep now.

"George?" He was still angry and his voice barked with hostility. "You don't like the way the goddamned campaign is going? Then spare me a few minutes of your valuable time. . . . Yes, right now. . . ."

17

"The first thing we need to know," George Sturdivant told his brother, "is, can we trust him?" The animosity between the two was swept aside in the excitement of the new development. "And if it's the real goods, how do we handle it?"

Tom, his adrenalin running too, nevertheless was cautious. He had, after all, experienced Al Hemmings at first hand. "Do we want to handle it at all, George? What if it gets out? It could backfire on us."

The senator was over the bathroom sink washing the sleep from his eyes. "Look, Tom, you heard the poll figures. You and your good news and bad news. We need something to turn this thing around, and fast. If we can prove Hacker's in the rackets, it's the perfect way to combat his pitch that we're just digging up old bodies."

"I don't like it," Tom said. "I don't like the money part, especially. Where are we going to get that kind of money? And how do we report it?"

"Getting it is easy enough."

"You sound like Nixon. Aren't you going to add, 'But it would be wrong, that's for sure'—just in case this room is bugged?"

"Tom, you played hardball as a reporter. Why do you back away from playing hardball as a politician?"

"I'm not a politician,"

"I'm not a politician," George mimicked. "I am not a crook. Now who sounds like Nixon?"

"Maybe there's a way we can get the stuff without Hemmings. If it's true, other people will know about it. Why don't I cut out from the campaign for a day and see what I can track down myself?"

"Because you're not a reporter anymore, Tom. Use your head. You know this sort of thing takes months to investigate. If anybody got a smell of you looking into it, I'd be dead. No; either we do business with this fink or we forget it. And we can't afford to forget it."

"Well, what about the money? We can't use regular campaign funds. The FEC would be onto us if we had any fake entry for anything approaching fifty thousand dollars in our next spending report. They're really watching the candidates this time."

"We don't use regular campaign funds," the senator said. "We use . . . Dad." He smirked as he said it.

Tom stared at his brother, eyebrows raised. "Hit up the old man for a payoff? Are you crazy?"

"Why not? He wants a Sturdivant in the White House at all costs. He told me that. Those were his very words."

"But he didn't mean it literally, George."

"You don't think so? What time is it?"

"Just after midnight."

The senator went to the phone and direct-dialed New York. He eyed his brother as he let the phone ring at the other end.

"Yes, hello, Henry," he said. "Is my father still up? . . . Yes, please." He put his hand over the phone's mouthpiece. "Listen," he said to Tom with a grin, "and you'll hear why, as they say in the papers, I'm the most persuasive voice in the U.S. Senate. . . . Hello, Dad? . . . Yes, fine. Nothing's the matter. Something's come up. I can't tell you about it. For your own protection. Do you know what I'm saying? . . . Good. Well, I may be needing some money in a few days. . . . Fifty thousand. . . . That's right. It's absolutely vital to the campaign. I think I can safely say it will assure the nomination.

. . . Don't worry, I know how to handle it. We've never had any trouble about it before. Okay. . . . Yeah, I'll be calling you, Dad. Thanks."

George hung up the phone and beamed smugly at his brother. "You see? Nothing to it."

"And you didn't even have to tell him what for."

The senator smiled. "Deniability, it's called in the CIA. So much the better for everybody that way."

"I have a feeling this sort of thing has happened before. The old man sure didn't need any convincing."

"Welcome to the real world, kid brother."

Tom stared at him. "I don't like it," he said, but without much conviction.

"Well, I'm the candidate, and I'm for it," George said.

The two brothers glared at each other. The hostility was creeping back in.

"You don't need me for this kind of thing," Tom said. "You can get one of your hacks to handle it."

"That's exactly where you're wrong," the senator said. "You're the only one who can handle it, for obvious reasons. We've got to keep this in the family, for my sake and for the old man's."

"Well, I didn't agree to do this to be your bagman, George."

"Look, Tom, don't start being an ass again. I had no way of knowing we'd get into something like this. But it's an opportunity we can't pass up. Anyway, maybe it won't come to a thing."

Tom agreed reluctantly to contact Hemmings in the morning. He went to his room and turned on the television set. But he was restless and soon switched it off. He walked to the phone, picked it up, hesitated, then hung up. He went over to the desk and poured himself a drink, then went back to the phone. He would make one more try. He dialed Nora's room and held the receiver nervously as the number rang six times. There was no answer. He slammed down the receiver and looked at his watch. It was now after one o'clock. He walked out into the corridor and to the bar, looking for Nora, but she was not there. As he returned to his room, he turned a corner and came upon her, and Mike.

"Hi, Tom," she said, with a nervous smile that sent a pang through him.

"Hiya, Tom," Mike said, evenly.

He nodded at them and continued on. In his room he watched an old movie on television for a while, not really following it. After about twenty minutes, he dialed Nora's room again. Again there was no answer. He jammed the receiver onto the cradle and lay across the bed, clothed except for his shoes. He tried to push away his concentration on her, telling himself he was jumping to conclusions. But he knew her. He forced himself to think of the information that was being dangled before him against Hacker. Through his mind raced scores of scenes about the campaign, and, his brother, and his father, and Mike Webb, and the column, and, unavoidably, at last about Nora and their four years together. He deliberately took himself from the first days to the present, painfully savoring the moments of discovery that had marked the beginning, that had captured him; above all else, the tantalizing contrast between her sober, public side and the private world of wildness and unpredictability to which she had admitted him then. The thought that these same scenes were now being played with Mike Webb consumed him, until he could not tolerate the torture of dwelling on it. Yet it was like a scab that he could not resist picking at before it could heal entirely. He worried it, resurrecting details with painful clarity, uncovering half-forgotten moments, then holding them before his mind's eye until they punished him with the hollow sense of his irretrievable loss. He got up, poured himself an exceedingly stiff drink, downed it, then refilled the glass and slumped into a chair, switching on the old movie again and watching. Not really watching, but rather letting the images dance before his eyes while he fought to keep those other piercing images from his insistent mind.

Nora moved closer to Mike in the semi-darkness of his room. He lay on his back with one arm over her shoulder in the silence.

"Did that bother you just now?" he asked.

"Did what bother me?"

"Seeing Tom. You acted a bit uptight, I thought."

"Well, yes, it wasn't the most comfortable moment."

"Do you think he knows?"

"I don't know. Probably not. We *do* work together. Or has it been so long since I've written anything that you forgot?"

"Don't be bitchy."

"I'm not," she said. "I just couldn't resist the opening."

"Well, if he does know, I hope he doesn't think it's any kind of quid pro quo."

"What difference does it make?" she said. "We know it isn't."

They lapsed into silence.

"One thing we do know," she said, putting her arms around his neck. "You aren't, as you put it, a mere observer of the passing scene."

"Yes, that's true, in one sense. But when I'm not with you like this, I'm still pretty much a scorekeeper on the sidelines."

All at once, she sat up in the bed. She held an imaginary microphone in front of her. "A Scorekeeper on the Sidelines of Life," she said, in the deep tones of a radio announcer. "Tell me, and our listening audience, Mr. Scorekeeper, how does Life look from the Sidelines?"

"Repetitious," he said. "If you've seen one presidential campaign, Miss, you've seen 'em all, I always say."

"Yes, you do. You do always say that. It makes you a terrible bore, did you know that?"

"Scorekeepers are supposed to be boring."

"Well, why don't you do something more exciting? Instead of being a Scorekeeper on the Sidelines of Life, why don't you be a Shaper of National Opinion? I hear the job's open."

"Because what people want from me is the correct score."

She let out an exaggerated groan. "Ladies and gentlemen of the listening audience," she said, "I'm afraid we're out of time. You have been listening to an exclusive interview with an exclusively terrible bore with a one-track mind. Good night, and good luck."

"Very funny," he said, in a tone that confessed he really thought so. "Was that good night for the listening audience, or for me?"

"It depends," she said, "on whether you're a scorekeeper, and a terrible bore, off the air as well as on." And she slid down and tightened her hold around his neck.

They did no more interviewing that night, and she had occasion to tell him later that he was not really a terrible bore after all. Afterward he slept deeply and well. This time it was she who lay awake into the night, thinking of the brief, unexpected confrontation with Tom Sturdivant, and recalling some of the same scenes that were forcing their way through his consciousness in another room down the hall. But for Nora, it was as if she were watching a film of her own life. The idea made her feel cold. How strange it was that she who was so determined to be a full participant in life was able to look back on times she had lived so fully and emotionally with such detachment.

Now that she was here with Mike Webb, it almost seemed as if the other had never really happened, or rather, had happened to someone else. And what of Webb? She could not mislead herself forever that she was merely playing the Good Samaritan to a lonely man. She had always looked up to him, even from the very first when she had met Tom. And she had never resented Mike's success the way she had Tom's. Mike had paid his dues. She could not help wondering whether part of the equation was that she wanted to get back at Tom Sturdivant, just as Mike Webb did, for abandoning what they had had together.

She looked over at the sleeping Webb. That kind of spitefulness did not do justice to how she felt about him. In revealing herself to him, she had discovered his own private side; with her, he was no longer the gruff, hard-bitten skeptic who had seen everything and dismissed everything. His sensitivity to her feelings, the vulnerabilities he permitted to surface only when they were alone, drew her to him. He had let her into a secret part of his life, as she had admitted him to hers, and that was enough for now.

The thoughts enabled Nora to justify her behavior to herself, without ever confronting the other element she knew was there. She was, suddenly, a syndicated columnist, sharing a byline with one of the most prominent American journalists. And he had hired her before she had extricated him from what they now jokingly called his interment among the pyramids. All that had happened between them afterward had nothing to do with that first decision he had made about her, she persuaded herself. She believed it, or at least told herself she believed it.

The coldness came over her again. Nora looked at this solid, dependable man sleeping next to her. She told herself that for all her professional shortcomings, which he had spelled out to her so straightforwardly, she was holding her own with him, woman to man. What she was doing was fair, and she did not have to apologize for it—to herself or anyone else. She needed him, yes; but he needed her, too. She looked away from him and lay on her side, staring into the darkness. Everything was all right. But that being so, she could not understand why it was she who could not sleep and who, indeed, began to sob quietly, yet uncontrollably. She pulled the covers over her head, so as not to wake him.

18

Approaching Concord on the expressway from Manchester, George and Tom Sturdivant turned off at a tollbooth. Tom lowered the car window, tossed a quarter into the coin receptacle, waited for the light to turn green, then drove off at the first exit, marked "Hooksett." The snow was piled high on either side as the road wound into the countryside. They crossed an old bridge over a stream frozen solid, and in about twenty minutes, after many turns, came to the China Dragon, a restaurant-motel set incongruously in the New Hampshire hills.

"I still don't like this," Tom said. "And I don't like you being here."

"It's okay," George said. "If the man insists, he insists. Don't worry. We're in the middle of nowhere. And it's better that there are two of us here with him."

The brothers went inside, across a small wooden bridge over a shallow pool of water filled with pennies tossed by hundreds of earlier customers.

"Let's hope we get lucky," George said, gesturing at the pool. "This is going to cost us a lot more than pennies."

It was early evening and the restaurant was nearly empty. Al Hemmings was sitting at a booth in a far corner, a drink and a small plate of egg rolls in front of him. He broke into a broad grin when he saw the Sturdivant brothers approaching.

"Ah," he said, "I knew you wouldn't disappoint me. How do you like my place? Best Chinese restaurant in New Hampshire."

"It must be the only one," Tom said, sourly. He looked around condescendingly at the garish decor, all bright reds and golds.

"No, just the best hidden," Hemmings said. "From prying eyes."

The newcomers joined him in the booth and ordered drinks.

"What are you having to eat?" Hemmings asked. "Better decide now. It takes time."

"We're not going to eat with you," Tom said. "There's a limit to what we'll do to beat Hacker."

Hemmings was unfazed by the crack. "Suit yourself," he said. "I'm used to eating alone."

"Let's get on with it," the senator said. "Let's see what you've got."

Hemmings reached into an old leather briefcase and pulled out a thick pile of papers. He handed the sheets one at a time to George, who examined each carefully, then passed them on to his brother. Neither said a word, making a strong attempt to be impassive. But as they read they could not completely mask their interest. One document caused the senator to suck in his breath. He handed it quickly to Tom. The three men sat there for perhaps fifteen minutes, Hemmings watching the other two like a patient jewel dealer, confident that the quality of his wares was his best sales pitch.

"How do we know these are authentic?" George asked at last.

Hemmings smiled tolerantly at him. "Please, Senator," he said. "You're not dealing with an amateur."

"You mentioned a tape the other night," Tom interjected.

"Yes," Hemmings said. "I have it right here. Would you like to hear it?"

"Here?" Tom said, looking around nervously.

Hemmings smiled again and withdrew from his jacket pocket a tiny cassette player equipped with an earplug. He handed it to the senator.

"This you don't get to keep," he said. "Just to listen to, by way of verification. I promised my source I would return it, with no copies made."

Tom looked at him. "Why would you make a promise like that?"

"Because, my friend, like you in your old line of work, I have to be able to go back to my sources."

"Honor among thieves, is that it?"

"Must you put it that way? Anyway, that's how it has to be. But listen."

The senator worked the plug into his ear and turned on the cassette player. One voice was irrefutably Hacker's, the other sounded like Leo Manasian's.

"Hello, Leo. How did you make out?"

"Fine. It's all set. Our friends in Trenton have delivered. The permits are greased to go through next week. They don't even know you're involved. Same as in Carson City."

"Good. And the, er, discounts?"

"They agreed to the same cut as in Vegas and Reno. They weren't hard to get along with, once they knew who we've got with us."

"Of course. And what about our other friends? Are they satisfied?"

"Why wouldn't they be? As I told you, all they care about are the liquor contracts and the freedom to operate without harassment on the rest. Don't worry, they're aboard."

There was more of the same, between Hacker and several unidentified voices. They talked always in a veiled fashion, with no names mentioned. That fact did not seem to disturb either George or Tom Sturdivant. The language of politics often was in code; pols spoke of "this guy" or "the other guy" or "the governor's friend," and the more cryptic the better. If you were inside you understood; if you weren't, you weren't supposed to.

The documents were more specific. They were confidential memoranda and legal papers that, pieced together, indicated a few conservative businessmen and bankers, fronting for a group headed by Hacker, had bought into major gambling casinos in Las Vegas and

Reno, and were preparing to do the same in Atlantic City. Some names prominent within organized crime appeared to be in the Hacker group, names that Tom Sturdivant as a former investigative reporter readily recognized. Reading the documents, his reservations steadily fell away.

"This stuff," he said to his brother, oblivious to Hemmings' presence, "is dynamite."

"I knew you'd think so," Hemmings said, rubbing his hands together. "Do we have a deal?"

As he said it, the waiter came over. George Sturdivant nervously looked up at him and shook his head, indicating he did not want another drink. When the man walked off, George got up.

"No sense in pushing our luck," he said. "I just came to see what you had. You'll have to work out the rest with Tom. Let's go," he said curtly to his brother.

Outside, as they got into the car, George said: "Offer him thirty thousand. He's going to hold some stuff out on us and try to hit us again. Maybe if we offer him thirty, he'll give us the tape. To get the rest."

"You sound as if you've done this before," Tom said.

His brother smiled. "How could you suspect such a thing?"

The senator waited in the car while Tom went back inside. In about ten minutes he came out again.

"You were wrong," he said. "He insisted on the full fifty and he wouldn't budge on the tape. He said he knew you were going to try 'that old caper'—that was the way he put it. He said you insulted him but he needs the money so he won't make a federal case of it."

"Big of him," George said. "What about the transfer?"

"I told him where to draw the money in the morning and he said he'll deliver the papers to me tomorrow at the Wayfarer."

Tom got behind the wheel and they drove off. It was quite dark but he made his way expertly back to the expressway and south to Manchester.

"It scares hell out of me, George," Tom said on the drive back. "What if it gets out that we bought this stuff?"

"Who's going to tell? Hemmings? Don't sweat it. The trick is to leak the information without our fingerprints on it. We've got to get it into the hands of a reporter of impeccable reputation." And he smiled again.

Tom looked over to see whether his brother was serious. "You don't mean Mike? He'll never run that stuff without going over it with a magnifying glass. I know how he operates. He'll want to spend weeks checking it out, and we don't have weeks."

"Well," the senator said, "we'll just have to find a way to get around that problem."

Mike Webb sat in the waiting room of the small private air terminal in Manchester, looking at the falling snow and joining in the general grousing among the press corps about the weather.

"I don't think we're going to get out of here today," he said to Barney Mulvihill.

"Don't bet on it," Mulvihill said. "When Ed Hacker says he's going to be someplace, he generally gets there. That's a big part of what he's got going for him. He delivers on the unimportant things, and the unwashed think he's great for it."

Hacker had not yet arrived. Webb and Mulvihill went into a small bar off the lobby and each ordered an eye-opener. Webb was not much for drinking in the morning but it looked, with the fierce weather, like a long hard day ahead, and Mulvihill seemed insistent. It was not the weather, of course. Mulvihill was a heavy drinker, snow, rain, or shine. Nor was he a "problem drinker." It was no problem for him or anyone else. He was just a hard drinker in the old Irish mold. But the fact was that on this morning he did want to get his old friend alone.

"Mike," Mulvihill said, "what the hell's going on with you?"

"What do you mean?"

"I mean what's with you and the broad? You're balling her, no?"

Webb looked into his drink. "I don't want to discuss it," he said.

"Suit yourself," Mulvihill said, shrugging.

"What makes you think that?" Webb said.

"I thought you didn't want to discuss it."

"What makes you think so?"

"Because I'm not stupid. Anybody with half an eye can see how you've changed toward her. You keep your hands off her in public, but you can't keep your eyes off her."

"I didn't think it showed."

"Reporter's trained eye," Mulvihill said.

Webb debated with himself for a moment, toying with his glass. Then he broke into an easy smile. "You got me, pal," he said. "If I told you how it happened, you wouldn't believe me."

"Try me."

"No, your weak heart couldn't stand the titillation."

"What about yours? You're not that much younger than me."

"I managed."

"Well, you sure look better the last few days. You were looking as if you hadn't slept in weeks."

"That was true."

"It must agree with you."

Webb just smiled now. He didn't want to joke about it.

Mulvihill ordered another round, but the conversation clearly was doing more for his alertness than the drinks.

"And what about the column? I take it this means you're going to carry her indefinitely, or at least until this thing runs its course?"

"She's smart, Barney. And she's determined. She'll get the knack. It was unfair of me to put her on the spot in the midst of a campaign. And the whole thing with Tom has been hard for her to handle. Hacker tried to box her in with it."

"That figures."

Webb looked at Mulvihill directly for the first time. "And she's good for me, Barney. I was hitting bottom. For a change I feel I'm in the game, not just watching it, not just recording it."

"You're in the game, all right. Just be sure the game you're in and the one you're supposed to be writing about don't get too mixed up."

"Thanks, coach," Webb said. "I'll try to remember that."

While they were talking, Hacker had arrived, accompanied by Greg Commager, the press secretary, and Bea Morrison. Mulvihill paid the check and they joined the group. Hacker was speaking directly to the pilot.

"Hell, man, I've flown in much worse weather than this," he said. "Those folks up in Berlin [he pronounced it BURR-lin in the local style] are expecting me."

"It's even rougher up there in the White Mountains, Mr. President," the pilot said. "I don't know whether we can get clearance."

"You get on the phone, or the radio, or whatever you have to use, and you get us cleared," Hacker said, in his most presidential tone.

"I'll try, sir," the pilot said.

Hacker turned, smiling broadly, and he and Commager approached the waiting reporters, some of whom showed signs of air sickness even before they were aboard the plane. They were not eager to make the flight, but the decision was out of their hands.

"Well, fellas," Commager announced in his condescending way, "this morning we're going to separate the men from the boys. The White-Knuckle Special to Berlin is about to depart. The president and I won't hold it against you if you don't care to come along. But you'll miss what he's going to tell the folks up there about the indomitable courage of the national press corps."

Hacker laughed uproariously at Commager's needling but not in a contemptuous way. Some of his targets even joined in.

In a moment the pilot came over and told Hacker he had managed to get the flight cleared.

"Let's go, boys and girls," Hacker said, taking Bea Morrison's arm and escorting her through the falling snow to the waiting plane. The plane was an old propeller job, a de Havilland Otter; it did not inspire great confidence among the dogged passengers, none of whom felt free to back out after Commager's remark. There were about twenty seats in the plane, and Hacker took one immediately behind the pilot, with Bea next to him. Webb and Mulvihill settled in just behind them, and within moments the plane was full and they were off. It was a

189

lumbering takeoff, up through the snow. All faces were turned to the windows, except Hacker's. He was busy pouring drinks into paper cups from a bottle an aide had brought aboard, and passing them back.

"Here, friends, a little dose of Doctor Hacker's elixir," he announced. "It has never failed to bring me and mine through the most fearsome moments."

The drinks were welcome. The flight was one of the worst the veterans aboard had experienced. The plane seemed buffeted by the snow, dropping precipitously every few minutes, as if falling off a cliff, then catching in a sudden updraft. As the White Mountains rose, the plane kept the same elevation, and it was more than an hour before they began to approach Berlin. By that time the snow had mixed with hail, and the sound of it pelting the fuselage intensified the apprehension in the cabin.

"This," Mulvihill declared loudly after one particularly heart-stopping drop, "calls for a song." He, Webb, and a few others, to screw up their waning courage and kill time, set about composing an instant parody for the occasion. Soon, after much patchwork, it was finished, and all, including Hacker, were belting it out lustily. All, that is, except those few—Commager among them, to the great satisfaction of the reporters—who were frozen with fear, gripping the arms of their seats until their knuckles were in truth white:

"He floats through the air, this dogged has-been,
The daring ex-Pres in his flying machine.
Ed Hacker's determined, his ambition's obscene,
To regain what was stolen away."

Other choruses, equally bad, were dreamed up on the spot and sung, but with waning enthusiasm as the flight dragged on. Hacker was compared in words and music to every famous flier from Orville and Wilbur Wright to the Red Baron, and always unfavorably.

During a lull, the pilot turned his head and said to Hacker: "Berlin's closing down sir. I don't think we can get in there."

"You just get us in there, boy," Hacker snapped. "We didn't come this far just to turn around and go back." He said this last a bit too loudly. The singing suddenly tapered off, and all braced themselves for the landing. The plane descended until the mountains could be seen close on either side—too close for comfort, the aircraft swaying and dropping sharply. Nobody spoke, not even the candidate, as eyes strained to see the ground through a heavy haze and the blinding snow. Webb noticed that Bea Morrison was clutching Hacker's hand tightly, and to hell with who saw it.

"I could lose my license for this," the pilot said, half to himself. The remark made Hacker smile through his teeth.

"I'm worrying about losing my goddamned ass," the former president of the United States said, "and he's worrying about losing his license."

All at once the ground came up, so suddenly that someone gasped, and then the plane hit the snow-covered runway with a jolt, rising slightly, hitting down twice more, and swaying badly. But the pilot held fast, and in a moment had the plane in firm control, taxiing to a swift stop. The passengers, led by Hacker, burst into applause and cheers.

"Good work, my boy," Hacker shouted to him. "Your courage and skill will not go unrewarded in the next administration!"

For the first time since the descent had started, everybody laughed. Everybody except the pilot, who said nothing, but simply shook his head from side to side, as if not believing he had done what he had done.

Webb let his breath out in a long, low rush.

"You weren't nervous, were you, Mike?" Mulvihill asked, grinning.

"Me? Don't be ridiculous. But is there a men's room in the terminal?" And they both laughed, a little more heartily than the occasion called for.

At the airport fence, perhaps fifty hardy well-wishers cheered Hacker as he emerged from the plane. He raised his arms in a victory sign and plowed through the snow to them. They were a motley bunch after the long wait, having braved the cold and watched the snow-filled sky with trepidation for the plane to break out of the whiteness and touch down safely. To Hacker, they looked at a distance like a long row of snowmen breathing great puffs of white smoke, calling his name and pressing forward against the fence to shake his hand. Up close, the candidate saw red faces framed with eyebrows, moustaches, and beards that caught and held the snow, but with happy grins shining through, radiating warmth.

The rest of the passengers, composed again, filed out of the plane. "You've just seen why you guys aren't going to keep Ed Hacker out of the White House," Commager said, having suddenly regained his chutzpah. Webb and Mulvihill glared at him with even greater contempt than usual.

As the Hacker party sought to drive from the airport to a small motel just outside the town, where a headquarters had been established, it was clear the weather would permit no campaigning. By this time, visibility was no more than a few feet, and pines and birches heavy with the accumulation of snow drooped and swayed precariously on either side of the road. A dozen times en route, the cars had to stop to help other motorists out of ditches or to wait while cars ahead attempted to climb steep and slippery hills. Nearly half a mile from the motel, the road became totally impassable. All passengers, including Hacker, were obliged to proceed on foot. When they arrived at the motel, they were informed that all phone lines were down and there was no hope of restoring service until the storm had subsided.

"Well, we might as well relax and enjoy it," Hacker said, grinning at Bea Morrison, somewhat to her embarrassment, and to the consternation of Greg Commager.

"Must he flaunt it?" Commager whispered to a Hacker advance man. "One of these clowns," he said, gesturing to the press corps coming up behind, "is going to start writing about it if he's not more careful."

"What's to write about?" the advance man said, deadpan. "She's his personal secretary. Everybody knows that."

"Right," Commager said, shrugging.

It was early afternoon by the time everyone was assigned to his room and had eaten lunch—sandwiches and coffee, which was the motel's only fare. The snow was so heavy that it was impossible to see anything but a white haze from the windows. The manager, who ran the motel with his wife and one teenage son, got a roaring fire going in the small combination bar and dining room. Somebody tried the one television set in the motel, a console in the lobby, but all he could find was more "snow." "The cable must be broken," the manager said. With little else to do, before long, a poker game was in progress among Webb, Mulvihill, and a few other reporters. It was exactly the way they liked to spend a snowbound afternoon. Webb had already written the next day's column, a lighthearted account of the flight into Berlin that conveyed the steely determination behind Hacker's ever-present façade of joviality. It made a good, readable piece and Webb was disturbed that there were still no phone lines open, and he could not dictate it to New York. He rolled up the copy and tucked it in the breast pocket of his old black tweed jacket, from time to time interrupting the card game to check on the phones.

"You'll never get it out today," Mulvihill told him. "You should have filed something before you came up here. You know how the weather can be."

"Yeah," Webb said. "I didn't really think we'd make it here, to tell the truth. Well, Nora will know enough to check with New York and file something from Manchester."

"After you benched her?"

"It's an emergency. She'll go ahead. She may not be the best writer in the world, but she's dependable."

"You seem to have raised your impression of her in the last few days," Mulvihill said, smirking in a kidding way.

Webb only smiled.

In a while, Hacker and Commager joined the card game, to Mulvihill's unveiled dissatisfaction. "I don't mind playing with a presidential candidate, but why do we have to deal the flack in?" he asked the group.

Commager, as usual, was totally insensitive to the remark. He took a seat vacated by another reporter. "Deal the cards," he said. "This is my game."

The first few hands were punctuated chiefly by Commager's sassy monologue about how he hated to take hard-earned money from low-paid reporters, which he was doing. But Hacker's buoyancy and endless store of political stories eventually lightened the mood. Throughout the long afternoon, the hands were dealt and played, as the motel manager's wife, tending the bar, kept a steady flow of drinks coming. Hacker got on the subject of presidential candidates, and told about the time in 1964 when, as a senator, he was in Scottsdale, Arizona, and paid a courtesy call on the Republican nominee, Barry Goldwater.

"I go to the door and his wife answers," Hacker said.

" 'Is Barry home?' I ask.

" 'Yes,' she says, 'He's out back in the swimming pool.'

"So I go out back, and no Barry. I go to the house again and tell his wife.

" 'Did you look *in* the pool?' she asks.

"So I go back out and look down. There, lying on the bottom of the pool in the deepest part, maybe ten or twelve feet, is Barry, with a long tube in his mouth extending up to the surface. Well, I call down a couple of times but he can't hear me. So I throw a few pebbles down and he begins to stir. He takes the tube out of his mouth and swims to the surface.

"I ask him: 'What the hell are you doing down there, Barry?' And he says, 'I'm getting a little rest. With the damn telephone ringing all the time, this is the only place I can get away from it.' "

Hacker swore the story was true. And he told of the time in 1967 when he was in Alaska for some Senate committee hearing. George Romney, then a presidential hopeful, gave a big speech at a dinner in Anchorage excoriating Lyndon Johnson and his Vietnam policy. "It was hard for a Democrat like me to take until Romney let his fervor get away from him," Hacker recalled. "Finally he said that Lyndon running the country's foreign policy was about as effective as a one-armed paperhanger. The trouble was, the host congressman sitting right next to Romney had only one arm."

One story inevitably triggered another. "Poor old George, always putting his foot in his mouth," Mulvihill said. "I was on that trip to Alaska and I remember that dinner. Later we went to Pocatello, and the Idaho governor, an ultraconservative, went out of his way to say nice things about George at a big Republican lunch. Mrs. Romney and the governor's wife—who were both attractive women—were seated at the head table. George felt obliged to repay the governor's compliments, but politically he had nothing in common with this old mossback. So he thought for a minute and finally said: 'The governor and I share one thing in common—our wives!' "

"Yeah, and he never understood why the remark brought the house down," Webb said. "The thing was, that kind of thing got to be Romney's trademark. He was really a conscientious, hard-working guy, but there were dozens of stories like that, making him out to be a bumbler, and that's all anybody remembered. I'll never forget Gene McCarthy's crack about him after Romney said he'd been brainwashed in Vietnam. Gene said: 'I would have thought a light rinse would have done it.' "

The stories rolled out, one after the other—from Hacker, from Webb, from Mulvihill and other reporters. In the campaign in which they were all involved, the politicians and the newsmen indisputably were adversaries, but they were all drawing on their mutual experience in political life; it was what they shared in common, not what separated them, that was striking. Had a stranger somehow managed to defy the paralyzing snowstorm, to make his way from another world and come upon this scene, he almost certainly would have taken them to be a pack of lodge brothers off on a winter-vacation lark.

"Good old Gene," Mulvihill said, picking up the thread. "The quickest wit in the business, but also the roughest. The kids called him 'Clean Gene' up here in the sixty-eight primary, but we always called him 'Mean Gene.' He said that Clifford Case of New Jersey reminded him of the soldier they sent onto the battlefield after the smoke had cleared—to shoot the wounded. Gene never hesitated finishing anybody off himself when he had the chance."

"But you had to hand it to Gene," another reporter said. "He always had a wrinkle. I remember in seventy-two, when he tried to take a run at Muskie in the Illinois primary. He had very little money, so he bought himself a coach ticket from Chicago to St. Louis and back on Ozark Airlines. Ozark stopped at every jerkwater town between the two cities, and Gene got aboard in Chicago, had himself a martini, got off at the first stop, held a press conference right there at the airport, then got on the next plane to the next jerkwater town. He spent the whole day like that, from martini to press conference and back to martini on the next leg. It was a fine, low-key day, just the kind of offbeat number Gene liked. He had a great time and, of course, won no votes."

The hands were dealt and the stories were told and the drinks kept coming. From time to time, when somebody had folded his hand early, he would go to a window and peer out into the whiteness, reporting back on the futility of their situation—thus permitting all of them to enjoy the leisurely afternoon in good conscience. The motel owners were not politically sophisticated people, and so the scene that surely would have been regarded as bizarre by the cognoscenti—a deposed president of the United States playing poker and swapping old campaign yarns with the reporter who had been instrumental in his downfall—was wasted on them. The interlude was like a movie film frozen on a single frame, or like one of those insane moments in an old Laurel and Hardy comedy when, in the middle of a life-or-death chase between the good guys and the bad guys, they all pass a particularly engaging street singer. The chased and the chasers all stop, listen to the end of the song, then resume with the same abandon as before.

The stories, of course, eventually got around to Richard Nixon. Webb told of the time, in the summer of 1966, when Nixon as a private citizen was campaigning frenetically about the country for Republican congressional candidates. "He figured—correctly—that if the Republicans made big gains in the House," Webb recalled, "he would be the party hero. Well, nobody was paying much attention to him then, so it was easy to travel with him. Most of the time it was just Nixon, his old friend Pat Hillings, who succeeded him in his House seat, and me. Every night, after the last speech, Nixon would go to his room, have a glass of milk, do some sit-ups and go to bed. After he was tucked in, Hillings and I would do a little harmless drinking, sometimes closing the bar. Invariably, the next morning, Nixon would call Hillings in. 'What did you do last night?' he would ask. 'Where did you go? Who were you with? Did you find any women? Did you score?' Well before his time, Nixon was a dirty old man."

The conversation ranged that way over the poker game, and the hostility that had been building up for weeks between the reporters and the candidate took a breather. Even Commager seemed tolerable after a while. "I always liked the story," he said at one point, "about the reporter going in to see one of Lyndon's press secretaries, at the time of the Bobby Baker case. The Baker connection was causing Lyndon great embarrassment because everybody knew Bobby was his chief gopher. The reporter asked what exactly was the relationship between the president and Baker. And the press secretary smiled benignly and said, 'To be perfectly candid, they hardly know each other!' "

"Yeah, Commager," Mulvihill said, "you *would* like that story. Your father probably told it to you every night before he tucked you into bed, so you would grow up to be a good little flack." Everybody laughed, even Hacker and Commager.

It was that kind of day, with nowhere to go and nothing to do but play cards, drink booze, and tell stories. In the late afternoon, Bea Morrison and some of the staff minions joined the party. The manager's wife made more sandwiches and brought them to the tables. Predictably, everybody was a little drunk, including the candidate. At one point he put his arm around Bea and pulled her to him, in full view of everyone in the room. Commager suddenly contracted a severe case of sobriety. He got up and put some change in the jukebox, then asked Bea to dance. She readily accepted. Soon, all the reporters were taking their turn. Hacker, not to be outdone, cut in. In short order, it was a general brawl, while outside the snow fell, and the wind blew, relentlessly.

"You know," a young reporter said to Mulvihill, "old Hacker isn't such a bad guy. Neither is Commager, when he lets his hair down."

"Sure," Mulvihill said, "I'll remind you of that the next time either of them sinks his teeth into your neck."

Webb was sitting alone in a corner, deep in thought. Mulvihill went over and sat with him. "I guess the world won't hear from Mike Webb tomorrow," he said, reaching in and pulling the typewritten column from Webb's jacket.

"Guess not," Webb said, smiling. "And the world will survive it."

"It's good to see you relaxed for a change, Mike," his friend said. "The fact is, the world *will* survive it, and so will you."

They ordered another drink and watched the heavy snowfall outside.

"There's something to be said for bad weather," Webb said. He did not bother to check the phones again. He knew it would be a waste of time.

19

The Sturdivant headquarters in Manchester was on the fourth floor of the Carpenter Hotel, a relic that had nondescript food and service but was cheap and centrally located, just off the main street. The management did not object to political campaigns coming in, knocking down walls and partitions, and otherwise contributing to the overall deterioration. Nora Williams was sitting in the press room nervously chain-smoking and trying to make a phone call to Berlin.

"Damn," she said heatedly, slamming the receiver down.

"What's the problem?" asked Ray MacIntosh, slouched in a chair.

"Oh, I can't reach Mike. He went up to Berlin with Hacker this morning and all the phone lines are down."

"So? Mike's a big boy. He's been stranded in a snowstorm before."

"It's the column. He was supposed to file for tomorrow from up there, and the syndicate hasn't gotten a line from him."

"He must really be snowed in," MacIntosh said. "Well, what's a partner for? Why don't you just write the column for tomorrow? Or isn't it your turn?"

"Never mind."

"What's the matter, Nora, won't he let you? Is that what's going on? I knew it was something but I had another thing in mind."

Nora did not smile in the way she usually greeted his gibes. "Why don't you drop dead, buddy?" she said. She picked up the phone and tried to call Berlin again.

"If you're not writing the column with him," MacIntosh persisted, "what are you doing with him?"

"MacIntosh, did anybody ever tell you you're obnoxious?"

"Why, yes, many people, many times. I write it off as jealousy."

She glared at him, got up, and stormed out of the room, almost crashing into Tom Sturdivant as she did. He grabbed her by the shoulders, as much in self-protection as anything else.

The sight of him seemed to jolt her. "Hello, Tom," she said, her voice low, an awkward, embarrassed smile creeping over her face. "How are you?"

"'How are you?'" he mimicked. "I'm just terrific. I don't have to ask how you are."

Her eyes dropped. "Excuse me, I have to go," she said, softly, and hurried down the hall.

"Ah, enter the columnist-turned-flack," MacIntosh said. "Right on cue. What's up?"

"I'm looking for Mike. Have you seen him?"

"Everybody's looking for Mike. He's up to his ass in snow in Berlin, with Hacker. That's what has Nora in a snit. The syndicate is screaming for the column and for some reason she can't fill in for him. I don't know what that's all about, do you?"

Tom did not answer him. He turned and walked down the corridor to his own office, where his brother was stretched out on a sofa, reading some papers in a folder, with great interest.

"Did you find him?" the senator asked, looking up as Tom came in.

"No," Tom said. "He's out with Hacker, in Berlin."

"Did you talk to Nora?" George asked.

"No, MacIntosh told me. But I ran into her for a second and I could see she was upset. Because no column's been filed, I guess."

"Well, let's help her out. Let's see if we can come up with a good one for her," the senator said, grinning.

"That's what I was thinking," Tom said. "But I don't know if she'll go for it, George. She wouldn't dare make a move on anything like this without Mike. Not on anything as sensitive as this."

"That depends on how much of a bind she's in."

"She's in pretty much of a bind. One of the guys told me Mike's been writing the column every day because he wasn't satisfied with what she was doing. She's not about to buck him now."

"Why not? What better time, when there is no column, and we lay a great story in her lap? A story that will break the campaign wide open."

"I don't know. . . . In any event, I don't want to deal with her on it," Tom said.

"Never mind that. Get her in here."

Tom did not move. "You do it, George. You call her."

The senator got up from the sofa and walked to a window overlooking the front of the hotel.

"I hate to put it to you this way," he said, looking out the window and speaking with his back to his brother. "But I think you're missing a hell of an opportunity."

"What do you mean?"

George turned and faced Tom. "I mean you can make Nora look awfully good. To the syndicate, if not to Mike."

Tom bristled. "What the hell do I care whether she looks good or not?"

"Because it's eating at you—the number she pulled on you. You haven't been worth a damn to me since it happened. As long as Mike is just carrying her, you're going to be out of it with her. But she's looking for the main chance and always has been. If she comes up with a story on her own as big as this one, she may start remembering you again."

Tom shook his head. "You're a dreamer, brother," he said.

"Well, have it your way," the senator said, going to the phone. "We've got to get her in here one way or the other."

Tom hesitated, then went over quickly and picked up the phone before George could take it. He dialed the press room, then the coffee shop downstairs. When Nora came on, he was all business.

"Nora? I'm sorry to bother you. I've been looking for Mike but I understand he's stuck up in the North Country. . . . George and I needed to talk to him right away, to show him something I know you'd both be interested in. . . . Well, could you come up to the office? . . . And Nora, don't take an ad in the paper about it. . . . The sooner the better . . ."

A few minutes later, she came into the room. Tom closed the door behind her. Their eyes barely met and she walked over to where the senator sat and offered her hand, rather awkwardly.

"Hi, Nora," George said, getting up and quickly kissing her on her cheek. "Sit over here." He led her to the sofa in front of which was a long coffee table with the contents of the folder spread out on it.

Tom sat down across the way. "Before we show you this stuff," he said, taking over, still businesslike, "we have to have your word that you didn't get it from us. And no direct quotations. You know the rules of the game."

She was interested, and she nodded her assent. Tom reached over, picked up one of the sheets, and handed it to her. "Start with this," he said. "It's the transcript of a taped conversation between Hacker and Leo Manasian. It lays out the nub of it." The two men sat in silence as she read quickly through the transcript, shaking her head from time to time.

"Where did you get it, and how do you know it's authentic?"

"Nora," Tom said, "we're locked in, but take my word for it as a reporter"—she looked up at him and smirked as he said it—"we've heard the tape. It's Hacker and Manasian all right."

"I want to hear it too."

"You can't. We don't have it."

"Well, why can't you get it?"

"Because our source won't let it out of his possession. And, besides, there isn't time. Read over these other papers," he said, gesturing over the table, "and they'll remove any doubts you have."

He began to hand her more documents and she read them carefully, again shaking her head.

"Where do these come from?"

"Come on, Nora. You know better than that," Tom said. "All we can tell you is that this stuff is solidly sourced."

Nora went carefully through all the papers they had assembled before her, picking them up and putting them down in little piles, studying each one carefully. Then she sat back on the sofa and let out a slow sigh. She looked at Tom, then over to George, who smiled, then back to Tom.

"Mike would insist on hearing the tape," she said.

"Not if he saw all this detail," Tom offered. "And not if I told him I had heard it. You're not talking to a novice."

"No, I'm talking to the campaign manager for the rival candidate."

George spoke up for the first time. "Look, Nora, we were planning to give all this to Mike. We were sure he'd realize what we have. We frankly would prefer to see it in your column. But yours isn't the only column."

She shifted uneasily on the sofa. "Don't try to lean on me, George," she said. "Maybe I can get through to Mike now." She got up and went to the phone at George's side, but the lines to Berlin were still dead—as the senator was sure they would be.

She sat down again. "You really think you have me, don't you?" she said to them.

"No," George said, "we don't have you. We're giving you first shot at this because it will have the most clout coming from you, and—because Tom wants it that way."

She looked over at Tom. He was staring intently at her. She seemed, for the first time since she had entered the room, to be a bit flustered.

"I appreciate that," she said, meaning it.

"Is your deadline the same?" he asked, knowing it was. "If it is, you don't have much time."

"I have two hours," she said.

"You can use that typewriter over there," George said. "We can't let any of this stuff out of this room."

Tom moved the coffee table, with the papers spread out on it, next to the small desk on which the typewriter sat.

George got up and walked to the door. "I've got a meeting," he said. "I'll tell the hotel operator on the way out that you're here, in case Mike gets through on the phone. Tom, why don't you stay to keep an eye on things?"

"Are you afraid I'm going to waltz out with all of this?" Nora asked.

"I don't know why you'd want to," George said, "but we gave our word we wouldn't let it out of our sight."

After George left, Tom took a chair in a far corner of the room and began reading some papers. For a long time, Nora sat at the typewriter, sifting through the documents and the transcript, but writing nothing. Tom glanced at his wristwatch, but made no comment.

"I'm stuck," she said finally. "I'm too tense," she added, as if she were alone in the room, talking to herself. "I don't know whether I should be doing this at all."

He said nothing.

"Mike will be furious," she said.

"How do you think he'll be if you let the deadline go by?" he asked.

"He'll think I'm stupid as well as incompetent," she said.

She shuffled through all the papers again, making notes on a pad, trying to organize the material before starting. Many times, she had seen Tom and Mike do the same when they were dealing with a mass of data to cram into a single 750-word column. She tried writing several leads but they were all too awkward, or they left out something important.

"Tom," she said at last. "Can you—help me? How do I get into this?"

Expressionless, he rose and walked over to where she was sitting. "I'll just get you started," he said, and waited. She frowned, but got up, and let him take the chair at the typewriter. He began at once to write:

Manchester, N.H., Feb. 16—Former President Edwin Hacker is deeply involved with legal and illegal gambling interests, including some major organized-crime figures, in Las Vegas, Reno, and Atlantic City, according to extensive documents examined by this column.

The information made available to us indicates that Hacker has been instrumental in obtaining gambling permits for his underworld friends in all three cities where legalized casinos operate. Also, his actions appear to have cleared the way for figures prominent in the illegal liquor, drugs, and prostitution rackets to flourish at the casinos in the three cities.

The papers examined by us suggest that Hacker's gambling friends have made extensive contributions to his campaign to regain the presidency, through dummy operations somewhat like those uncovered in his successful campaign four years ago, which in part led to his resignation under fire from the office. . . .

Tom got up from the typewriter. "Now you just have to fill in the details." he said.

"Thank you," Nora said, her voice barely audible, her eyes avoiding him as she replaced him at the desk.

"There's no need to mention this part to Mike," Tom said.

"No, I won't," she whispered, still not looking up. "Thanks."

There was not too much more to write, but she labored under the pressure. Just at deadline, she finished and rushed to the phone to call the column in to the syndicate. Tom listened unobtrusively as she dictated and then discussed the story with an editor at the other end of the line.

"Yes, I'm sure. . . . Well, Mike's snowed in. I tried to get him. . . . No, I can't tell you, but I'm satisfied it's solid. I saw the stuff myself. . . . There's a transcript of Hacker and Manasian's conversation—and a tape."

At this, Tom shook his head, but she held up her free hand. "Yes," she said. "I did."

At this, Tom smiled just perceptibly, then caught himself. She was too engrossed in her conversation to have noticed. "Okay," she said. "And thank you very much. I appreciate your saying that. I'll talk to you in the morning."

Nora hung up the receiver with a dazed smile on her face. "They thought they weren't going to hear from me. They're a little nervous, but they're ecstatic about it."

"Who was on the other end? Bill Evans?" he asked.

"Yes. . . . He liked it. He really did. He said it was Pulitzer material, for God's sake."

"Maybe so," he said. "I hope he's right."

She went over to her purse, took out a cigarette, and lit it. She drew on it, then turned to him. "Tom," she said, "I appreciate what you did. Especially—especially under the . . . circumstances."

"Forget it."

"I've been pretty crummy to you."

"Yes, you have."

"I couldn't help it."

"You couldn't?"

"Well, I was so disappointed in you quitting the column and all."

"It's worked out okay for you, hasn't it?"

She didn't answer him. She walked to the window and looked out. "I think," she said haltingly, "I might have liked it better the other way."

He moved over behind her. "What about Mike?" he said.

"He's been wonderful to me," she said. "I can never repay him."

"Well, you just scored a big one for him."

"I hope so."

"Don't worry. The source is highly reliable."

"Who is it?"

"I promised George I wouldn't say."

She looked at him over her shoulder but did not press him.

"It was Al Hemmings," he blurted out, not understanding why he was telling her.

"Hacker's old buddy?" she said, startled, turning to face him.

"Yeah. He got shut out at the White House and didn't like it."

She let her breath out. "Well, that makes me feel better about the story. But why didn't he come directly to Mike or to some other reporter?"

"Why do you think?" he said, smiling.

"I have no idea."

"Because revenge wasn't all he wanted."

"What do you mean?"

He put his hands on her shoulders. "I've told you too much already. I always tell you too much. If you can get information out of others the way you can get it out of me, you'll be one hell of a reporter."

"I'm trying," she said. the nervous smile breaking out. "With a little help from my friends."

"And you do have a way of making friends," he said, trying to hold her.

"Please, Tom, don't," she said, moving away. "I have to go. Thanks again."

"Sure," he said, as she turned and went out the door.

"Sure," he said again, to himself, when she was gone.

20

A decidedly hung over Mike Webb walked into the motel lobby. The snow had stopped during the night, making it possible for Hacker to resume his campaign schedule. As Webb awaited the candidate, he went over to the manager at the desk.

"Any contact yet with the outside world?"

No, sir," the manager said. "They're hoping to get a line or two cleared sometime this morning, but you never know up here."

Barney Mulvihill came into the lobby, his face bearing the imprint of the long night in the bar. "What do you hear?" he asked Webb.

"Not a word."

Presently, Hacker appeared, sporting a hooded fur parka and his customary confident grin, and looking none the worse for wear. Bea Morrison was with him, similarly attired and similarly clear-eyed.

"Let's go, boys," Hacker said, "I'm after the frostbite vote today. 'Dogged President Braves Blizzard,' the headlines will say tomorrow. And I'll be very big on the evening news in this getup. I told you, Barney, that little plane ride would be worth it."

"For you, maybe," Mulvihill said.

"That's what it's all about, my friend," the candidate said.

The entourage filed out and got into four waiting cars. One main road into Berlin had been cleared, but that was all. They drove about two miles, then pulled off to the side and went on foot to a school.

"The kids have school today?" one Washington reporter asked in disbelief.

"Up here they go no matter what," Hacker said. "That's why I'm going to get all the votes here. Because I'm the only candidate not afraid of the weather."

Inside, the children waited expectantly in the gymnasium, where a homemade banner of colored paper was strung across a stage at the front, reading: "Welcome President Hacker."

"*President* Hacker," Mulvihill said. "He's even got the innocents saying it."

Hacker strode into the gym, shedding his parka as he did, handing it to an aide, and plunging into the crowd of perhaps a hundred pre-teen boys and girls. Rather than going to the stage, where faculty members sat expectantly in their Sunday best to greet him, he took a folding chair, dragged it to the middle of the floor, and stood on it. Putting aside his customary antipress tirade, Hacker played inspirational father-image. He talked about America the Land of Opportunity, tracing his own humble beginnings as a Minnesota farmboy, braving his share of bitter winters, working his way through high school and college, advancing in politics as a mayor, governor, senator, and finally president of the United States.

"Ripe corn in the husk," Webb whispered to Mulvihill. But it clearly went over with the kids, who sat perfectly still on the gym floor, enraptured.

"In the words of the immortal Mario Procaccino," Barney replied, invoking the old New York mayoral candidate and shameless master of the maudlin, "corn is in the ear of the beholder."

The ingredients of success, Hacker said, were hard work, long hours, and overcoming obstacles like the winter weather in the north country of New Hampshire. Life could be hard, Hacker told the children, but that didn't mean it couldn't be fun, too.

Out of the corner of his eye, Ed Hacker spied a set of parallel bars along a far wall. To the astonishment and glee of the children, he sprang off the chair, over to the bars. In a second, he was up on them, twisting high until his head was pointing directly down and his feet up at the ceiling. As he did, a great number of coins fell from his pockets, and hanging thus upside down, the former president of the United States shouted two words that sent all the kids scurrying. "Finders, keepers!" he yelled, red-faced. The children scampered beneath him, scrapping among themselves for the pennies, nickels, dimes, and quarters that rolled over the gym floor. Mulvihill and Webb stood watching, shaking their heads in grudging appreciation of a showman at work.

"Where do you suppose he got all the change?" Webb asked, smiling in spite of himself.

"Out of his piggy bank," Mulvihill said. "Where else? No doubt he carries it with him wherever he goes."

Commager sidled up to them. "Not bad, eh?" he said. "Good advance, that's all. The president never goes anywhere without knowing what the opportunities are. We learned that from Nixon."

"That's not all," Mulvihill said.

"Nixon was a tightwad," Commager replied in all seriousness, selling his man hard. "And he could never do that on the parallel bars. Nixon could hardly even walk in sync. This man's an athlete. And at his age."

"Screw off, flack," Webb said, putting the camaraderie of the previous day behind him.

At last Hacker left the parallel bars, still red-faced but grinning broadly, immensely pleased with himself, and again mounted the chair as the last kids scrambled for unclaimed coins.

"Let's play a little question-and-answer game," he said. "How many of you here are old enough to vote? Raise your hands." Of course, no hands went up.

"How many of you have moms and dads old enough to vote?" All hands went up.

"How many have grandmas and grandpas old enough to vote?" Most hands.

"How many have sisters and brothers old enough?" Many hands.

"How many have aunts and uncles?" More hands.

"Now, how many of you are going home and asking your moms and dads, your grandmas and grandpas, your sisters and brothers, and aunts and uncles, to vote for me?" Every single hand in the crowd shot up, as the kids grinned and shrieked.

"But do you know what my name is?" he asked.

"Yes!" they screamed.

"What is it?"

"*President* Hacker!"

He stepped off the chair again, and in a second the children were swarming all over him, the smaller ones stretching their arms to be picked up. He reached down, hugged a little girl to him, set her down carefully, picked up another child, and another, and another. The place was bedlam.

"Conning little children," Mulvihill said. "I've seen everything."

"And their parents, and their brothers and sisters and aunts and uncles, when they all hear about this at the dinner table tonight," Webb said, unable to suppress another smile at Hacker's audacity.

It took nearly half an hour for the kids to settle down, so that Hacker could make his way out of the gym. The entourage plowed through the snow to the road, climbed into the cars, and drove back to the motel.

As they approached, Webb and Mulvihill saw Leo Manasian, who had not made the trip the day before, standing expectantly at the entrance, clutching a newspaper. Manasian went to Hacker's lead car, stuck his head in through an opened side window, and in a moment Hacker came bounding out. He took Manasian by the arm and led him vigorously inside. By the time Webb and Mulvihill could leave their car to pursue them, the two men were already out of the lobby, presumably in Hacker's room. Bea Morrison, left behind for once, was hurrying in that direction.

"What's that all about?" Mulvihill asked a young Hacker aide standing in the lobby.

"I don't know," he said. "All I know is, Manasian just came in on a charter plane from Manchester all worked up. Something about a column in *The Boston Globe*. Somebody said it was yours, Mr. Webb."

Webb went quickly to the desk. "Are the phones in yet?" he asked.

"No, sir. Not yet. No word when they will be."

Mulvihill walked into the men's room off the lobby and was surprised to find Manasian and Hacker there, huddled over the open newspaper. When they saw him, Hacker turned and suddenly pushed Manasian into a stall with him and closed the door. It was a ludicrous sight, but they were not laughing. They were whispering, and as they talked, Hacker repeatedly flushed the toilet so that Mulvihill could not hear what they said. Presently the two men came out, Hacker solemn-faced. Manasian waved Mulvihill off and he and the candidate went out and down the corridor to Hacker's room.

"Something big is up," Mulvihill told Webb. "It's something in this morning's *Globe*. Manasian brought it up from Manchester and they were poring over it in the can when I walked in."

"Well, if it's that big, it'll be on television," Webb said. He went over to the console in the lobby.

"Sorry, sir," the desk clerk called over. "That's still out. We have trouble getting good reception anyway, even in good weather."

By this time, word was around that something had happened. The desk clerk suggested they might catch the news on his car radio. He gave his keys to Mulvihill, and he, Webb, and several other reporters went out into the parking lot. After much shouting back and forth they located the car, which as luck would have it was an old Volkswagen beetle. They pushed the heavy snow off the doors and crowded in. There were so many of them, and they were so raucous, that a passerby might have speculated they were rehearsing the famous circus routine. Mulvihill turned on the radio and twisted the dial until he found an all-news station. Some local stories came on, and then what they were listening for:

There's a sensational development in the presidential primary campaign in New Hampshire this morning. Syndicated columnists Michael Webb and Nora Williams report that former President Edwin Hacker has connections with organized crime figures in gambling and associated activities in Las Vegas, Reno, and Atlantic City. The columnists say they have seen evidence documenting the association. Hacker, snowbound in Berlin, New Hampshire, where he flew yesterday for a day of campaigning, has not been reachable for comment because all telephone contact has been disrupted in that area. In Manchester, Hacker's two opponents, Senator George Sturdivant and Walter Grafton, said they knew nothing of the allegations. But Sturdivant said that if there were any substance to them, pressure would surely mount for Hacker to withdraw from the race. As soon as we have more details, we will pass them on to you on this all-news station.

Mulvihill looked quickly at Webb. He was ashen. The other reporters in the car turned to him.

"What about it, Mike?" one of them said. "Give us a fill."

Webb looked blank. "That's . . . about it right there," he said. He pushed his way out of the car and headed into the motel.

"I get the first phone hooked up," he said to the clerk, menacingly. "Understand? I'll be in my room." And he headed down the corridor, the other reporters behind him, uncomprehending. He rushed into his room and slammed the door behind him.

"What's bugging *him*?" another reporter asked. "I've never seen him stonewall the troops before." The reporters went on down the corridor toward Hacker's suite. When they had turned the corner, Mulvihill went back to Webb's door and rapped quietly. "Mike? This is Barney. Let me in. Hurry up."

After a moment, the door opened. Webb motioned his friend inside, saying nothing, then closed the door behind him.

"You didn't know anything about it," Mulvihill said, reciting a fact, not asking a question.

"Sure I did," Webb said.

"Bullshit. Nora must have gotten hold of something and she ran with it."

"You know I couldn't file yesterday."

"So it was Nora. She got onto a good one. You were right about her, after all."

"God, let's hope so. This is either a grand-slam home run or a triple error with the bases loaded. But why the hell would she go with such a blockbuster when I'm snowed in up here? Why didn't she just write some crap and let it go for one day?"

"Would you sit on that kind of a story, Mike? Give her credit for some judgment. . . . You might as well. The fat's in the fire anyway."

"Barney, if anybody asks you, you don't know whose piece it was."

"Everybody will assume it's yours, of course."

"Fine. If it works out, I can straighten out the credit."

"And if it doesn't? You eat the whole rotten apple, is that it?"

Webb didn't answer. The discussion was terminated abruptly by a clamor outside, and Mulvihill went to check on it. Leo Manasian had come out of Hacker's room and was walking to a small meeting room where television cameras had been set up for a press conference. Manasian went to the microphones with a prepared statement. He waited for the reporters to get settled in their seats.

"I will read a statement," he said. "There will be no questions. President Hacker will not be coming out at this time. The rest of the day's events are canceled. Here goes:

"President Hacker has asked me to inform you that the allegations made by columnists Michael Webb and Nora Williams are news to him. He will have no formal reply or comment until he has had an opportunity to examine them and discuss the matter with his attorneys. He has authorized me to say, however, that he intends to remain in the race for the presidential nomination of his party."

Some aggressive reporters tried to press Manasian, but he waved them away and walked out of the room, returning to Hacker's suite, closing the door, and locking it behind him.

"It wasn't a denial," one reporter said. "It doesn't sound good for old

Eddie. Looks like Mike caught him with his hand in the cookie jar again. Webb may be getting old, but he's still got his stuff. He doesn't miss Sturdivant."

"Mike sure played this one close to the vest," another said. "Not a ripple. I don't think even Mulvihill knew about it."

"Well," a third said, "if I had one like that, I wouldn't tell my grandmother about it until I had it in print. And what a break for Nora! Barely broken in and she latches a ride onto a story that could win a Pulitzer."

"Maybe *she* got it," the second reporter said. The others laughed.

In Manchester, the evening news was on television, and George and Tom Sturdivant hovered eagerly over the set in George's room at the Wayfarer. There were film clips from Berlin of a somber Ed Hacker, his personal secretary, and Leo Manasian ready to board a charter plane, and the three leaving, close-mouthed, for "an undisclosed destination" as reporters peppered them with questions, in vain.

"We've got him!" Tom said triumphantly, pacing the room but not taking his eye off the set. "The bastard is as guilty as sin. You can see it all over his face." He had put his doubts and any indecisiveness behind him and seemed in control.

"What's your next step?" George asked his brother.

"Now we wait for the great American press to stick its collective nose into the records of the Nevada and New Jersey gambling commissions. It shouldn't take more than a few days to come up with the documentation."

"What about us springing some of the stuff we showed to Nora?" George suggested.

"That's the last thing we want to do. There isn't a fingerprint of ours on this story—and we have to keep it that way. Let the boys dig it out now."

But the loose ends bothered the senator. "What about Mike?" he asked. "Aren't we going to have to show him the same stuff? You know Nora will tell him where she got it."

"Sure," Tom acknowledged. "But the column is out there with it now. What can he do? We'll just tell him we had to give the stuff back." The instinct for the kill that had made Tom a tough investigative reporter was surfacing.

"He'll never buy that," George warned. "Suppose Mike threatens to write another column saying where Nora got the information?"

Tom smiled. "Take it from me, George," he said. "He's not going to blow the whistle on her. Not now."

"What do you mean, not now?"

"Mike Webb is currently under the magic spell of Nora Williams, and I know what that's like."

"Oh, is he? And doesn't that bother you?"

The question did not get an answer.

The planes were flying before phone service could be restored to Berlin. So Webb, Mulvihill, and the other reporters chartered one to return to Manchester. When they got back to the Wayfarer, Mike went immediately to Nora's room. She opened at his knock, and as soon as he had closed the door behind him, put her arms around him. He held her for a long, warm moment, and then broke away.

"What the hell happened yesterday?" he asked, with just a trace of an edge in his voice. He lit a cigarette and sat on the windowsill, away from her, waiting.

"Mike," she said defensively, studying his eyes, attempting to read his mood, "I tried to reach you, but it was impossible."

"I know that."

"Well, you hadn't filed, and the syndicate was giving me a hard time. . . ."

"So you just plucked this fantastic story out of the air?"

"No, of course not."

"Well, where did it come from?"

"Tom . . . and George . . . gave it to me."

"And where did they get it?"

Nora hesitated. "They wouldn't say."

"What?" His eyebrows shot up. "You went with a story like that without knowing the source? And no direct quotes?"

"They wouldn't permit that, either. But they had papers and a tape, and everything. They showed it all to me."

"They had a tape? Of what?"

Nora bit her lip. She didn't care for this third degree but she had expected it. "Of Hacker and Manasian discussing the whole gambling deal."

"How did you know it was Hacker and Manasian? Did you recognize their voices?" Webb was asking all the questions he would have posed to the Sturdivant brothers.

She hesitated again. "Yes," she said.

"Well," he said, letting up. "It looks okay. Hacker has been behaving like he's been caught breaking into Fort Knox."

"He's admitted it?" Her face brightened.

"No, but he's stonewalling it. It looks to me like he's scrambling around for an explanation."

He sat down heavily in an armchair. She came over and sat on the arm, and he pulled her into his lap.

"Then it's all right?" she asked. "I did all right?"

He laughed. "Pending further developments, I'd say you did all right."

She breathed a sigh of relief. "I've been so nervous about it. Especially because I knew you didn't want me writing any of the columns at all for a while."

"We were in a spot and you bailed us out," he said. He kissed her, and she held on to him.

"You're so good to me," she said, very quietly.

"Well," he answered, "you're good to me, too."

"How am I good to you?"

"You mean, besides writing the column when I'm snowbound?"

"Yes."

"You take my mind off myself."

"How do I do that?"

"You're doing it right now. By being here."

She let him go, leaned back, and looked at him. "I can do better than that," she said, and she pulled her sweater up over her head and off, tossing it on the floor. He laughed and sat there.

"What's the matter?" she asked. "Isn't that better?"

"Yes, it is," he said. "I just get a kick out of how you constantly try to shock me."

"Is that what I do?"

"All the time. To see if you can get a rise out of the old man."

She smiled. "Oh, a little play on words there, huh?"

"Not intentionally. I sometimes think you're trying to practice some kind of sexual medicare."

She frowned. "We're back to the old-enough-to-be-your-father thing, are we? I thought we had settled that. Well, Methuselah, I guess you're going to have to take that course over again."

She pushed herself up out of his lap and went over and climbed up on the bed. She stepped out of her skirt, and stood there, legs astride, hands on hips, mischievously looking down at him—until he got up from the chair, came over to her, and pulled her down.

"I hope I'm not late for class," he said.

Once, during the night, the phone rang, but she told him to let it ring, and he did, and eventually it stopped. Ordinarily he would not have shut the outside world out like that. He was, after all, in the midst of a presidential campaign, in the midst of a sensational development that cried out for more digging. Well, tomorrow would be time enough. There, in the quiet and the darkness, with her even breathing the only punctuation, he reflected on how quickly he had changed in the last days; how the depression and the brooding had suddenly ebbed, and the professional compulsion too, as if he had undergone some surgery of the emotions. He found himself chuckling aloud, and she stirred at the sound of it.

"What's so funny?" she murmured, only half awake, reaching over to touch his face.

"I was thinking," he said. "All this, and Ed Hacker's head on a plate, too."

"Mmmmmmm," she said. "Now go to sleep."

"Okay," he said, as if it would be the easiest thing in the world for him to do. And he knew now that it was.

21

The next day, with Hacker incommunicado, George Sturdivant enjoyed the heaviest press coverage of his campaign. The reporters hung on his every word, anticipating an attack on the latest revelations. But through the first three stops, the senator declined to accommodate them. As he and Tom had planned it, the strategy was to lay off. At a plant gate, a visit to a home for the elderly, and a long and tiresome tour of an insurance-company office in Concord, he contented himself with handshaking and small talk. Because it was the only show in town—Grafton had been written off as a serious contender—both partners of the Webb and Williams column went along, each wearing a Cheshire-cat smile to inquiries from their colleagues about the source of the latest charges against Hacker. Nora was bouncy and even flirtatious toward the male reporters. She displayed a new sense of acceptance, of belonging to the fraternity, and at the same time she allowed herself occasional displays of possessiveness toward Webb, absently holding on to his arm as they talked to other reporters. It embarrassed him slightly but lifted his spirits and ego.

In the cold light of day, however, Webb's professional skepticism took hold. He got Tom Sturdivant aside at the fourth stop, and they stayed on the press bus while the others followed the candidate.

"You were shooting fish in a barrel, laying that story on Nora—you know that, don't you?" Webb asked his former partner.

"You weren't reachable, Mike."

"Fortunately for you."

"What difference does it make? You got the story."

"Oh, come on, Tom, are you kidding? You never wrote a story or a column without knowing the source, did you?"

"Well, there's a first time for everything, as the farm boy said to the virgin."

"Who was it?"

"Can't tell you, Mike. I gave my word."

"And why no direct quotes?"

"Those were the conditions."

"I want to see the papers and hear the tape."

"What tape?"

"Come on, Tom. Nora told me about it."

"What did she tell you?"

"That it was Hacker and Manasian. How do you know? How can you be sure?"

Tom frowned. "Do you think after all this time I can't recognize Ed Hacker's voice and speech patterns?"

"It could have been a good imitation."

"It was no imitation, believe me."

"Well, I want to hear it, and see all the papers," Mike said. "And quote from them. We can't just let the story sit where it is."

"It won't," Tom insisted. "The *Times,* The *Post,* The *Star, The Wall Street Journal,* and the newsmags all have their people in Carson City and Trenton. Poring over the records, talking to the local pols. They'll break it out in a day or two. Either that way or by coming up with some hood who's facing a stiff term in the slammer and won't mind selling out a pol to save his own skin."

Webb grew increasingly impatient. "You would never let the opposition overtake you on your own story when you were working with me," he said. "Why do you expect me to? Why don't you want me to pursue this?"

Tom could see the situation getting away from him. "I'll tell you what," he said. "Maybe I can spring some of the papers for you. But the tape is out. We don't have it."

"Get it."

"I can't."

"It hasn't been destroyed, has it?"

"Not to my knowledge. What difference does it make anyway? It's not admissible in a court. The main thing is that the story's out. Hacker's up against a wall, and he knows it. He's going to have to get out."

"Well, we'll see," Webb said. "In the meantime, show me your basis for convincing Nora to stick both of our necks out."

"Okay, as soon as we get back to the Wayfarer tonight."

"Let's go back now."

"Mike, how will that look? It'll be like advertising on television where you got the first story."

As they talked, the rest of the press corps came bounding excitedly onto the bus.

"What's up?" Mike asked Nora, who was beaming.

"George finally let go. An old woman in there asked him about Hacker and he unloaded. Said he was a crook before he got into the White House, while he was there, and now. He said Hacker should quit, and he's asking the Justice Department to consider criminal action."

Tom was clearly chagrined. "He shouldn't have done that," he said, as if to himself.

"Why not, if Hacker's guilty?" Nora asked.

"Because it makes George look like a ghoul. It would have been better just to let it happen."

"I don't know what difference it makes," she said.

"Nora, your fangs are showing," Mike said, smiling. "You've

caught the scent of blood. It's not an attractive trait."

She looked at him, puzzled.

"You've got to try to be a bit more magnanimous in triumph," he said.

She seemed momentarily censured, then broke into a dazzling grin. "But," she said, "it feels soooo good!"

George Sturdivant's remarks dominated the early-evening news, as everyone knew they would. But at the very end, they were unexpectedly overshadowed. As the network shows were about to go off the air, Cronkite and the other anchor men were handed bulletins that each immediately read. "Former President Edwin Hacker," Cronkite intoned, "has asked for network-television time tonight to make what his campaign calls a critically important announcement. There are no further details, but it sounds as if Mr. Hacker may be preparing to withdraw his candidacy for his party's nomination for the presidency, only eight days before the New Hampshire primary. I've just been told that CBS will air the former president's statement live at nine o'clock tonight. His political aide, Leo Manasian, informs us that Mr. Hacker will speak from the studios of Television Station WBZ in Boston, where the former president, Manasian now says, has been in seclusion since the story broke of his alleged ties to organized crime and gambling."

When the announcement came, Mike heard it in Tom Sturdivant's room at the Wayfarer as he was going over the documents Nora had seen and taking notes. "I've got to get down to Boston," he said, handing the folder back to Sturdivant and heading for the door. "I'll have to look at the rest of this when I get back tonight. Okay?"

"Okay," Sturdivant said. "But this sounds like the ball game."

"Yeah," Webb agreed. "I can still get there in plenty of time if I leave now. I'll phone you when I'm back."

Mike, Nora, Barney Mulvihill, and—unavoidably—Ray MacIntosh decided to share a car for the one-hour drive to Boston. Nora was buoyant now, and MacIntosh was morose. He plainly did not enjoy having been so thoroughly beaten on this major story, and he horned in on the trip to Boston because he was uneasy about being whipped even more badly. He could not bring himself to ask Mike and Nora directly where they had gotten the story, and so Mulvihill spent much of the drive south taunting him.

"It's a good thing for you Hacker's pulling out tonight—if he is," he said. "Because Mike and Nora have three more columns backed up on this thing that would knock your socks off. Either Hacker gets out and stops the flow of his and your blood or your desk is going to have you on the police beat in Queens."

"What about you?" MacIntosh asked. "You don't look so good on this one yourself."

Mulvihill maintained his usual you-win-some, you-lose-some demeanor. "I've been to the top of the mountain, son. I know what it looks like from up there."

"Yeah? How does it look?"

"All you can see is a pack of hungry guys like you, trying to climb over each other to get where I was twenty years ago."

Through all this banter, Mike, who was driving, and Nora, beside him, sat in quiet amusement. She busied herself fiddling with the radio dial, picking up repeated announcements of Hacker's scheduled statement. For all their joking, they could sense the feeling of a public execution about the anticipated withdrawal; the reporters would have had to admit, had they been forced to be frank, that they felt a certain exhilaration at the prospect of being present when the ax fell.

At the studio, they showed their credentials and were ushered into a compact viewing room, separated from the actual studio by a ceiling-to-floor glass wall. Most members of the political press corps had elected to remain in Manchester to watch the statement on television, but these four wanted to experience this bit of history at first hand. To be able to do so was one of the windfalls of their trade, one that too many reporters took for granted. The better ones liked to be sure that in their stories they conveyed the sense of a real event, with real people. Mulvihill said that when he was an old man he wanted to be able to tell his great-grandchildren about all the great moments in American history to which he bore personal witness—"like Milton Shapp's announcement that he was running for president in seventy-six, things like that."

About five minutes before air time, Hacker strode onto the set. He was as Webb and Mulvihill had last seen him flying out of Berlin—grim-faced. Mildred Hacker was at his side, expressionless. Leo Manasian was whispering to his boss, and with about a minute to go, Greg Commager came onto the set and said something briefly to Manasian. Then he walked over to the viewing booth, where the reporters sat, their eyes glued on Hacker. Nobody bothered to greet him and he took a seat in the rear of the booth, for once at a loss for words. Bea Morrison could be seen standing in the studio's wings, out of camera range, with Amos Cormier at her side.

Hacker sat in an easy chair, with Mildred Hacker on a sofa to his right. He wore a dark-blue business suit and had no notes. He watched the set director, an attractive young woman, with great intensity, until she held up her ten fingers to indicate the number of seconds to air time. Then he turned full-face to the camera directly in front of him. Presently the director dropped her hand and an announcer's voice from off the set introduced him: "Ladies and gentlemen, the former president of the United States, Edwin Hacker." He said "former" of course, but it sounded presidential nonetheless. It was what Hacker always had going for him.

Hacker put aside his customary joviality. "My fellow Americans," he intoned, as if he were about to declare that a state of war existed somewhere. "The day before yesterday, serious allegations were made against me in the climactic days of the New Hampshire presidential primary campaign. I was accused of being connected with gambling activities in the three American cities where casino gambling is legal, but where—we all know—organized crime has achieved a foothold for a variety of associated illegal undertakings. I was accused, first, of having influenced the acquisition of gambling licenses in all three places and personally profiting thereby. And, second, of assisting key members of the criminal underworld to obtain advantageous arrangements for the pursuit of these associated undertakings, from extortion in the sale of liquor, to drug traffic and prostitution.

"These are grave charges against anyone, but particularly against a candidate for the highest office in this land, and one who has already held that office and has been forced from it. I would point out that these charges have come initially from the very same quarter that levied those other allegations against me that cost me the presidency; the high office that you, the American people, bestowed upon me in the secrecy of the ballot box. They have come from the press, and specifically from the newspaper column that led the witch-hunt against me scarcely two years ago. No proof, no witnesses, no documents have been offered in substantiation—only the same cowardly roundhouse blows."

Nora listened with a mixture of fascination and apprehension as Hacker spoke these words. She looked nervously at Webb. He reached over and took her hand in the semi-dark, a gesture that no one noticed, so intent were they all in watching the stern, determined man before them. Hacker went on:

"At first, I vowed to follow the counsel of my political advisers and say mothing. 'Don't lend dignity to the charges by denying them,' my friends told me. But today one of my opponents, Senator George Sturdivant—also acting with no proof, no witnesses, no documentation—not only repeated the allegations but demeaned my character and good name in public, put the FBI and the Justice Department onto me, and demanded that I retire from this contest. And so I must hold my peace no longer.

"Here and now, before this great television audience, I deny the charges—all of them. I challenge those who accuse me to prove these most serious and destructive allegations, or admit the great wrong they have done me. I welcome the inquiries of the FBI. I call on my foes, in language we can all understand, to fish or cut bait. Those who make these accusations owe you, the American people, as well as me, one of two things—proof or a public apology. That is the fair way, the American way."

Hacker turned and looked over at his wife.

"A man in public life," he said somberly, "does not endure this sort of thing alone. He shares it with all of his loyal followers, and most of all with his family. My dear wife sitting here with me has already been asked to endure much more than any one person should have to, merely to remain loyal and at the side of her husband. And tonight, as in the many dark days of the past, she is beside me still. I want you all to know that not once in the last days, since these latest unfair and untrue allegations have been leveled at me, has she questioned my innocence. That is the kind of steadfastness a man in public life needs if he is to persevere."

Nora stole a glance at Bea Morrison in the wings. She was, incongruously, grinning.

"Yet, it is not reasonable to expect that those outside my close family circle will accept what I say on faith. These are times of great cynicism toward those who hold the voters' trust, or seek it. In every political campaign since 1974, we have heard politicians say that Watergate is behind us. Yet the aftertaste of that deplorable national tragedy lingers. The American people want proof; and they are right. They are entitled to it. So it is in this case."

Webb glanced at Mulvihill, sitting on his left. "Here it comes," he said. Mulvihill nodded. The studio was deathly still, all eyes glued on the figure before the camera.

"More than a quarter of a century ago," Hacker said, "another man, a man destined to become president of the United States, stood before a nationwide television audience pleading his case against a much less serious allegation. That man was Richard Nixon. I know it is not in vogue to invoke that name these days. But I do so deliberately. When Richard Nixon as a candidate for vice president in 1952 faced an attempt by the press and his political enemies to force him from the Republican ticket with Dwight D. Eisenhower, he stated his case forthrightly. He asked the American people to cast their votes, through telegrams and phone calls to the Republican National Committee, on whether or not he should remain on the party's ticket. He vowed to accede to their judgment and they told him, and the country, overwhelmingly, that he must not knuckle under to those few who would have substituted their will for the will of the people."

Webb watched and listened with a look of deep apprehension. The certitude—or the gall—of the man was unnerving.

"I do not ask tonight for such a demonstration of public support," Hacker concluded. "The allegations that have been placed on the public record are much more serious than those Richard Nixon faced in 1952. They cannot be resolved by an unofficial mandate. I ask instead that you join me in demanding that the press and Senator Sturdivant present proof or apologize.

"I say to you tonight that I will not retreat. I will not surrender. I was driven once from the presidency and have lived to regret it. I will not be driven this time from the pursuit of an office that was rightfully mine, that you bestowed upon me legitimately and overwhelmingly four years ago. I intend to fight this malicious smear. I intend to continue my campaign to vindicate myself and all the millions of Americans whose votes sent me to the White House in the first place. If you needed any more evidence of what I have been saying to you, my fellow Americans, about the circumstances that precipitated my resignation two years ago, you have it tonight. And this time, I assure you with all my heart, I do not intend to be thrust aside. This political crusade on which I have embarked will go forward until I am back where your votes and your trust placed me four years ago—as your president. Thank you and good night."

Hacker sat grimly, without smiling, staring into the camera until the red light went out, signaling he was off the air. Then Cormier, Manasian, and other associates on the set rushed over to him, shaking his hand, while Mildred Hacker continued to sit alone on the sofa, still expressionless. Bea Morrison came out and gave her boss a playful hug. In the booth, the lights were flicked on and Commager, who had been silent throughout the performance, came bounding down the aisle to the front where the reporters sat numbed.

"So much for another resignation," Commager said, grinning broadly. And looking directly at Webb, he asked: "And will there be a rejoinder from the Fourth Estate?"

Webb stared back at him, but said nothing.

"How about you, Miss America?" Commager asked mockingly of Nora. She looked to Webb to somehow extricate her, but he did not notice. He was already up the aisle and heading out of the studio. She brushed past the smirking Commager and caught up with him, grabbing on to his arm like a child fearful of being left behind in a hostile crowd. He did not even look at her to acknowledge her presence, but kept right on going.

22

Mike and Nora left Barney Mulvihill and Ray MacIntosh behind in Boston to file their stories and took the car back to Manchester. En route, they said little; he was deep in thought and the silence was broken only occasionally when he would ask her a question about the column she had done, about the papers she had seen. And the tape she had heard.

"Are you sure it was Hacker?" he asked.

"What?"

"His voice. On the tape."

". . . Yes."

"How could you be sure?"

". . . Well . . . Tom said there was no question about it, and he's heard him in person much more than I have."

She did not know how to cope with him under these circumstances. She had of late treated him almost as a personal plaything, but she regarded him professionally with a sense of awe. This clearly was not an occasion for any sort of levity. "Is everything . . . all right?" she asked him.

"I don't know," he said. There was no hostility toward her in his voice, or even impatience. It was more that he was distracted, that his mind was not on her. She had seen him this way at times when Tom was still with the column, but not in the last month. She reached over and put her hand on his knee, and when he looked over at her, she smiled her nervous smile. He did not smile back, and in a moment she took her hand away.

"We've got to find out the source," he said. "Hacker's put the ball in our court. We can't let it sit there. We can't wait for somebody else to move the story ahead. I knew that from the beginning."

She said nothing.

"Do you have any ideas?" he asked her.

"About what?"

"About the source. About who it could be who laid all that stuff on Tom and George."

"No . . . yes." She paused, watching him out of the corner of her eye. "It—" she stopped, then started again. "It was Al Hemmings."

He took his eyes off the road and stared at her. "Al Hemmings? The old Hacker hack?"

"Yes."

"How do you know that?"

She hesitated again, then went on: ". . . Tom told me."

"Well, why in hell didn't you say so?"

"He asked me not to. . . . He told me in confidence."

He stared again at her, unbelieving. "In confidence? Listen, sweetheart, you and I have no confidences when it comes to work, understand?"

Nora was surprised by his use of the old, grating familiarity, the intentional invoking of the male chauvinism. She felt a sense of desperation come over her.

"Well," he said, not dwelling on why she had not volunteered the vital information earlier, "that makes sense. Hacker milked Hemmings dry in the last campaign and then dropped him. He was considered too unsavory to have around the White House. What a laugh. *Anybody* too unsavory for that crowd. 'Don't get mad, get even.'

The old Boston Irish motto. Hemmings would be the kind to follow it, that's for sure."

"But why take all that stuff to George and Tom?" she asked. "Why not bring it to you?"

He looked at her and smiled, the first sign of warmth. "For somebody who's been around politics as long as you have, you're awfully naïve. Money. Hemmings no doubt held them up for a nice piece of change."

He thought for a moment of what he had said. "Say, maybe that's how we go. Maybe that's where we take it next. Sturdivant pays for the goods on Hacker. Beautiful!"

She squirmed in her seat. "But how does that help?" she asked. "It only supports what Hacker was saying."

"So what? It's a hell of a story if it's true."

"You mean you'd blow the whistle on George and Tom after they leaked all that stuff to us?"

He looked at her again, harder this time. "Did they tell you they bought the stuff?"

"No. Tom just said Hemmings wanted something more than revenge."

"Then we're not locked in on it. They obviously were using you, anyway."

She didn't quite know how to say the next thing. "And you'd blow the whistle on . . . me? On us?"

He reflected on that. "Yeah," he said finally, "I see what you mean. And the real question is what Hacker was doing with the rackets, what he got out of it."

"Yes," she said, relieved that he was on another track. "So what do we do?"

"We find Hemmings. And then we squeeze him."

"What does he look like?"

"He's a boozy, obese guy—probably in his early sixties. He looks like he'd sell his mother into white slavery. Red-faced, squat, walks like a longshoreman."

"I haven't seen anybody like that around."

"He's probably out of the state by now. As soon as we get back to the Wayfarer, I'll start calling."

"Couldn't Tom put you in touch with him?"

He shook his head at her, incredulous. "Sure, he's going to drop the guy in our lap when he probably just finished paying him off. Tom knows enough to try to keep his fingerprints off all this. I'm surprised he even told you about Hemmings. How did that happen anyway?"

"It just . . . slipped out. He didn't mean to tell me. . . . Will you have to tell him that you know? I wish you wouldn't."

"I'll see. First, I'll try to get to Hemmings on my own. I don't want to be caught in any three-way conspiracy between the two of them. We have our own fingerprints to worry about now."

"I don't understand."

"You heard Hacker. He'd love to be able to say the press and his chief opponent were in league with a disgruntled office seeker to do him in."

When they drove up to the Wayfarer, it was nearly midnight. Tom Sturdivant was standing out front and he came up to the car as Webb was parking it.

"I called down to the press room at WBZ," he said. "Barney said you were heading back up here. George wants to see you right away." He talked only to Webb. Then, almost as an afterthought, he turned to Nora. "You, too, Nora, of course."

The columnists went with him to the senator's room. George Sturdivant opened the door and flashed the two a confident grin. "Well," he said, motioning for them to sit down, "it looks like we've got him."

"Yeah?" Webb said.

"Now's the time to spring the documents. We've decided to turn them over to you."

"George, we've already written about them," Webb said, suspicious.

"But now you can quote directly from them. You can produce them to satisfy the doubters."

"Why don't you do that?"

"Don't you want them? I thought we were doing you a favor."

"Before we write any more from this stuff," Webb said, "we need to know the source. And we need to talk to him."

"That's not possible," Tom interjected, looking nervously at Nora.

"And I have to hear that tape."

"No go," Tom said. "I can't get it. But it was Hacker all right. No question about it."

"Try to get it," Webb said.

"All right, but I don't think it can be done. Why is the tape so damned important?"

"For credibility. You can throw all the papers at the voters and they won't mean a thing if people don't want to believe. The tapes were what got Nixon."

"But they weren't made public then. There were only transcripts."

"But Nixon acknowledged that there *were* tapes. And he put out a printed version himself that was damaging enough. This time we need the real thing. It's the only way. With the documents we could develop witnesses, but we don't have the time. If this thing is going to be nailed down before the primary Tuesday, you've got to spring that tape."

"Mike's right," the senator said. "You better get back to our source."

Tom nodded. "We'll let you know," he said to Webb, still acting as if Nora was not there.

For the first time since Nora had been with him, Webb had difficulty sleeping. He lay awake, looking at the outline of her beside him in the dark. His mind raced over the whole story, and the tumultuous events of the last few days. He got up, taking care not to wake Nora. He moved the room's one armchair into a far corner, away from the bed, and settled into it, lighting a cigarette. He felt uncomfortable with the story's untidiness. He did not like getting into it as late as he had. He would not have handled it as Nora had—as they had pushed her into handling it. And Hacker was one of the great bluffers, one of the great political poker players. He had the nerve to bet the sky on a pair of jacks. He was doing no more than he had done in the past—crying dirty press and unfair tactics when he was caught red-handed. In his television talk he had taken the case away from the purely factual into the realm where he was most effective—the emotional, the suspicious, the biased; the realm of the haters, the conspiratorial minds, the put-upon, the bad losers who always looked for a scapegoat.

Webb sat in the dark and tried to put the problem in focus. Hacker had always been the high-priced lawyer from uptown in the court of public opinion. The only way to nail him for sure, to cut through all the razzmatazz, was to get him cold—with the tape in his own unmistakable voice, unwarily confessing all. It could all be confirmed later by other means, but by that time the primary would be over—maybe several primaries—and until then Hacker could play the victimized innocent, and there was no telling how the voters would react to that.

As Webb mulled over the situation, he accepted that Hacker's thinly veiled plea for telegram and telephone support would generate an overwhelmingly favorable response; such blatant pitches always did. It was hard at such times to believe in government by the people. Webb did have to admit to himself that in comparison with Nixon's famous "Checkers" speech, to which Hacker had alluded, Hacker's presentation had been much tougher, much more polished, much less fawning. But it sought to tap the same prejudices, the same feelings of the man of the people being unfairly pummeled by the Larger Forces over which the little people had no control. In a day or two, the whole matter of whether this presidential candidate had been in bed with bigtime gamblers, pimps, dope and illicit-booze peddlers might be buried in an avalanche of public sentiment for a persecuted underdog.

He looked over at Nora. He wondered how she could sleep so

soundly when her neck was on the line. Outside of their editors, only the Sturdivant brothers and Barney Mulvihill knew for certain that she had written the column. It was easy for him to protect her. Before going to Berlin he had put a hell of a lot of pressure on her, and with him stranded that pressure had certainly intensified. Maybe she hadn't asked all the right questions, but she got the column out and she had a former president hanging by his fingernails. She was fragile on the surface, but she had nerve. And she had him; she knew she could count on him, and he liked that. As he thought about her, watched her in the stillness, he was able finally to put the story out of his mind. He squashed the cigarette, went back to bed, and let sleep overtake him.

Al Hemmings had dropped out of sight. Tom Sturdivant checked all the motels and even called the China Dragon in Hooksett, to no avail. He was not surprised, nor did he expect that Hemmings would agree to hand over the tape without another large "commission." He was confident that they already had enough material to hang Hacker, and he much preferred having some totally independent source, like the investigating press, finish him off. George Sturdivant had already been guilty of a misstep in baiting Hacker, but maybe that would prove to be beneficial in the end. It apparently had goaded Hacker into his television address, denying wrongdoing. Tom liked the idea of playing out the line against Hacker a little at a time; let him really get the hook in his mouth before he was brought in.

Webb had no better luck tracking Hemmings down. From his room at the Wayfarer, he also placed calls to the governors of New Jersey and Nevada, both of whose campaigns he had covered, but he was just going through the motions. He knew both men well, and they were a matched set—both scared of their own shadows and certain to run as far away from this controversy as they could. He would get no helpful information about the gambling situation in their states from either one of them.

Next he called veteran reporters he knew at the *Trenton Times* and the *Las Vegas Sun.* They were, he was sure, already digging into the story.

He gave them the names of some of the organized-crime figures mentioned in the memos, which Nora had left out of the column, fearing libel. They were obvious names, and the two local reporters had already begun to look for any connections they might have had with Hacker. The former president was no stranger to the gambling cities, both reporters told Webb, but that meant nothing in itself; it was in keeping with his fun-loving, gregarious nature.

Webb wasn't getting far. Still, these were necessary bases to touch; he had to do the work—the way a conscientious pilot runs down his checklist before takeoff.

Hacker was back on the campaign trail again, and Nora went along with him. It was an extremely difficult time for her, because in the old style of George Wallace, he took to pointing her out in the crowd as part of the team that had written all those lies about him. He was shameless about it:

"Yeah, folks, it's the same old story. The press didn't like you electing me president in the first place. They didn't like it all the while I was in there; they did their best to get me out, and now they're pulling out all the stops to keep me out. There's a very pretty young lady over there in the press section you ought to meet. Look around, back there. The one with the dark hair and the bright-green blouse. Ain't she something? Hiya, Nora, honey. Her name is Nora Williams, and she writes that syndicated column with Michael Webb that printed all the drivel about me and those gamblers. She never said where they got it, and I'm waiting to hear. Maybe she'd like to come up here and tell us. . . . No? . . . I didn't think so. Well, it's nice to have her with us anyway. She sure is good to look at. . . . Too bad she can't get her facts straight."

This harangue, always met first with surliness in the crowd and then derision and ridicule, unnerved Nora, but she steeled herself against it. Hacker's frontal attack, bolstered by more heavy-handed Cormier editorials, caused the other reporters to adopt a defensive attitude toward her. Most never really associated her with the pertinent column in the first place, and thought she was bravely carrying part of Webb's burden for him. She said nothing to disabuse them of the notion. She marveled at how Hacker could so boldly declare his innocence, after all the documentation she had seen. But as Webb had told her, he was one of the world's great con men.

George Sturdivant, for his part, was determined this time to keep quiet and let the press work its will on the story. He tended to agree with Webb that there was a danger that the thing could drag out past primary day. But he was more concerned that his role in creating the story might be discovered—and damage him—so he said no more about it. He told inquiring reporters that he had been assured the FBI and the Justice Department were investigating the matter, and he was confident something definitive would be coming from them "soon." Senator Grafton, meanwhile, simply held on and went along his own dogged, do-good way, silently hoping the controversy might somehow leave him untouched, so that when the smoke cleared he would be the one major figure still standing.

But the smoke did not clear. It hovered over the campaign for the next two days. Nothing was coming out of New Jersey or Nevada to substantiate the allegations; nothing was coming from the FBI or the Justice Department. Hacker, fairly crowing over the nondevelopments, kept up his incessant taunting of George Sturdivant and the press, with special focus on the Webb and Williams column. This was all turning out to be very different from Hacker's White House demise. Then, the Webb-Sturdivant column, after its initial revelations of wrongdoing against Hacker, had delivered one day upon another of more information and more testimony, until the case against him was so overwhelming that he fell under its weight. This time there had been just a single boulder hoisted onto Hacker's back; he had flipped it off and dared his opponents to lift it there again and make it stay.

Webb chafed in the new situation. When he was among his colleagues, uncommon embarrassment prevailed. He was too good at what he did, too proven, to be doubted on any such major story; yet they also knew he was no one-shot artist, so they were waiting for him to break another piece of the story. The atmosphere on the press bus worsened. Everyone made a point of saying hello each morning, but few chose to engage him in conversation. Even MacIntosh, who usually could be counted on to join in a verbal sparring match, stayed clear.

Nora, squirming under Hacker's jibes, at last sought relief. "Hacker is killing me," she told Mike. "At every stop he singles me out and works me over. Why can't we write a piece about the tape?"

"Without having it? Don't be crazy."

"Well, it exists," she said. "It's not as if it didn't exist."

"I'd have to hear it myself first."

"Well . . . I heard it."

"But I didn't."

"If we don't write about the tape, Mike, Hacker could win the primary."

"Maybe."

"You don't want that to happen, do you?"

"Nora, that's not my prime concern. What I'm worried about right now is the credibility of the column."

"Why can't we quote directly from the memos? And maybe release some of them?"

"I want to check them out with the source first. You should have done it yourself the first time." Webb knew he was going over old ground.

"There was no time, Mike. You know that. . . . Are you going to start on me now, too?"

He looked at her and backed off. "No. Forget it. You did what you thought was best."

"But you wouldn't have done it, is that right?"

"I don't know. I probably would have done the same thing in the same spot," he said, not believing it.

"Well," she said, "we're beginning to look foolish. I'm beginning to look foolish. We have the memos and all that, and we're just sitting on them. If we quote them it will reinforce our position, show we weren't just making up the first column, and it might generate some reporting by somebody else. And it might provoke Hacker into making a mistake."

Webb mulled over the idea. She watched him intently, saying no more, but looking rather desperate.

Finally, he shrugged. "You buy a ticket, you take the whole ride," he said. "We're already fully committed by the first column. We might as well go ahead. We can lead with the Watkins memo, and meanwhile you'd better check out the court records in Carson City." She knew at once to what he was referring, and went to work on the phone, enthusiastically.

From the notes Webb had taken from the Sturdivant file on Hacker, he wrote the second column on the former president's alleged activities. It appeared the next day—five days before the primary:

Manchester, N.H., Feb. 20—Former President Edwin Hacker's connection with the ownership and operation of two large Las Vegas gambling casinos, in conjunction with four prominent organized-crime figures, is documented in memoranda and court records obtained by this column.

In a memo dated November 23 of last year, Roger Watkins, a well-known Denver insurance broker and longtime contributor to Hacker campaigns, informed the former president that arrangements had been made with Dolph Newfield, the owner of the two casinos, for participation by what is referred to as "the Hacker group." The four organized-crime figures are mentioned by name in the memo as members of the group. They are Leonard "Ace" Walters, Myron Levinson, Rocco Talesi, and August Ehrhardt, all of Las Vegas. Other documents indicate "the Hacker group" is also involved in casino gambling in Reno and Atlantic City, N.J.

Court records in Carson City, Nev., disclose that on November 26, three days after the memo to Hacker was written, Watkins, president of the Colorado Mutual Insurance Company, filed notification of controlling-stock purchase in his own name in the two casinos in question, the Desert Sands and the Gold Oasis. Because the organized-crime figures listed in the memo as members of "the Hacker group" are familiar names to law-enforcement agencies, that fact would appear to explain why Watkins did not list them in the papers filed in the Nevada court.

Other papers indicate that Watkins and several of his business associates also served as front men for the same group of gamblers for the purpose of making heavy contributions to the current Hacker presidential campaign. Attempts by this column to contact Watkins and each of the four organized-crime figures were unavailing. Their secretaries reported all were "out of town" but declined to say where they could be located or when they would be back in their offices.

The column produced the expected reactions. George Sturdivant renewed his demand that Hacker quit the race, and Hacker, crying foul, reiterated his denials and his determination not to be driven out "by the vultures of the press."

"Mike, are you okay on this?" Mulvihill asked. "This is dynamite stuff. If you had it all along, why did you wait so long to let it go?"

"I just wanted to be careful," Webb told him.

"And now you're being careful?"

"As careful as necessary."

It was midafternoon on the Saturday before the primary. Webb and Mulvihill had just returned to the Wayfarer after a long and liquid lunch with an old New Hampshire friend who had managed the ill-fated Romney campaign in 1968. They were in high spirits, laughing about that campaign, and specifically about the candidate's slogan that year. "Romney Fights Moral Decay" had always reminded them of an advertisement for a fluoride toothpaste. As they came into the lobby, Ray MacIntosh and several other reporters walked quickly by, obviously headed toward the room where press conferences were held. They had that anticipatory manner about them that told Webb and Mulvihill that some new development was breaking.

"It's Hacker," MacIntosh told Mulvihill. "He's called a press conference and he's requested network TV again. He says this time it's really big."

Webb and Mulvihill fell in with the group, entered the room and took seats before the battery of microphones. Nora was there, and she came over and sat next to Mike. In a moment Ed Hacker strode in, stern, with Leo Manasian on one side and a fat, red-faced man in a rumpled green suit on the other. Mike recognized him at once as Al Hemmings.

23

"Ladies and gentlemen," Edwin Hacker began. "I know you're all familiar with the latest attempt to smear me, including the escalation of that effort in a newspaper column today. The latest column purports to quote from a memorandum to me from Mr. Roger Watkins of Denver, an old friend, informing me that he had arranged to purchase shares in two Las Vegas casinos for myself and four notorious members of the criminal underworld. It quotes also from the official court record of a stock purchase by Mr. Watkins. And it claims to have evidence that crime figures have contributed to my campaign, with Mr. Watkins and some of his friends fronting for them. I have here a telegram from Mr. Watkins that, with your indulgence, I will now read:

"'To President Hacker: I categorically deny making any deal for casino stock on your behalf or on behalf of any of the four men listed in today's Webb-Williams column, or writing you any memorandum to that effect. It is a complete fabrication and I am referring the matter to my attorneys for possible libel action. The record of stock purchase on file in Carson City notes a personal transaction of my own with the owner of the two casinos in question, as the clerk of the court, Mr. Warren Beekman, will attest. Nor have I or any of my associates ever received any money from any of the four men to contribute to your campaign, or for any other purpose. I have never met nor spoken with any of the men mentioned. I regret profoundly that my name has been used in this way in an intentional effort to destroy your campaign for the presidency, and I pledge my complete support in holding the perpetrators to account. Roger Watkins, president, Colorado Mutual Insurance Company.'"

Hacker stepped back from the microphones to let the effect of what he had just read sink in. Nora bit her bottom lip and turned to Webb. He took a deep breath but said nothing, keeping his eyes on Hacker, who was now staring directly at him, the slightest curl on his lips.

Hacker stepped up to the microphones again. "For those of you who want to talk directly with Mr. Watkins, I am advised he is in his Denver office right now, and as soon as we are through here, you may call him. Leo Manasian, my aide, has his direct-dial number."

Hacker looked over his shoulder and nodded to the man in the rumpled green suit.

"To go on: I have a gentleman with me today who has something to say to you. Some of you may remember him from my first campaign. His name is Albert Hemmings, and he was in charge of special events. Some of you rather ungenerously referred to his bailiwick then as 'dirty tricks,' and in fact it was that reputation—not entirely deserved—that obliged me after winning the presidency to reject Mr. Hemmings for a post that he coveted on the White House staff. I had not seen Mr. Hemmings for several years until he came to me this afternoon with a story that I would now ask him to convey to all of you. Mr. Hemmings."

Al Hemmings coughed nervously and smiled at his old boss. As he hoisted his bulk to the microphones, his eyes flickered over the crowd of reporters, all of them busily scribbling. Then he looked down at his feet, sheepishly, as if he were a guilty man in a police lineup.

"Well, I don't know just how to begin. First I guess I should say I never intended to be here. I wouldn't have been, except that about a week ago I got a phone call. It was from the campaign of Senator

Sturdivant, and they asked me if I would like to go to work for them. I was out of a job, and to tell you the truth I was still unhappy with President Hacker about how I was treated after the last election. So I said okay. I met with Tom Sturdivant, the senator's brother, and he asked me to do my specialty—that's how he put it, 'do your specialty'—on Mr. Hacker.

"Well, I had been out in Denver and a friend of mine told me about the deal in Vegas Mr. Watkins had just made, and it seemed to me the perfect hook. So I worked up the memo Mr. Hacker just referred to. And I prepared all the supporting papers, including references to Reno and Atlantic City, and the campaign contributions, and I turned them over to Tom Sturdivant, for a fee. You can figure out the rest. I guess I didn't anticipate the reaction it would have. I certainly never wanted Mr. Hacker destroyed. I was angry about not getting the White House job, sure, but I never intended to ruin the man. I worked hard for him in his earlier campaigns. He's a good man, and when I realized what I had started, I guess I couldn't live with myself. So I went to him today and told him all about it. And that's why I'm here."

The reporters were stunned. It sounded preposterous, especially that a professional dirty-tricks artist like Hemmings would tell all like this. But there he was. His recital finished, Hemmings dug into a trouser pocket and pulled out a handkerchief. He mopped his perspiring brow and looked over expectantly at Hacker, as if seeking a sign of approval. The candidate studiously avoided his eyes, instead looking straight ahead at the reporters, intent on their reaction.

Barney Mulvihill, predictably, was the first on his feet. "Mr. Hemmings," he said, "are you telling us you faked that memo and the rest, sold it to the Sturdivant campaign, then decided to put your own neck in a noose by parading out here to inform us about it?"

"I know the price I'll probably have to pay for this," Hemmings said with a straight face, "but I couldn't live with myself if I didn't do it."

"How do we know you gave the stuff to Tom Sturdivant? Where did you give it to him, and when, and how much money did you get for it?"

Hemmings turned to Hacker, as if inquiring whether he should go on. Hacker nodded smugly.

"I met Tom Sturdivant here at the Wayfarer the night of the debate and I told him what I had," Hemmings said, sweating profusely again. "He wanted his brother, the senator, to see the material, so we arranged to meet the next night at the China Dragon, a restaurant over in Hooksett. It's out of the way, so we wouldn't be seen. They came and I showed it to them. You can ask the owner. His name is Charles Lee. He was there. He saw them. They offered me fifty thousand dollars for it. I drew the money from a dummy account they keep down in Boston. I can give you the name of the bank. It's the First National of Boston and the account is under the name of Philip Patterson. I understand that's the senator's brother-in-law. You can check."

Hemmings was nervous but he had the chapter and verse memorized perfectly.

Mulvihill was right back at him. "You mean to say they offered you fifty thousand dollars for this material and it came as a surprise to you later that it would be such a bombshell in the campaign? You expect us to believe that?"

Hemmings allowed himself a wry smile. "Well, you get all you can in this business, all the traffic will bear. I knew they needed something. I knew what the polls were showing. Mr. Hacker was hanging on to his base strength and Sturdivant needed something to shake it."

MacIntosh joined in. "Do you realize, Mr. Hemmings, that you could go to jail for this?"

"Yes, sir, I know that. But, like I said, I have to live with myself."

"Why didn't you think of that before?" MacIntosh asked. "Have you gotten some 'consideration' from Edwin Hacker or his campaign staff that you'll be taken care of after all this is over?"

"No, sir. I've always been a Hacker man—until this happened. I guess because I was sore, I just didn't realize what I was getting into. As soon as I did, I decided I'd better come forward. I may be a dirty-tricks artist, as you gentlemen like to call me, but I have my loyalties too. I never meant any real harm to Mr. Hacker. He's a fine man, and I wouldn't want anything I did to keep him out of the presidency."

There were more questions from various reporters—all except Mike Webb and Nora Williams, who sat there completely subdued. Hemmings answered each inquiry fully; about how he had faked the memos and other documents, about the contact with Tom and George Sturdivant, and above all about his own sudden seizure of conscience. The rest of it was believable, but the spectacle of this tired hack being forced by pangs of wrongdoing into publicly confessing his transgressions went down hard with this seasoned audience. Still, Hemmings stuck to his story, and no amount of questioning, or needling, could shake him from it. At the end, Hacker stood next to Hemmings, put his arm around his shoulder, and thanked him for doing "the honest thing, the right thing, in this most serious matter."

Hemmings took his seat, and Hacker approached the microphones a final time. "You have heard what you have heard," he said, soberly. "All during this campaign I have told the American people that the same unholy alliance of a predatory press and ambitious politicians that smeared me and drove me from the White House two years ago was determined to defeat me again."

He was speaking past the assembled reporters, to the audience that would see him on television on the evening-news shows. "Now you have the stark proof of it, in the words of the agent of that alliance. You have heard how the material against me was fabricated, and who bought it. None of us needs to be told how that material found its way from the campaign manager of my opponent, Senator Sturdivant, to the Webb-Williams column. There could be no better example of press irresponsibility.

"I do not believe I am unreasonable to demand a public apology from Senator Sturdivant and from the columnists who so willingly did his dirty work for him. If Mr. Hemmings has broken any laws, I am sure he will be prosecuted. But I would ask at the same time that the Justice Department examine the activities of Senator Sturdivant and his campaign manager, and of Mr. Webb and Miss Williams, in determining who must share the responsibility for this whole sordid affair.

"Senator Sturdivant only this morning renewed his demand that I withdraw from the race. I will not reply by demanding the same of him. But I wonder how a man can hope to win the public's support for the highest office in the land when he stoops to the kind of activities you have heard described here. For myself, I intend to resume my campaign with renewed vigor, knowing that at last I have been vindicated and that the people know the truth. I look forward to their judgment here in New Hampshire on Tuesday. Thank you."

Hacker walked off without taking questions. Most of the reporters raced for the telephones. It was doubtful that many of them bought Hemmings' story completely, but it was out there now, on the public record. Barney Mulvihill came over to Webb and put his arm around his shoulder, but said nothing. There was, both realized, nothing to say. After he had left, Mike and Nora went directly to Webb's room. He locked the door behind them and they sat on the bed.

"I'm . . . sorry," she said, weakly. "For getting you into this mess . . . But I don't understand. I didn't know Tom had recruited Hemmings, honestly."

"He probably didn't," Webb said. "I know Tom. He might take something like that if it came his way. But he wouldn't think of going after it. George might, but not Tom."

"Then what happened?"

"It's simple. Hemmings sold out. He collected from Tom and George and then went over and sold the idea of blowing the whistle on them to Hacker."

"But why would he do that? And risk going to jail?"

"Same reason. Money. He can do a few years and come out set financially for the rest of his life."

Webb leaned over, took the bottle of scotch from his night table and poured himself a drink.

"Want one?" he asked.

"No, thanks." She watched him, then quietly put her face in her hands and began to sob. He said nothing, and did not make a move to comfort her.

"Oh, God, I've botched things," she said.

"Forget it," he said, putting his arm around her. They sat there, quietly, for several moments.

"Wait a minute," Webb said suddenly.

"What?"

"The tape. What about the tape? With Hacker's voice on it."

"Maybe there wasn't any."

"What? Nora! You said you heard it!"

She hesitated, and he took his arm away and looked at her. "I mean," she said, "maybe it really wasn't his voice."

Webb took her by the shoulders. "You never heard any tape, did you? . . . Did you?"

"No."

"Then why in hell did you say you did?"

She avoided his insistent eyes. "I didn't want to admit I had bought the story so easily. We needed a column badly that day. . . . And I needed to prove something to you."

"Yeah, you proved it all right," he said. It was the first time he had permitted himself to utter even a trace of disappointment in her. She leaned against him again and sobbed harder. He held her and said nothing. Her body was shaking uncontrollably; he lay back with her in his arms, and almost without realizing it, he was stroking her hair. She moved against him, still sobbing, as if she were trying somehow to seize a transfusion of his strength. Then she held him fiercely, and captured him in the one way in which she could always have the upper hand; in which her judgment as a journalist meant nothing, and in the end she could comfort *him*.

"Mike," she said afterward, lying still, "what are we going to do?"

He did not answer her, as if he resented being brought back to all that so quickly. He seemed miles away. Abruptly, he sat up and dialed the phone.

"Tom? This is Mike. Yeah, well, there's no use going over all that. What about the tape? Was there a tape or wasn't there, and did it have Hacker's voice on it or didn't it?" . . . You're sure? . . . Well, I don't know what difference it makes anyway. We'll never get our hands on it now."

Webb hung up and poured himself another drink. "Tom insists he heard it, and it was Hacker," he said. "But it doesn't make sense." He was talking more to himself than to her. He put on his shoes, got up and started pacing. Before he could say more, the phone rang. When he heard who it was, he held the receiver with both hands.

The voice of Edwin Hacker jarred him. "Sorry I had to drop that little megatonner on you, Mike," Hacker said. "All's fair in love and politics. But no hard feelings. How about coming over to my room for a drink? Right now." The invitation had the force of a command.

"That son of a bitch," Webb said as he hung up. He was at rock-bottom, and he knew that Hacker was not about to extend a helping hand. But his curiosity was whetted. One thing he had to give Ed Hacker: he was a tantalizer. Something in Mike Webb rose to the bait. He was totally oblivious of Nora now, and he was out the door before she could ask him what was going on.

In the candidate's suite, Webb not surprisingly found Hacker celebrating in grand style. He had a bottle of champagne in his hand, ministering to the thirst of his wife, his personal secretary, his chief political aide, and—of course—Al Hemmings.

"You know all these folks," Hacker said, as graciously as if he had not seen Webb for months, though less than an hour before he had been castigating him viciously before the television cameras. "And you know my good friend Al Hemmings over there." There were no handshakes, not even nods of recognition.

"What do you want, Hacker?" Webb demanded. He stood in the center of the room, a trapped, frustrated bear, his fists clenched.

"Take it easy, Mike," Hacker said. "I just want to crow a bit. You don't mind, do you? Do you have any questions? You were awfully quiet out there. Anything at all?"

"I have to hand it to you, Hacker," Webb stormed. "That was a pretty smooth performance. How much did you have to ante up to your good friend Al to take a dive?"

Hacker raised his eyebrows. "Mike! You surprise me! Al has been a loyal friend of mine for many years. You didn't believe all that crap about me turning my back on him when we were in the White House, did you? It's just that you don't have your best dirty-tricks man operating from the State Dining Room."

"You mean he's been with you all this time?"

"A riot, ain't it?" Hemmings put in, laughing. Mildred Hacker gave him a look of massive disgust, but said nothing.

"And you cooked this whole thing up yourself?"

"Mike," Hacker said, grinning, "what a wild imagination you have. It's just a matter of knowing what bait the fish will go after."

Webb smiled in spite of himself. "And the tape. There *was* a tape, wasn't there?"

"Sure," Hacker said. "Would you like to hear it?" He motioned to Bea Morrison, who, without comment, picked up a tape recorder on the table next to her. She took a small cassette from her purse, inserted it, and let it run:

"Hello, Leo. How did you make out?"

"Fine. It's all set. Our friends in Trenton have delivered. The permits are greased to go through next week. They don't even know you're involved. Same as in Carson City."

"Good. And the, er, discounts?"

"They agreed to the same cut as in Vegas and Reno. They weren't hard to get along with, once they knew who we've got with us."

"Of course. And what about our other friends? Are they satisfied?"

"Why wouldn't they be? As I told you, all they care about are the liquor contracts and the freedom to operate without harassment on the rest. Don't worry, they're aboard."

Hacker, Manasian, and Hemmings laughed uproariously. Webb, desperately, lunged across the room at Bea Morrison, grasping for the tape recorder. But Hemmings was out of his chair remarkably swiftly for a man of his size. He simply fell in front of Webb, cutting him down. As Webb lay helpless, Hemmings blocking his way, he could hear the tape rewinding in Bea Morrison's hand—being neatly erased.

"The old college try," Hacker said, laughing still. "I don't blame you, Mike. It was your last shot. It's too bad the business about the tape will die with all of us. A nice touch, don't you think? We probably couldn't have gotten the Sturdivant boys to buy the whole package without it. We really ought to send a small check to Nixon and that gal of his, Rose Mary Whatshername. They were my inspiration."

Webb picked himself off the floor and headed for the door.

"Aren't you going to have a drink?" Hacker asked. "Don't be a bad loser."

Webb turned and was about to reply, but Hacker cut him off. "Because you *are* a loser, boy," Hacker said, not laughing now. "It took me a long time to even the score with you, but now you're finished. Dead. You, and your old partner, and that hungry little bitch you replaced him with. Now get your ass out of here, and let the winners celebrate. See you in the White House."

24

The New Hampshire primary was less than twenty-four hours away. Tom Sturdivant stood at his brother's side in the Wayfarer conference center as the senator read his statement into a battery of microphones. They were no longer the picture of confident American aristocracy. George Sturdivant's shoulders sagged and his younger brother wore a vacant, distracted look. Two months earlier, when Tom had embarked on the enterprise of making his brother the next president of the United States, he had not dreamed it would bring them so quickly and so painfully to this point.

"Ladies and gentlemen," Tom heard his brother say in a flat, weary voice, "I am today withdrawing my candidacy for the presidential nomination of the Democratic party. The events of the last few days leave me no recourse. For the sake of the record, let me say that no one in my campaign recruited Albert Hemmings to practice 'dirty tricks' against former President Hacker. The fact is, Mr. Hemmings approached us with the material that subsequently was made public, admittedly through a leak from my campaign headquarters. We proceeded on the belief that the material was authentic and the allegations correct. But I appreciate now that this belief did not justify the manner in which my campaign participated in obtaining and disclosing the information."

Tom Sturdivant knew how he, as a reporter, would have dealt with this dissembling claptrap, especially the characterization of the intentional plant with Nora Williams as a "leak." That he had helped his brother write the statement only underscored how far his folly had brought him. He knew it didn't matter that Hemmings had lied about the original contract; that the brothers believed Hacker was indeed in the gambling rackets; even that they really had recognized Hacker's voice on the tape. All that mattered was that they had bought bad goods, and that they had been caught red-handed peddling it.

The rest was a formality. "I regret deeply my own actions and those of members of my campaign in this entire matter," Tom heard his brother intone. The senator argued one last time, lamely, that Hacker still was not fit to occupy the White House again. He did not, however, endorse Walter Grafton, for which Grafton doubtless would be grateful. "I know I have forfeited the right to suggest to others how to vote tomorrow," he said in colossal understatement. "I ask only that they try to look at the real issue of the campaign—Edwin Hacker's record—and vote accordingly."

The Sturdivant brothers turned and strode quickly from the hall, their heads up, their jaws set, but the old jauntiness gone. Some of the reporters in front jumped from their seats and trailed after them, shouting questions, but in vain.

"At least George had the good sense not to give Grafton the kiss of death," Ray MacIntosh said to Barney Mulvihill as they walked toward the press room.

"George will be lucky to keep his Senate seat for the rest of his term," Mulvihill said. "The Republicans want the Ethics Committee to investigate this whole mess."

The two reporters studiously avoided any mention of Mike Webb and Nora Williams, who, to nobody's surprise, had not attended the press conference.

Webb was in his room reading the morning newspaper, an open

bottle at his side, when he heard a knock. "It's Tom, Mike. Do you have a minute?"

Webb let his former partner in.

"I guess you've heard," Sturdivant said, as Webb closed the door behind him. "We're out of it."

"Yeah. Too bad," Webb said, standing with his hands in his pockets, not sounding as if he cared about it one way or the other.

"Mike, what can I say?"

"Nothing. Forget it."

"You were right. I should have stayed with you. None of this would have happened."

"Swell. That and a dime will get me a cup of coffee."

"I'm sorry, Mike."

"Sure. Who isn't?"

There was a very awkward pause.

"You think we took advantage of Nora, don't you?" Sturdivant asked.

"Look, Tom, I'm not putting it off on anybody," Webb said.

"Well, don't be too hard on yourself."

"Thanks."

There was another, longer, and even more awkward pause.

"Well," Sturdivant said at last, "I'll see you around."

"Sure."

Sturdivant left Webb's room and walked down the corridor. He tapped lightly on Nora's door. There was no response at first and then he heard her voice, softly. "Who is it?"

"Tom. I need to talk to you."

He stood there, waiting, and finally heard the latch snap.

Nora opened the door, then turned and walked to the far side of the room. It was evident she had not slept much in the last days.

"I just wanted to tell you that you were right," he said. "You and Mike. If I had stayed with the column there never would have been this mess."

"It's too late for all that," she said.

"You think I used you, don't you?" he asked.

She shrugged. "Everybody uses everybody," she answered.

"You'll be all right," he said. "You can depend on Mike."

She looked down at her hands but said nothing.

"I'm sorry, Nora. Genuinely sorry."

She turned her face to him at last, her eyes brimming. "So am I, Tom. For . . . everything."

He started over toward her, but she shook her head and he stopped. "Well," he said, "see you back in Washington."

She did not reply, but watched him forlornly as he left the room.

"The Yalie," she said aloud after he had gone, apropos of nothing.

On election eve, Mike and Nora skipped a press party at the Wayfarer given by the Dunfey brothers, owners of the hotel, and had a quiet dinner at a place called The Daffodil up the road. She seemed not to grasp the severity of the situation for the column, but he knew. He had already received phone calls from the syndicate informing him of newspaper client cancellations, but he had said nothing of it to her. Though they tried to talk of other things, it always came back to what had happened.

"You never should have taken me on," she said to him, for what seemed like the fifth time.

"You did what you thought was right," he said. "You had no way of knowing what was really going on."

She looked up at him. "You're too good to me," she said. And then: "You're too good, period, to let this set you back."

He reached across the table and took her hand. "No, Nora," he said, "it's all over. The column is dead. The cancellations have been pouring in to New York. You only get one chance on that kind of story. It's like the AP reporter who broke the embargo on the German surrender in World War Two. He had his military accreditation lifted and he wound up in the boondocks. You play in the big leagues, you have to expect the stakes will be high."

"The column is dead? Just like that? After four years? You built it up to three hundred papers."

"More than a hundred have pulled out already."

"But you have a contract."

"Yes, with the syndicate. But the papers can get out anytime they want, from one month to the next. We cut the pie with the syndicate, fifty-fifty. Fifty percent of peanuts is peanuts."

She put her head in her hands, there at the table. "Oh, Mike, I'm sorry. All those years behind you . . ."

"I'll make out all right. It's you I'm concerned about."

She looked up, uneasily, then the nervous smile crept across her face. "Don't worry about me," she said, softly.

"But I do."

She looked away from him and intently studied her own hands on the table. "Well, I . . . I think I've got something else," she said.

"Oh?"

She bit on her lower lip, still avoiding his eyes. "Paul Ostrow of ABC came by to see me this afternoon. They're looking desperately for a woman with news experience who looks . . . looks good on camera, as a traveling political correspondent for their early-morning show. I have to go to New York tomorrow for an interview."

"I see."

"It's a great chance for me, Mike. I don't think I can turn it down. Especially now."

"Of course not."

"And . . . you won't have to worry about me. You can take care of yourself."

"Right."

There was another long silence. She took the menu, though they had already ordered, and read it through several times. She asked him how his favorite hockey team was doing, and whether he planned to see the New York City Ballet when it came to the Kennedy Center in the spring, and anything else she could think of to try to combat the tension and the awkwardness. But he gave her one-word answers and volunteered nothing on his own. Dinner came and they ate with only an occasional word between them, then drove in complete silence back to the motel. He walked her to her room, and she paused at the door.

"Mike," she said quietly.

"Yeah?"

She started to reach out to him, then let her arms drop to her sides. ". . . Nothing, I guess."

He watched her eyes, tried to hold them with his own, but she would not allow him to. "You really don't care about anyone, do you?" he said, finally.

She would not look directly at him. "I know you won't believe it, but I do," she answered.

Abruptly, she turned to leave, but he held her arm. "You think you can just move into people's lives and walk away when you want without leaving a trace," he said. "Like some hit-and-run driver."

She looked up at him suddenly as he said the last, then dropped her eyes again, turned, and slipped into her room, not looking back at him as she closed the door.

Mike Webb went to the bar and took a seat alone in a corner. Other reporters in the place observed his arrival, whispered among themselves, but did not intrude on him. In a few minutes, however, Barney Mulvihill came in from the press party and dropped down heavily next to Webb. He obviously had consumed a considerable quantity of alcohol.

"Rough," he said.

"Amen."

"What now?"

"The column's in the ashcan. They're yanking it from Bangor to Berkeley."

"What the hell," Mulvihill said, "you're a reporter, not a pundit."

"I'll be lucky if I can be even that," Webb said. "Would *you* hire me now?"

"I would. But I'm not so sure my editor would. There's no sense conning you."

"I've been thinking," Webb said. "Maybe I can go back to writing sports."

"Sports?" Mike, don't be funny."

"I'm not. I was a damn good sports writer when I was a kid."

"Politics is your beat, Mike. You're still the best in the business. Everybody knows that."

"Yeah, I sure proved it. didn't I?"

"It wasn't you. You know that. And I know that."

"That's all who know it, and I want to keep it that way, Barney."

"Okay, that's up to you. But you're a damn fool, you know that, don't you?"

"She wrote the first story, but after that I should have cut it off. I went along, and that was suicide."

Mulvihill looked at Webb. His friend was as tired and drawn as he had ever seen him. "Well, what now?" Mulvihill said, slurring his words. "Are the two of you going to open a Mom-and-Pop grocery store somewhere, or what? Are you going to continue to carry her? You're going to have a hard enough time making it yourself, pal."

Webb stared at his drink. "She's . . . moving on," he said. "Television."

Mulvihill groaned. "After what's happened? How did she swing that? . . . No, don't bother with the details. She's been in the news several days running, and she's good-looking. And she won't have to write much. The perfect formula for the boob tube. They can persuade themselves she's been the innocent victim in all this."

"You've got it," Webb said.

Mulvihill reached over and put his meaty arm on Webb's shoulder. "I don't like to rub it in, Mike, but why are you so passive about it? You pay for it while she goes onward and upward. Doesn't that make you want to do something?"

Webb looked at Mulvihill with irritation. "What do you suggest?

No, it just makes me wonder about myself. All my adult life I've been in the business of judging people. Ruth was forever berating me because I settled for being an observer. Some hell of an observer I turned out to be."

Mulvihill motioned to a waiter to bring drinks. "When you stop being an observer, as you put it, Mike, and start being a player, you see things, and people, from a different angle. What did you expect? Making a cold, analytical judgment about her was not exactly what you were focused on the last few weeks."

"If you saw what was happening," Webb asked, "why didn't you tell me?"

Mulvihill allowed himself the slightest grin. "Look, friend," he said. "You were getting your battery charged. Who was I to disconnect you? Even if I could have. You would have told me to bug off."

"I suppose so," Webb said, toying with his glass. The two friends sat there, neither one speaking.

"But it was more than that," Webb said at last. "At least I thought it was. At least for me." He looked at Mulvihill. "You think you know somebody. And suddenly you find out how little you know."

Mulvihill nodded. "Now that it's over," he said, "you have to level with yourself. Don't think you have to pay for it the rest of your life. It will pass. Don't let it eat at you. Why don't you take some time off? Go someplace. Call Ruth and ask her to go with you. When you get back, call me and we can work on something together. A good magazine piece, or a book, maybe. I've always wanted to try a book. If you wanted to, you and I could start a new column."

Webb knew how Mulvihill abhorred the idea of writing a column. But even this demonstration of friendship failed to lift his spirits. When he spoke again, he acted as if the last few minutes' conversation had never taken place. "Sports and politics are not that different," Webb said, reaching back to what he had been saying. "You have winners and losers. You have a contest that begins and ends. You lose once, you go on and play again. And whoever wins and loses, it doesn't matter. It doesn't make any difference in the scheme of things."

"You don't believe that," Mulvihill said.

"As you always say, Barney, the only way to look at a politician is down."

"I never really thought that, Mike, and I know you don't."

"Right now I do."

"Well, you'll get over it. You can't wash out a whole career over one bad story."

"Tell that to your editor when you hand him my job application."

Webb and Mulvihill had three or four more drinks and then, when the bar closed, they went their separate ways. Webb walked down the corridor to Nora's door and then beyond, to his own. He let himself in, not bothering to switch on the light. He knew where everything was. He stripped off his shoes and socks. Then he removed his jacket and his trousers, draped them carefully over a chair, and climbed into bed. He lay quietly for a moment, then reached his hand out to the other side. He did not quite know why; he knew no one would be there. He lit a cigarette and lay smoking in the darkness, watching the small red glow from the tip as it lengthened and turned to ash. He did not leave a wake-up call. He did not expect to get to sleep, and he was not going anywhere in the morning.